"I'm sorry, Dusty."

He knew his wife was staring at him; he could feel the intensity of her gaze. He stopped to pick up the toy bear that his niece had just hurled, and he tucked it back in the stroller.

She was leaving him in a few days. That was the deal he'd agreed to. June first. He had agreed to buy her a plane ticket out of Alaska, to let her walk out of his life without trying to stop her.

June first.

He had five days to save his marriage.

Dear Reader,

What better way to start off this month—or any month—than with a new book by *New York Times* bestselling author Nora Roberts? And when that book is the latest installment in her popular Night Tales series, the good news gets even better. I think you'll love every word of *Night Smoke* (which is also this month's American Hero title), so all that remains is for you to sit back and enjoy.

With *Left at the Altar*, award-winning author Justine Davis continues our highly popular Romantic Traditions program—and also brings back Sean Holt, a character many of you have suggested should have his own book. *Annie and the Outlaw*, by Sharon Sala, is another special book. This one boasts the Spellbound flash to tell you it's a little bit unusual—and as soon as you meet hero Gabriel Donner and discover his predicament, you'll know exactly what I mean. Our successful Premiere program continues this month, too, introducing one new author in each line. Try Kia Cochrane's *Married by a Thread* for a deeply emotional reading experience. And don't forget Maggie Shayne—back with *Forgotten Vows...?*— and Cathryn Clare, who checks in with *The Angel and the Renegade*. All in all, it's another wonderful month here at Intimate Moments.

I hope you enjoy all our books—this and every month—and that you'll always feel free to write to me with your thoughts.

Enjoy!

Leslie J. Wainger
Senior Editor and Editorial Coordinator

Please address questions and book requests to:
Silhouette Reader Service
U.S.: 3010 Walden Ave., P.O. Box 1325, Buffalo, NY 14269
Canadian: P.O. Box 609, Fort Erie, Ont. L2A 5X3

MARRIED BY A THREAD

Kia Cochrane

Silhouette®

INTIMATE™MOMENTS®

Published by Silhouette Books

America's Publisher of Contemporary Romance

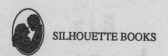 **SILHOUETTE BOOKS**

ISBN 0-373-07600-2

MARRIED BY A THREAD

Copyright © 1994 by Kia Jurkus

This edition published by arrangement with Harlequin Enterprises B. V.

® and TM are trademarks of Harlequin Enterprises B. V., used under
license. Trademarks indicated with ® are registered in the United States
Patent and Trademark Office, the Canadian Trade Marks Office and in
other countries.

Printed in U.S.A.

KIA COCHRANE

reads anything she can get her hands on. "I love books with happy endings," Kia says, "especially romances." Kia, who has been writing since she was nine years old, was born and raised in Virginia and now lives in North Carolina with her husband, their white miniature poodle and their golden retriever.

Dear Reader,

I'm so excited to have my first book published by Silhouette Intimate Moments. I always knew I wanted to write books like these, because they're my kind of books—with romance, adventure and happy endings.

I've been writing since I was old enough to turn words into sentences and sentences into stories. I have two passions—reading and writing. I love reading romances, both contemporary and historical, and I also love mysteries and science fiction/fantasy. And I like to quilt, bake bread (kneading by hand is very soothing to the soul), crochet and do Fair Isle knitting.

Some of my favorite authors are Sue Grafton, Terry Brooks, Heather Graham Pozzessere and Danielle Steel. And my favorite book is *The Prince of Tides* by Pat Conroy.

I love to watch the old movies from the thirties and forties, and new ones such as *Ghost* and *Pretty Woman*. I also enjoy war movies, and since I was born and raised in the Blue Ridge Mountains of Virginia, my favorite television series has always been *The Waltons*.

Married by a Thread came to be written, in part, because I've always been fascinated by Alaska and the life of a bush pilot. I hope you enjoy reading the book as much as I enjoyed writing it.

Sincerely,

Kia Cochrane

Chapter 1

Tori McKay pushed open the door of McKay Air Service and sat down at the desk. She was going to miss this place, she thought as she stood and restlessly paced the small office.

But she wasn't going to miss waiting around for Dusty to come flying in, late and cocky as hell, with some outrageous story to share with Tanner. Both men were third-generation bush pilots who lived by the adage: *There are old pilots and there are bold pilots, but there are no old, bold pilots.*

And neither of them intended to grow old, it would seem.

Where was Dusty? she asked herself with considerable irritation, annoyed that she was peering out the window and praying for some sign of his floatplane. One was landing at this very moment, but her hopes died quickly when she recognized the red and silver gullwing SR-9.

McKay Air Service had four planes: a red, white and blue Cessna 185 Skywagon ski-plane, a blue and white Dornier DO 27, and two gullwing SR-9 floatplanes.

Dusty's was the green and silver SR-9.

Tori stood at the window a long time looking up at the darkening sky, her thoughts flying up among the clouds, so self-absorbed that she jumped when the door opened and then slammed shut.

She turned around. Her brother-in-law, Tanner, entered the office, and he looked tired. "Dusty's not back yet, huh?"

"No."

"Did he tell you why he wanted the Nome-Fairbanks run?"

She shook her head. "Sandy brought him a message from our lawyer but I don't know what it was about." Sandy was one of their pilots.

He straddled a chair, propped his arms on the back and sat there watching her for a long moment. "Are you still planning to leave us?"

"I have no choice."

"And Dusty—what about him?"

"I'm not leaving him. I'm leaving Alaska."

"It's the same thing."

Tori stared silently into the kind and gentle silver-gray of his eyes. Tanner was her friend, but he couldn't possibly understand.

She had lost so much; now it was time to move on and make a new and better life for herself.

She heard another plane land outside, and she glanced out the window toward the hangar. It was the green and silver SR-9, and her heart fluttered in relief.

And she resented even this smallest of feelings, resented the way her heart had a mind of its own when it came to Dusty. She had to get out of here, out of Alaska and back to the main part of the United States.

Before Dusty discovered her walls were crumbling down around her.

A few minutes later, the door burst open and he stood in the doorway, his forest green eyes skidding across the distance between them and landing on her face. He was dressed in boots, jeans and flight jacket, his honey-colored hair lit up by the sun. And in one arm he carried a sleeping baby in a pink jacket, in his other he carried a diaper bag.

Tori stared at him in alarm. "That's Dakota Grace!"

"Yeah," Dusty said briefly, and gently kicked the door shut with his foot.

Tori's attention was fixed on her husband as he moved silently into the room, his green eyes finding hers. His eyes always had a way of touching down on hers, his gaze hot and sexual at all the wrong moments.

It had been that way from the first moment they met.

She watched as Tanner took the sleeping baby out of Dusty's arms, and she forced back a memory that was coming too close to the surface. She burst out, "But what is she doing here?"

Dusty dropped the diaper bag on the desk. "We're her legal guardians."

"What?" Tori was startled.

"Matt wanted us to raise her if anything happened to him."

Matt was Dusty and Tanner's foster brother, a Yup'ik Eskimo who had been taken in by Dusty's parents when Matt was three years old and given an English name.

Matt and his wife Laurie had died two weeks ago in a car accident, leaving their one-year-old daughter an orphan.

"But I thought Laurie's sister Emily was taking care of her," Tori said.

"Just for a couple of weeks," Dusty explained. "She has to get back home to Seattle."

"But...but..." Tori stammered.

"And Emily's expecting her own child. She told me that today. She said she can't raise two babies."

"I take it you don't believe her," Tanner put in quietly.

"Her husband doesn't want Laurie's half-breed Indian kid in his home."

"Is that what she said?" Tanner demanded.

"Not in so many words, but that's what she meant."

"But Dusty, we can't raise her—" Tori stopped midsentence when the forest green eyes touched down on hers again.

"Why not?"

"Because I'm leaving."

"So you said."

"Dusty—" She broke off when she heard her voice beginning to rise. The idea was absurd—giving a baby girl to two bush pilots, to be raised in northwest Alaska? "Are you telling me Matt gave his infant daughter to you and me and Tanner?"

"Not exactly." His eyes tangled with hers. "He gave her to us. To you and me," he added softly.

Tori's eyes widened, and then narrowed drastically. "But I'm moving to Arizona."

"Not for a few days. Can't you help out until then?" When Tori looked at him doubtfully, he hastily added, "We did talk about it the night Matt and Laurie told us she was pregnant, and sort of agreed—"

"That was nearly two years ago," Tori interrupted. A lot of things had changed since then.

"But you and I *did* agree to raise their baby if anything happened to them."

"It was a verbal agreement," she burst out. "I don't think it would hold up in court."

Dusty shrugged. "But they trusted us to come through for them, and I've already accepted the responsibility for Dakota." He paused. "And it's partly your responsibility to take care of her, at least for the next few days."

Her responsibility? Tori seriously considered wringing his neck for getting her into this. But, reluctantly, she had to admit he was right.

"And Tanner and I will help out all we can."

"Right." Tori didn't believe that for a moment. Dusty and Tanner's rugged flight schedule would make that nearly impossible—and the bulk of responsibility would fall to Tori.

And it was none of her business. She was leaving for Arizona as soon as she could.

She knew it, and so did Dusty.

Before she could stop herself, she reached for Dakota. "Did you feed her?"

"Of course."

Dakota was warm and dry and waking up. Her dark eyes opened wide as she looked up at Tori, and her mouth formed a perfect pink O of surprise before spreading into a happy grin, causing something to shift painfully deep inside Tori.

"I'll keep her with me until I'm ready to leave. Then you're on your own," she stated briskly, scooping up the diaper bag with one hand, and adjusting the baby to a more comfortable position on her hip. At the door, which Dusty hastily opened for her, she added tersely, "Just don't go getting any of your half-baked ideas about playing on my maternal instincts. Because it won't work."

Dusty obliged her by slamming the door shut behind her.

"What the hell are you grinning about?" Dusty snapped.

"Nothing." Tanner was still grinning, and making no effort to hide it.

Cursing beneath his breath, Dusty wandered over to the window. His gaze followed Tori as she made her way next door to the log cabin they'd shared for the past five years....

The home they no longer shared.

His attention was riveted to the thick mass of red-gold hair that streamed down her back in mermaid waves. Each lock was a tapestry of natural color: russet and deep polished gold and a warm golden brown. She was tall at five feet seven, only three inches shorter than he was, and from the moment he saw her, he'd wanted her. Back then, she was all heat and energy and strength and courage.

Only lately, she seemed to have lost all her courage.

One finger reached out to gently touch the window-pane, as if tracing the outline of her. *Damn it, Tori,* he thought painfully. He watched until she was inside the cabin and the lights were on, and then he allowed himself a heavy sigh.

"Do you think your plan will work?" Tanner's voice broke into Dusty's misery, and he turned.

"What plan?"

"Getting Tori to take care of the baby."

He shrugged and wandered over to sit on the edge of the desk. "I had no choice. I had to honor Matt's request and take the baby. Tori has nothing to do with it."

Tanner laughed. "Yeah, right. And there's no snow in Alaska."

He eyed his brother. "What was I supposed to do? Put Matt's child into some bureaucratic system, and have her bounced around from one foster home to another? Adoptive parents stand in line for white babies, not Native American Indians. And certainly not half-breeds. Dakota belongs here, with us." He fished an envelope out of his shirt pocket and handed it to Tanner. "Matt left a letter."

Tanner quickly scanned the contents of the envelope, and glanced up. "He wrote this the night Dakota was born," he said slowly.

"And his feelings are clear," Dusty said.

"He wants you and Tori to raise her," Tanner pointed out.

"Yeah," Dusty agreed softly.

"You and *Tori.*"

"Yeah."

"But she's leaving," Tanner reminded him, his voice low and gentle.

"So she said." The silence stretched between them for several minutes before Dusty changed the subject. "Zach Jordan won the Nenana Ice Classic."

"It figures." Only the hardening, tightening expression in Tanner's silver-gray eyes gave anything away.

The Nenana Ice Classic was a yearly event, where bets were taken as to when the Tanana River would break—and spring would officially arrive. A tripod was frozen into the river ice in such a manner that when it first moved, the exact moment was recorded. This was legal gambling in Alaska, and it involved a great deal of cash.

And this year the winner was their archrival, Zach Jordan, of the Jordan Air Guides in Nome.

"We sure could have used that cash," Dusty remarked.

Tanner looked at him for a full moment, then vaulted to his feet with a kind of helpless fury that made Dusty flinch. His gray eyes burned into Dusty's. "I shouldn't have come back. When I got out of prison I should've kept on going."

"This is your home—and our family business."

"Aw, come off it, Dusty. You built this air service almost from the ground up. After I was sent to prison and Skylar left for Miami, the whole thing fell on your shoulders." Skylar was their younger sister. "Dad might have left it to the three of us, but it was you who made a thriving business out of it. You and Tori."

"We've gone through rough times before," Dusty reminded him.

But Tanner was shaking his head. "It's different this time. It's not a matter of professional competition with Jordan Air Guides—it's damned personal. It's not enough that I spent five years in prison, paying for Kyle Jordan's death. His family wants to crush me into the ground."

"You didn't kill him."

"You're the only one who believes that."

"Tori believes you're innocent."

"Okay, so two."

"And Skylar—"

"It doesn't matter. I was convicted and sent to prison. In the eyes of the world I'm as guilty as sin."

Dusty grew still. Tanner had been released from prison six months ago, and the Jordans were out to get him— there was no doubt about that. Evidently prison wasn't enough punishment; they had to harass him and try to intimidate him into leaving.

"I could handle it if all I had to worry about was myself," Tanner was saying. "But I'm not the only one involved here. I have to think about you and Tori, and now Dakota...."

Dusty slid off the desk. "Forget it. We're having a cash flow problem, that's all. We'll just tighten our belts and get through it. But you're *not* leaving," he said definitely. "I need you here."

"Dusty—"

"We have four planes and only three pilots since Tori retired from flying. If we need to, we can let Sandy go, but that's only if things get worse. If we had to, you and I could do it alone, the way we did after Dad was killed."

"Dusty, you're losing business because no one wants an ex-con for a pilot—especially one who was in prison for beating a man to death with a baseball bat," he said evenly.

"Kyle died due to a single blow to the head."

"Not according to the rumors flying around. Hell, I took four men into the bush today, and one of them was actually beginning to shake and sweat."

"Maybe he was afraid of flying."

"We were still on the ground."

"I need you here," Dusty stubbornly repeated. Everyone was trying to leave him, it seemed, and he was doing his best to try to keep his life intact. "Things will pick up."

"McKay Air Service has been going steadily downhill ever since I got home," Tanner said.

"We can handle it," Dusty insisted.

"I don't want you taking this kind of heat because of me."

This was getting to be an old argument between them and it was wearing thin. Dusty knew his brother was innocent despite the overwhelming evidence that said otherwise. Tanner had threatened Kyle in a bar in Nome, and later that night the police had found his mangled body—along with a bloody baseball bat in Tanner's red and silver SR-9.

He knew his brother was innocent and he had no problem standing by him. But Dusty had never found out what the fight in the bar had been about, and it looked as though Tanner would go to his grave before he told anyone.

Dusty wandered over to the window and stood looking at the cabin, and his attention shifted from his problems with his brother back to his problems with his wife.

Tanner joined him at the window. "Tori's as much a prisoner as I ever was," he said softly. "Only her prison is inside herself."

Dusty stood there in bleak silence, knowing Tanner was right. She'd poured all her rage and grief and guilt into a place deep inside herself, and boarded it up tight with indifference and silence... and no one could get in.

He also knew that Dakota could slip unseen into that boarded up place, and start the healing.

Or cause her so much pain he'd never get her back.

Chapter 2

"Mama."

Dakota had fallen asleep while eating her dinner of mashed potatoes and peas, and again while Tori was giving her a warm bath. Tori had made a bed for her out of several folded quilts, and covered her with a soft, worn, pink-and-green quilt, but the child was awake again.

And crying softly, her little arms stretched out. "Mama," she whimpered.

Tori picked her up, and a lightening bolt of pain shot through her when Dakota's arms went around her neck. Tori grew still, scarcely able to breathe.

Damn you, Dusty.

She changed her, dressed her in a clean, dry sleeper she'd found in the diaper bag and sat down with her in the antique rocking chair. The huge dark eyes stared up at her intently, and from time to time a heartbreaking sleepy grin would light up her tiny, heart-shaped face, and Tori had to fight back her own tears.

"I can't love you, Dakota," she whispered. "I can't let myself love you so please don't ask me to. Please don't look at me like that," she begged, gazing down into the innocent, trusting dark eyes.

I can't bear this. I can't. Tori rocked gently back and forth, the solid physical warmth of the toddler tunneling through her, deep and penetrating and chipping away at some of the ice around her heart and soul.

It's not fair, she railed inwardly. *It's not fair for Dusty to do this to me. He's asking the impossible, even for a few days.*

"Mama," Dakota said fretfully, her dark eyes searching Tori's, the child's puzzled expression sending arrows of grief straight to her heart.

Tori closed her eyes tightly, blocking out the sight of the baby she held. But she couldn't block out the warmth of the child. Or the baby-powdered scent of Dakota that filled the room with painful memories.

I can't do this, a tiny voice inside her whispered. *I won't do this.*

Dusty was Dakota's legal guardian. It was his responsibility to care for the child—not hers. He could make other arrangements for Dakota.

Like what? a voice inside her demanded. *What is he supposed to do? Stay home and let the air service go to hell?*

Tori knew he could hire someone to care for the baby during the day, but what about at night? What was going to happen to this child? she wondered uneasily, opening her eyes to gaze into the tiny face. Dakota was sleeping now, the gentle rise and fall of her breathing sending a flood of relief through Tori.

She appeared to be sleeping peacefully, but who could tell? Did babies have nightmares? Was Dakota searching for her mama in her dreams? Was she crawling after her daddy, unable to find him?

Tori took a deep, unsteady breath and let it out slowly. What kind of life was Dakota going to have now, with only Dusty and Tanner to look after her? A little girl needed a woman, a mother, to love her and teach her and look after her.

Dusty would undoubtedly teach her to fly, to soar, to spread her wings. He'd give her the moon and the stars and the bright blue Alaskan sky.

But would he be there, to pick up the pieces when she crashed and burned?

Tori curled up on the couch with her quilting hoop, her newest creation spread out over her lap. She made several quilting stitches, only to find she couldn't concentrate. Her attention kept drifting to the sleeping child on the floor.

The poor baby was exhausted. But now she was asleep, clutching her teddy bear with one slender arm, and Tori was relieved that the child hadn't awakened other than that one time.

But the baby's steady, gentle breathing unnerved her. The room was too quiet—and too full.

Tori took three more quilting stitches and tried not to sigh. It was frustrating having a baby here—frustrating and painful.

And it was just like Dusty to play a dirty trick like this on her.

As soon as Dusty popped to mind, the front door opened and those deep green eyes touched down on hers, then dragged themselves over to the sleeping baby.

"I brought a crib for her to sleep in."

Tori set her quilt aside and stood up as though an alarm had gone off inside her. "A crib..." Her hands were trembling and she quickly put them behind her back so he wouldn't see. "Dusty, you didn't—"

"I bought one in Fairbanks." His voice was soft and low, and his eyes never left her face. "Can I bring it in and set it up?"

She nodded and turned away, not trusting herself to speak as she tried to compose herself. Unwanted visions floated through her mind, and she quickly steeled herself against them.

She ran to hold the door open for him, grateful for something to do. The box was large and awkward, and he struggled through the door with it and headed down the hall. The cabin had three bedrooms: the small one on the left was her sewing room, the large master bedroom at the end of the hall...and the bedroom on the right.

She didn't go into that room any more than she had to.

Tori took a deep breath and followed him. He already had the lights on, and was in the middle of the empty room opening the box. She stood in the doorway remembering another night like this one...another night when she had watched him set up a crib.

Somehow, it seemed a long time ago.

He must have felt her presence because he looked up and their eyes met and held, and she saw the green of his eyes deepen and soften. He held out a hand and she walked slowly toward him, sliding her hand into his. His fingers squeezed hers briefly and after a moment he released her. She was grateful to him for reaching out...and then pulling back.

"Hold this end up."

Tori nodded. Just like last time, she thought. Only last time when they set up a crib, there wasn't this deafening silence between them. And when the crib was up and in its place against the southern wall, there had been joy and laughter—not this unnerving tension that was there now.

"What about the mattress and the... the bumper pads?" she said.

"I left some stuff on the porch. I'll get it."

Tori didn't want to stay in the room alone, but she couldn't bring herself to leave it, either. She wandered over to the window and stood looking out at Norton Sound. The ice was breaking around the edges and she flinched, remembering a night this past winter when Dusty had blurted out something about how her heart was as frozen as any part of Alaska, and he was sick of waiting for the spring thaw.

He had moved out the next day, quietly, and he hadn't been back. He was staying with Tanner in the smaller cabin behind the hangar, and it was a relief to be alone here at night, alone with her thoughts and with her memories.

No doubt Dusty had it in mind to distract her, to force her to look ahead instead of back. But it was easier to do it her way.

Dusty's way took too much effort.

He returned with a box that held a baby mattress, pink bumper pads, a set of crib-size sheets and a small pillow. He also had several suitcases. "Dakota's clothes are in here." He looked at her. "Did I forget anything?"

"Blankets."

"But—" He broke off and glanced away, and Tori grew still. She knew he was thinking about the stack of baby quilts she had stuck in the back of the closet. "Did she give you any trouble?" he asked after a moment, and

Tori shook her head, her mouth curving into a grudging smile.

"She was too sleepy."

"She was wide-awake in the plane, looking around at everything with interest." His grin was fleeting. "I guess she's her father's kid."

Tori nodded. Matt had been a pilot, too.

"Thanks for keeping her here."

"It's your house," she answered hastily. "Why shouldn't she stay here?"

"You know what I mean."

She was suddenly busy making up the crib. And then a thought hit her. "Can Dakota walk?" When this question was met with absolute silence, she glanced up and noticed the blank expression in Dusty's green eyes.

"I don't know."

She smiled at him. "I guess we'll find out tomorrow."

A few minutes later, with Dakota safely in her new bed, Tori turned out the light and went into the living room, only to find Dusty poking at the fire in the fireplace.

"I added another log."

She watched as he closed the screen. "I'm perfectly capable of keeping a fire going," she reminded him. "And it's not as though I've never lived alone before. I've been living in Alaska since I was eighteen, remember?"

"I remember." He stood up, his eyes reaching across the chasm between them, and she looked away.

"It's getting late," she said.

"Are you asking me to leave?"

"Dusty—" He was suddenly in front of her, close enough for her to feel the heat from his body, the heat from his gaze. She had a sudden yearning to get away from him, to turn and run.

Only she couldn't move.

"We have to talk."

She met his gaze and held it tightly. "I've said all there is to say."

"Not quite." He moved in closer. He was sinewy thin, his body condensed power. His jeans, fitting as if they were painted on, showed off the lean muscles in his thighs and narrow hips. Five foot ten was perfect for Dusty. "You announced you were moving to Arizona and I asked you why. You never answered me."

"My parents live in Phoenix."

"But you don't get along with them," he reminded her.

"And I can get a job teaching."

"And a divorce?"

Tori swallowed hard, not knowing how to answer him. Divorce was such an ugly word, and she couldn't bear the idea. To divorce Dusty? It was unthinkable.

But she *was* leaving, and she had to make him understand there was nothing he could do to change her mind.

"What are you going to do in Arizona?" Dusty asked tightly.

"I...I already told you." But she had no definite plans, and he knew it. She could tell by the challenging look in his eyes. And she could see he was about to launch into his favorite subject again. "I'm a grown woman—"

"Who has stopped loving her husband."

Her eyes stung with unshed tears. "You know that's not true."

"Do I?" His forest green eyes were endlessly deep, a void she could once again stumble into and never escape.

She turned away from him, fiercely holding back her tears. But he caught her hand, his grip gentle but firm.

"Let me go."

Dusty was like some exquisite paralyzing drug and she had to stay away from him. She had to.

"Not until—"

"Let go of me!"

His eyes were suddenly as cold as frost on a window-pane, and he turned and headed for the door. Crossing the room, he moved as if the wind had been knocked out of him. Then the door closed gently and she was alone.

Dusty carried his plate of food to the table, and dropped down next to Tanner. He didn't feel like social-izing—or eating or drinking, for that matter—but Mooseheart was for all three. It was a bar, a diner, a community center, store and post office all in one, with low ceilings and plank floors and log-cabin walls. Mooseheart was a well-established gathering place, and a favorite hangout for the McKay family.

Dusty ate his steak sandwich and greasy fries, and fin-ished his cup of coffee. He wanted a beer—or something stronger—but he had a flight tomorrow morning, and alcohol was prohibited a minimum of twenty-four hours before a flight. He held back a sigh. For once Dusty was tempted to ignore the regulations.

He was in a bad mood, and he was grateful that Tan-ner was reading, so Dusty didn't have to talk to him.

It'd been so long since he'd held Tori. Somewhere in that endless corridor of time, he'd lost her. Or she had lost him.

She had stopped loving him.

And now he had to let her go.

He didn't know what else he could do. He'd done everything he could think of to help her this past year, but she wasn't cooperating with him.

He'd even suggested counseling for both of them—but she was totally disinterested.

They'd been married five years, and up until a year ago their marriage had been perfect—a blending of respect and passion and friendship, a merging of minds and bodies and souls.

He desperately needed her back. Tori meant everything to him, but she was slipping through his fingers and he couldn't stop it from happening.

He'd offered to take her on a second honeymoon, to someplace warm and sunny, where they could be completely alone, without all the memories tearing at them. Two weeks on the beach, alone with Tori, had sounded like a great idea to him, but Tori had flatly refused.

She didn't want to be alone with him.

He'd just about given up hope until he'd discovered that Matt and Laurie had made them the legal guardians of Dakota Grace. But was it going to work? Could Dakota break through Tori's grief?

A child's love was a powerful thing, but sometimes fear was even more powerful.

Dusty barely acknowledged the waitress who cleared his plate away and brought him another cup of coffee. He was filled with memories of Tori, and slid easily back in time....

Tori was the only daughter of two stuffy, conventional professors, but she was nothing like them. When Tori was eighteen, she decided to go to the University of Alaska in Fairbanks, defying her parents. Eager to be on her own, fiercely independent and stubborn as hell—that was the Tori he'd fallen in love with.

He'd never forget the first time he saw her on campus, surrounded by guys and fending them off with ease and assurance. He decided he had to have her for himself.

But it hadn't been easy. He had to move heaven and earth—and bribe her with flying lessons—to get her to even *think* about going out with him. But it'd been worth it. They'd had one perfect year together before he had to leave school in his senior year and return home.

His dad had been killed in a plane crash, and Dusty had to look after Tanner and Skylar and McKay Air Service. The separation from Tori had been hell, but they had survived.

So why couldn't they survive what happened last year? he wondered for perhaps the thousandth time. Tori had heart and guts and more inner strength than any ten men he knew, yet she couldn't seem to find it within herself to go on, here in Alaska, with him.

And what about Dakota? If Tori left, he'd have to raise the baby by himself.

He had to honor Matt's last request. He and Matt had been close growing up, his foster brother a major part of the McKay family. Dusty didn't know if the letter Matt had written was legally binding, but it didn't matter. It was morally binding, simply because Dakota was Matt's daughter.

Dusty hadn't spent much time with Dakota since she was born. This past year had been rough on him, and his visits to Matt and Laurie in Fairbanks had been infrequent. He'd meet Matt for lunch sometimes when he took the Nome-Fairbanks run, but he'd rarely been out to their house. And Laurie's sister had been caring for Dakota since the funeral.

Would Dakota be able to adjust to him? he wondered. The baby barely knew him. To her, he was just this strange man who had taken her out of her home this afternoon, and dumped her into a strange cabin with a strange woman.

And was he capable of making a home for Dakota without Tori?

He'd managed to take care of Tanner and Skylar after their dad was killed. Matt had been living in Seattle at the time, and unable to help on a day-to-day basis. But Tanner and Skylar had been nearly grown, he kept thinking. And Dakota Grace was a baby.

Dusty shook his head. He was determined to raise Dakota as his own daughter, but it wasn't going to be easy. Especially alone.

"How 'bout a piece of pie, Dusty?" He glanced up and noticed Suzi hovering near his elbow. He shook his head. Suzi and her husband owned Mooseheart, and they were like family to the McKay kids—especially since their dad had died. "It's chocolate," she said, trying to bribe him. "Your favorite. I made it this afternoon."

His grin was fleeting. "Sure."

"Comin' up."

Dusty sat back in his chair and looked around the room. Being here, without Tori, brought back too many memories of the years when he was single. There'd been girls, but no one special, no one he could talk to, no one he could count on.

Until Tori.

She'd burst into his life, turned it upside down, turned *him* inside out . . . and made a permanent place for herself in his heart.

She was twenty-four when they decided to get married, and he was twenty-six. And he thought he'd known her, known all the colors and shadings of her personality. She was fire and light and sunshine—and she'd lit up his world.

But it was the light inside her that had gone out.

He'd met Tori on his twentieth birthday, and he'd tried to con her into going out with him to celebrate, but she had looked him over with those big, golden-brown eyes of hers, and told him to get lost.

He'd been hooked on her ever since.

Tanner and Skylar thought he was so attracted to the aloof redheaded freshman because she was a challenge, the first female who hadn't immediately fallen for his charms—or his line of bull.

And he couldn't bring himself to tell them the truth—that he had fallen in love with her the moment he saw her.

He wasn't going to let Tori go without one hell of a fight. Matt's letter had given him what he'd been searching for, a tangible way to pull Tori out of herself and start feeling again.

They had a second chance with Dakota, and the baby had a second chance to grow up with two loving parents. That is, if Tori had the guts to go for it.

Dusty's attention suddenly shifted away from his problems with Tori and toward the front door, and he felt the tension inch its way down his body. Zach Jordan and two of his buddies had entered Mooseheart, and they were looking for trouble. He could smell it.

And damn it, he wasn't in the mood.

"Hey, Tanner, I didn't know you could read," Zach called out, and Dusty stiffened, his eyes on his brother's face.

The room had grown still. Everyone in the area knew about the growing feud between the Jordans and the McKays.

"Where'd you learn? In prison?" one of Zach's companions guffawed, and Tanner's silver-gray eyes lifted to meet Dusty's. Tanner shook his head slightly, his eyes asking, begging, for Dusty to let it go.

"Tanner learned a lot of things in prison," the second one added. "Like how to weave baskets and make license plates...."

Dusty shifted in his seat. They had to stay cool—Tanner was on parole and he couldn't afford any trouble. McKay Air Service couldn't afford it, either.

"Tanner probably learned several new uses for a baseball bat, too," Zach said, laughing.

Dusty stood up and the silence in the room was deafening.

Suzi had paused several feet away, holding the slice of chocolate meringue pie, her eyes troubled, her wrinkled face worried and disapproving. Dusty turned to her, took the small pie plate out of her hand and crossed the room to where Zach and his cronies stood. Tanner was right behind him.

"You know, Zach," Dusty said as he dipped one finger into the slice of pie and sucked idly at the chocolate cream filling and snowy white topping, "rumor has it that Tanner's the one with the short fuse in the McKay family, but—" he dipped two fingers in the pie this time and flipped it into Zach's face "—actually, mine's a hell of a lot shorter."

"Why, you little—"

"You mess with my brother, you answer to me," Dusty growled. One of Zach's cronies edged closer and Dusty flipped the plate into his face, and then ducked. Throwing his weight into Zach, Dusty took them both through the front door and into the street. Everything Zach had ever said about Tanner spun through his head, and his blows were swift and sure.

And then Dusty was lifted off his feet by the pie-smeared, outraged, big-mouthed friend of Zach's, and he felt a hard fist slam into his eye ... and he saw stars.

Tanner was having trouble of his own, handling the third, much-larger man, so he was no help at the moment. Zach was now coming at him. Dusty sent a well-placed kick in the direction of his adversary's groin and Zach doubled over in pain, muttering a low, strangled oath.

"Dusty—behind you!" Tanner shouted, and he whirled. The guy with the pie on his face had drawn a knife.

He swung at Dusty's midsection, slicing his shirt, the tip of the blade raking across bare skin. Dusty kicked the knife out of the man's hand as several patrons of Mooseheart hurried out to break up the fight. Dusty sank to his knees. Clutching his stomach, he felt the blood oozing into the waistband of his jeans, but it was the blow to his head that was causing him the discomfort.

Lord, his head hurt.

The men helped him and Tanner inside, and Dusty swore softly as he bent over the bar, but he jerked away when Suzi's hands pulled his torn shirt apart and inspected the knife wound.

"All I need is a bottle of whiskey—"

"You need a doctor," she scolded, and he sent her a grin.

"Just give me the bottle... and some aspirin." He put his head down on the counter as the room started to spin, and he heard her muttering to herself as she did what he asked.

"Dusty, you might need stitches," Tanner said, his voice low.

Dusty shook his head, and struggled to straighten up, but he still felt woozy and disoriented. "It barely broke the skin," Dusty said weakly. Suzi slammed a pint bottle of whiskey down in front of him, and a bottle of aspirin.

Cradling the bottles of whiskey and aspirin, Dusty walked out of Mooseheart. Maybe he'd been in the mood for a fight, after all.

Chapter 3

"Dusty!" Tori flew into his bedroom at Tanner's and slid to a stop beside his bed. "Oh, my God..."

He knew what he must look like. He was sprawled out in the middle of the bed, wearing only his jeans, his head and shoulders propped up on several pillows, a bottle of whiskey in one hand, ice pack in the other. And a long, thin cut starting just below his left ribs and ending at the waistband of his jeans on the right side... a long, ragged slice that seeped blood every time he moved or coughed.

He lowered the ice pack. "Don't yell," he said weakly, and her eyes widened at the ugly bruise around what used to be his eye. It was nearly swollen shut, and his head felt like a moose was thundering through his skull.

She sank onto the bed, shifting her body to face him, and she looked scared and vulnerable. "Tanner told me you were stabbed with a knife."

He started to grin, but thought better of it. Tanner wanted them back together, and wasn't above stretching the truth to get her over here. "It's just a scratch," he said. He followed her gaze as it raked down the length of his wound, and watched as she shuddered.

"It needs to be cleaned and bandaged."

"It's okay."

She shoved him then, her brown eyes flashing angrily. "Damn it, Dusty..." When he groaned, she looked surprised. Her gaze softened but it was still wary. "You're faking."

"Does it look like I'm faking?"

"Well, no, but Tanner made it sound as if you were hurt—"

"I *am* hurt," he broke in defensively.

"Then the wound needs to be cleaned." She grabbed the bottle from his hand and held it over the jagged cut. When the whiskey hit his skin, he jumped, clenching his teeth as he glared at her.

"I could kill you for this, woman!" he said when he could speak.

"Oh, stop being such a wimp."

"A wimp?"

"Yes, a wimp." She set the bottle of whiskey on the nightstand. "A wimpy macho stud—out looking for a fight."

"I wasn't out looking. I got handed that fight on a silver platter." He was about to say more, but decided against it. His head hurt, he had bruises all over his body, he was sick to his stomach and the knife wound was stinging like hell. But he did add, "Next time you have a tiny little cut on your finger, I'm going to get vicious pleasure out of sticking your finger into a bottle of alcohol."

She laughed and started to stand up, but he reached for her hand. "Dusty," she said warningly.

"Don't go," he said softly, and their eyes met and held.

"Was all this some sort of sick joke, just to get me over here and into...into..."

"Into bed with me?" His eyes looked deeply into hers. "Do I look like I'm capable of making love tonight?"

He followed her gaze as it drifted slowly over him, and he realized that, yeah, he probably did look like he was ready, willing and able. He saw her eyes linger on the place where he could feel himself straining against the zipper on his faded jeans—the result of having her so close to him after such a long time.

His arousal had been swift and immediate at the precise moment when she'd poured the whiskey on his cut. This was the Tori he'd fallen in love with—not the faded, nervous, pale, depressed *shadow* of a woman that she'd become.

"You could always manage to make love," she answered his question, her voice even. "Nothing ever bothered you."

"Damn it, Tori." The words were choked out of him, even as his fingers tightened around hers. "How can you say that to me?"

She lowered her eyes. "I'm sorry. I'm just tired. And I'm worried about you."

"I thought you didn't care."

"I care."

"Yeah." He closed his eyes as he tried to think. She hadn't pulled away from him yet; her hand was still in his, her fingers warm and still and soft. He remembered other nights...the butterfly softness of her fingers on his hot skin, stroking, caressing, closing around him....

He groaned when she pulled her hand out of his. "Are you in pain?"

He nodded. He was in pain, all right, but not the way she meant. "I'm okay."

"Did you take anything?"

"Aspirin."

"The ice pack should help your head and ease the swelling around your eye." He grunted, keeping his eyes tightly closed, hoping she wouldn't go away. And then Dusty heard her sigh, a small, soft, resigned sigh. "I'll get some bandages and disinfectant—"

"The whiskey took care of it," he broke in, opening his eyes . . . or rather his one good eye. His left one was swollen completely shut at the moment.

"It needs to be properly cleaned."

She returned shortly with the necessary equipment and set to work. Dusty watched as she gently cleaned the skin around the cut with a warm, damp cloth, and then carefully dabbed disinfectant on the wound. She started under his rib on the left side, where the cut was the deepest, and worked her way across his midsection. She paused at the waistband of his jeans.

The cut stopped there, but she could feel the sticky blood and dried whiskey on his belly. She unbuttoned his belt and partially unzipped his jeans . . . just enough for her to reach him.

She was fast and efficient, cleaning him with the damp cloth, but he could feel her hands trembling, and Dusty noticed how she kept her head bent, her long hair shielding her face from his steady gaze.

"Tori." His voice was husky with desire.

"That should do it," she said briskly. "You should be stiff and sore for a few days, but you'll live."

He was stiff and sore now, Dusty thought. He was aching for her... wanting her... needing her.... It had been so long. Too long.

Twelve months to be exact.

"I'll take your flight tomorrow," she offered. "You just get some rest." She eyed the whiskey bottle distastefully.

Dusty watched as Tori placed the cloth on the nightstand and stood, preparing to leave him. He struggled to sit up. "Tori, wait—oh, Lord," he muttered as his head started to swim and the room spun out from under him. "Tori..." He sagged back against the headboard, her name coming out of him in a low groan.

If the damn room would just stop spinning...

"Are you okay?" He could hear the concern in her voice, and he nodded. "Dusty?"

"Yeah." He could barely get the word out, and it occurred to him that he could be drunk. He'd been gulping down whiskey ever since Tanner brought him in here.

This was no time to be drunk, he decided. Or dizzy. He took a deep breath and let it out, and the room slowly straightened. Not entirely, but enough for him to focus on Tori's face. She was once again sitting on the bed, facing him, her hip an inch or two away from his, her hands folded in her lap. She looked flustered, uncomfortable, but she was obviously worried about him.

"You need to get some sleep."

"In a few minutes. Right now, I'd just like to look at you... be close to you...."

"Dusty, go to sleep." She sounded tired, and their eyes met.

He reached down with his right hand and zipped up his jeans, and he saw the faint stain of color on her cheeks. His eyes never left hers as he fastened his belt with one hand. When he was finished, he asked her softly, "Does that make you feel more comfortable?"

"I've seen a lot more of you than that."

His grin was gentle. "Not for a long time."

She was halfway off the bed when he caught her hand and drew her toward him. "Why are you doing this to me?"

Her words cut him deeper than any knife. "To make you see," he said.

"See what?"

"That it's not over between us."

Her hands were sandwiched between both of his now, and he thought she looked like a trapped animal... lost... scared... disoriented. He struggled to sit up, all the while keeping a firm grip on her. His head hurt like hell but this might be his last chance.

"Lie down," she ordered.

"No." He sat all the way up and grew suddenly still, until his stomach settled, and he could look at her without seeing *two* people he loved and was crazy enough to want.

"This isn't going to work," she chided.

"What?"

"Playing on my sympathies like this."

"We can work it out, Tori, if—"

"Stop it!" she cried, wrenching herself away from him and jumping up. "I don't want to hear any more of your talk about the future, about love and trust and survival! I lost a child, damn it, a son—"

"And so did I."

Her brown eyes helplessly stared into his. "How am I supposed to forget him? Can you tell me *how?*"

"I don't expect you to forget him. But I do expect you to face up to what happened and not run away from it."

"I'm not running away!"

"Yes, you are. You're running from me." His voice was sharper than he intended, but he had her complete attention now. He'd been walking on eggshells around her for a year...afraid to raise his voice...never venting his feelings...desperately afraid she'd break if he pushed too hard. "I've never had *anything* hurt me as much as when Shawn died," he told her fiercely. "Not when I lost my mom or when my dad was killed, or even when Tanner was sent to prison—nothing! So don't you stand there and tell me how much *you* hurt. *I* hurt!"

"Stop it!"

She had her hands over her ears, her breathing labored and shallow, and he relented, the brutal pain in her eyes quelling his anger as fast as it had hit him.

Dusty sagged against the headboard feeling drained, empty, spent. His stomach was churning now as much from frustration as from the blow to his head, and he reached for the bottle of whiskey. Taking a long, deep swallow and flinching as it went down, Dusty leveled his gaze into hers. "I love you," he stated softly, evenly. "And I need you. But you're so wrapped up in your own grief, you don't know, or care, that I'm alive. That you're alive. So get outta here and leave me alone." He took another swallow of whiskey and prayed that he'd pass out soon.

Tori turned and ran from the room. Seconds later he heard the door of Tanner's cabin open and close behind her, and he picked up the dripping ice pack and set it on his swollen eye, swearing softly.

Tori ran inside the cabin, the back of her throat choked with tears, and skidded to a stop in the living room. Tanner was sprawled on her couch sound asleep, a bruise on his cheek, a scratch on his chin, his dark blond hair falling over one eye, his shirt and jeans rumpled and torn. His left arm was flung against the back of the couch and his right hand was resting on his chest. Tori could see the bruised and swollen knuckles on both hands.

He shouldn't be fighting, she thought as she threw a quilt over him. She felt both irritation and affection for him, with the affection ultimately winning out. She'd known Tanner since he was seventeen. He was twenty-eight now, a year younger than she was, and a close friend.

She looked down at him and smiled gently. If her parents knew she had an ex-con asleep on her couch, they'd have a fit. She shook her head. Her brother-in-law was a sweet guy, and the thought of him killing a man with a baseball bat was preposterous to her.

He'd spent five years in prison for a crime he hadn't committed and yet, somehow, he had managed to survive with grace and style, his sense of humor still intact. He was a survivor, in every sense of the word.

Like Dusty.

Tori turned abruptly away. She didn't have the rugged pioneer spirit of the McKays. She wasn't a third-generation Alaskan, brought up on guts and glory.

She headed down the hall toward her bedroom, pausing to look in on Dakota. The baby was peacefully asleep, snoring softly, her little hand cupped under her chin. Tori stood next to the crib studying her a moment.

Dakota Grace had no idea of her loss, or the magnitude of what had happened to her. She was an orphan, the two people who meant the most to her dead. The next few weeks weren't going to be easy. She was exhausted tonight, unaware of her surroundings, but tomorrow, or the next day...

She didn't want this sweet baby in the cabin with her. Oh, God, she really didn't. It hurt too much, she felt too much. How easy it would be to become attached to Dakota. Here was an innocent child who had suffered a terrible loss, who would, in all probability, respond immediately to any show of kindness, and soak up every ounce of affection.

But she had nothing left inside to give Dakota. She was wiped out, physically, mentally and emotionally.

Tori tiptoed out of the room, only to linger in the doorway. She placed her hands on her ears, as she'd done earlier with Dusty, desperately trying to shut out the sounds in her head.

A baby crying... a baby laughing...

She stumbled down the hall and entered her bedroom, but the sounds kept getting louder.

Tori quickly undressed, went into the bathroom and got into the shower, turning the water on full force. She waited until the rushing water drowned out those sounds in her head. Then she scrubbed herself vigorously, rinsed, and dried herself with a big, soft towel.

But she couldn't block out the fact that Dakota was an orphan. The baby was virtually all alone in the world, with only Dusty and Tanner to care for her. She couldn't easily dismiss the fact that an innocent baby needed her.

In her bedroom, wearing a yellow terry-cloth robe, she brushed out her hair until it shone. She caught a reflection of herself in the mirror. She looked tired and pale, her expression pinched, her eyes dim.

Where was that woman who could do anything? she wondered. Who could handle anything that came up?

She threw the hairbrush down on the dresser. It was easy for Dusty, she thought savagely. He was a man. He hadn't carried Shawn inside his body for nine months. Shawn hadn't been part of him, part of his flesh....

A sudden vision almost blinded her with its clarity: Dusty in the rocking chair, cradling a six-week-old Shawn on his chest, both of them sound-asleep at five in the morning. This scene occurred on a regular basis, because if Dusty heard the baby before she did, he'd get up and feed him and change him, then rock him back to sleep.

She knew she was being unfair to Dusty. She knew he had loved their son...only...only he seemed perfectly willing, perfectly content, to go on with his life without him.

And she wasn't.

She couldn't.

Tori turned off the light and got into bed, clutching her robe tightly around her. And when she closed her eyes, she saw Dakota's heart-shaped face superimposed over the tiny face of her son. There was no escaping either infant.

She shivered and snuggled deeper into the covers. The bed seemed huge without Dusty in it. And cold.

But not as cold as she felt inside.

Chapter 4

Tori paused outside Mooseheart to rip open her package and peek inside at the fabric her mother had sent from Arizona, the earth tones, turquoise and sunset colors of the Southwest momentarily forcing her to remember what it was like to live in the desert heat.

A far cry from Nome, Alaska, she thought wryly, hugging the package to her chest and looking around. Nome had a rugged, rustic charm all its own, and at one time she had loved living here.

Nome was the regional center for communities on Norton Sound and the Seward Peninsula. With less than three thousand residents, it was one-tenth the size it was during the gold rush of the early 1900s, but at times it was still laced with intense excitement. People came in droves every March for the annual 1,049-mile Iditarod dogsled race from Anchorage to Nome, an event that usually gave Tori a great deal of joy.

But not this year. This year, the Iditarod had been the catalyst for painful memories.

This year, she hadn't bothered to come out of the cabin to see who had won the event. She'd been disinterested and even annoyed at Dusty's and Tanner's detailed account of the last minutes of the race.

This year, the Iditarod had brought about her decision to leave Alaska and move back to Phoenix, where her parents lived.

Because all she could think about was *last* year, and how happy she was then, with a brand-new baby and Dusty.

She'd driven him out of their cabin and into Tanner's ... driven him out of her bed ... and out of her life with cold, detached, calculated determination.

Because Dusty made her feel things she had no intention of ever feeling again.

He was like a magnet to her body and soul, drawing her to him against her will, and her only recourse was to fight back. To fight him as she'd never fought before.

Because Dusty didn't really understand. He had no concept of what it was like to carry a child inside your body for nine months, only to have that child ripped out of your life without warning.

He wanted her to share her feelings with him, to share her grief. But how could she? Sharing meant thinking, it meant *feeling*. And talking about it made the loss of Shawn too unbearable for words.

Dusty wanted another baby—and that was the biggest insult of all. It was an insult to the baby who had died, and it was an insult to her. Why couldn't he understand that you couldn't replace one baby with another? Why couldn't he understand that *one simple fact?* She'd driven him out of her bed—and he turned around and brought home Dakota Grace.

She'd worked very hard to drive him away. She'd put what was left of her heart and soul into breaking free of Dusty.

Breaking free of the past.

But he hadn't been convinced. Even though he'd been sleeping in Tanner's cabin for several months now, he continued to act as though it was only temporary. He'd moved out to give her the space she said she wanted, but it was obvious he had every intention of moving back in with her.

Her moving back to Arizona would make things clear to him once and for all.

She wandered down the street toward the cabin, her arms full and her heart empty. She was quite used to feeling numb; it was almost a physical part of her now, and the stone walls she had methodically built around her since Shawn's death were solid and high and strong. Nothing got through.

Except Dusty's grin.

Or a certain look in his eyes.

Or the sound of his voice.

She wouldn't be safe up here, not with him around. He was actively trying to tear down her walls, and she couldn't let him do that.

She just couldn't.

She was so intent on her own thoughts that she wasn't watching where she was going until it was too late. Until she realized she'd bumped into someone on the street.

And that someone was Zach Jordan.

"Good afternoon, Tori." He said it politely and without malice, but Tori was too aware of his hands on her shoulders. She knew he was only trying to steady her, that she had probably surprised him by running smack into him, but she didn't want him touching her.

"Good afternoon." Her voice was chilly, her chin coming up a fraction of an inch, and she made no attempt to apologize. After what he'd done to Dusty and Tanner, she didn't feel like apologizing. For anything.

"How is Dusty?" he asked slowly and her head snapped up.

"Am I supposed to believe you care?"

She watched as the deep blue eyes cooled in response to her attitude.

"I have nothing against your husband."

"Just my brother-in-law."

He released her and she stepped back, away from him. "I didn't mean for Dusty to get hurt the other night."

She studied him a moment. "If that's true, Zach, then maybe you should stop hanging around with a guy who carries a knife."

"That was a mistake."

"Was it?"

"Yes."

Tori gave an inward shake of her head. This man had sent flowers when Shawn died—this sworn enemy of the McKays. Zach was a gentle, thoughtful, caring man, and he'd been one of Tanner's closest friends since high school.

But Kyle's death had devastated him—and changed him.

Zach walked around with his grief smoldering inside. She'd thought he was healing, that he was getting on with his life after his brother's death—but Tanner's release from prison had set him off again. And opened old wounds.

And Tori knew from experience that some wounds never healed.

She brushed past him, but he caught her arm, his hand sliding down to grip hers. "I have nothing against you or Dusty. You know that, Tori. But Tanner murdered my brother—"

"No, he didn't." The hate and bitterness shimmered through Zach, providing a distraction, an outlet, for the pain he felt at losing his brother, and part of Tori envied him. At least he felt something. "Tanner didn't kill anyone."

"A jury thought otherwise."

"They were wrong."

"I want Tanner to leave town."

"Have you ever heard the expression 'fat chance'?"

"Zach, let her go," a voice said behind Tori and she jumped. Zach released her instantly and she turned. Zach's oldest brother, Caleb, stood there, along with another man, Joey Arnett.

"Are you speaking as my brother or a cop?" Zach drawled lazily.

Caleb shrugged. "Both." Then he turned to her. "Are you all right?"

"I didn't hurt her," Zach protested mildly. "Who in their right mind would hurt Tori?"

Tori ignored him and looked at Caleb with relief. "I'm fine. We . . . we were only talking."

Caleb nodded, his eyes searching her face for a moment. All the Jordans had dark hair, and those same deep blue eyes—the color of fresh blueberries.

When he seemed satisfied that she was unharmed—either physically or emotionally—Caleb looked at his brother. "What if I buy you a beer and you can tell me why you were harassing a citizen," he stated calmly, laying a hand on Zach's shoulder.

Caleb guided Zach toward Mooseheart as Tori watched them in thoughtful silence. Caleb had also sent flowers when her baby died. Only he had written a note saying how sorry he was, telling her not to hesitate if she needed him to do anything for her—or for Dusty.

"Don't mind Zach," Joey Arnett said gently beside her. "He's having it rough these days."

She watched Zach and Caleb disappear into Mooseheart. "All of us used to be such good friends."

"You and I are still good friends," Joey said.

She laughed and looked at him. "The best."

"That Dusty's one lucky guy. If you ever get smart and decide to leave him, remember, my offer still stands." And then he looked at her more closely. "Hey, I was only teasing," he said when she didn't respond.

She barely managed a smile. His "offer" had been made long ago, when Joey was Dusty's roommate in college. The three of them had been close, and it was a running gag that if Tori ever decided to get smart and dump Dusty, then Joey was more than willing to take his place.

She'd always liked Joey, he was easy to be with, and he would never do anything to hurt her relationship with Dusty. In fact, if she told him what was going on, he'd move heaven and earth to get them back together—not break them up.

Joey took her package from her. "Let me walk you home. As a police officer, it's my duty to keep young ladies from being accosted on the streets of Nome."

She laughed. And as they made their way toward her cabin, Tori asked, "When are you going to make an honest woman out of Kathy?"

"Maybe sooner than you think."

"Where have I heard that before?"

He grinned and put an affectionate arm around her shoulders. "You've been trying to get me married off since the day I met you."

"That's because I want to see you settled and happy."

"Those two things don't necessarily go together," he said. "You and Dusty were lucky to find what you have together. But for the rest of us . . ." His voice trailed off meaningfully, and Tori grew still, her thoughts subdued.

It was true—they had been lucky. Too lucky. But did people actually believe her relationship with Dusty could survive the loss of their child? That they could continue as if nothing had happened?

"Tori, why did you give up flying?" Joey asked her suddenly and she glanced at him, startled by his question. He shrugged. "You're a commercial pilot, but you don't fly."

Her steps slowed as she tried to think of the best way to answer him. She had retired from being a bush pilot nearly two years ago when she discovered she was pregnant. She'd planned to go back to work after having Shawn to herself for three months.

But that had never happened. Her time with her son had been brief.

"I take some of the mail runs," she explained to Joey. "Or if there's an emergency, or they need a fourth pilot. But I'm content being the dispatcher."

He shook his head. "If I had a college degree, I'd be damned if I'd work in an office," he stated flatly.

"You sound like my mother," Tori said. "Only with her it's 'You have a degree in education and you're wasting it by being a bush pilot in that godforsaken place.' End of quote," she said with a laugh.

"Parents. With you it's your mother, and with me it's my dad. No matter what you do or how hard you try, you're always wrong."

There was an unusual edge to his voice that alerted Tori. "What is it this time?"

He flashed her a grin. "Same thing. He's never forgiven me for flunking out of college. Or becoming a cop." They had reached her cabin, and he handed her package to her. "Being a lawyer is the only thing that will ever satisfy him."

Tori stood on the porch and watched him head down the street. She didn't know what to say to him—her parents had never approved of her life either.

She shrugged and pushed open the cabin door.

She found Dusty in the living room giving Dakota her bottle. She stood in the doorway and watched the gentle way he held the baby...and the way he searched the child's tiny face.

She wasn't so immune to him that she didn't see the hurt in his eyes when he looked at Matt's baby daughter in his arms.

But he should be holding his own son, not someone else's daughter, she thought as she closed the cabin door with a thud.

"Where's Eleni?" Eleni was Tori's friend, a retired schoolteacher who had agreed to take care of Dakota when Tori had to be out of the cabin.

"I sent her home. She's having company for dinner." The deep green eyes landed on her face, and Tori glanced away quickly.

In the doorway to the kitchen, she turned. "Do...do you want to stay for dinner?"

"Sure."

She nodded once and turned away. "It'll give you a chance to spend time with Dakota."

Dusty listened to her as she dragged out pots and pans, and shook his head slightly. This tension in Tori was something he'd been living with for a year, and it seemed to be a living, breathing part of her existence—and growing on its own.

Why couldn't she let go of it? Why couldn't she set aside her pain and her grief long enough to let other feelings in? he wondered, gazing down at the toddler he was holding.

He was taking such a chance bringing Dakota Grace into this cabin. And it hurt. It hurt like hell having her here. She was a constant reminder of what they'd lost.

But Dakota was also a comforting presence, a bright spark of life after months of darkness and solitude.

He studied the baby girl in his arms, and grinned at the intense way she was watching him, and the way her fingers clutched her baby bottle as though it were a lifeline. He wondered what she was thinking. The dark eyes—so much like Matt's—were a bit puzzled, but they were also filled with interest and curiosity.

He shifted into a more comfortable position in the rocking chair, and leaned back. He enjoyed the warm, solid weight of the baby on his lap, the way she felt in his arms. This was a tiny life he held—a life that had barely begun. And he found that he was looking forward to seeing her grow up and become all that she could be.

Suddenly, he was immensely grateful to Matt for giving him this chance to maybe, just maybe, make a difference in Dakota's life.

* * *

Dusty surveyed the area outside the hangar. He liked this time at the end of the day, when the planes were lined up like little soldiers waiting for his inspection.

Dusty circled the two SR-9s with McKay Air Service printed on the sides. The green and silver one was his—given to him by his father on the day Dusty obtained his private pilot's certificate. He was barely seventeen at the time—the minimum age allowed for a private pilot. The SR-9 belonged to him, as his personal property, instead of being part of McKay Air Service.

And the red and silver SR-9 was given to Tanner three years later.

Dusty leaned against the door of his plane and gazed up at the sky. A blue and silver SR-9 had belonged to their father—and was totally destroyed when he'd crashed in the Endicott Mountains ten years ago.

Both the pilot and the plane had burned.

Dusty pushed himself away from the door and wandered over to the hangar where the Curtiss JN4D Jenny was housed. This was the type of airplane that the barnstormers used, that made a generation aware of airplanes and aviators.

This one had been his grandfather's plane. His grandfather, Dustin Tanner McKay—called Dusty for short—had moved to Alaska and became a bush pilot in the late 1920s at the age of nineteen.

And Dusty had been named for him.

The plane was not licensed to fly, but Dusty held on to it for the same reason his father had held on to it—because it was a part of aviation history... and the McKay family's past.

Dusty's thoughts darkened. When his son was born, he'd bought him a toy airplane to set on his dresser, and had talked to Tori about taking their son up in a plane and teaching him to fly as soon as Shawn was old enough.

And maybe, one day, having enough money to get the Curtiss Jenny up and flying again so he could give something special to his son, as his father had given something special to him.

All he'd wanted for Shawn was for him to grow up safe and happy and free. He'd never force a child of his to become a pilot, or to work for McKay Air Service. Or do anything he seriously didn't want to do.

Dusty didn't believe in kids living their parents' dreams.

His dad had never forced any of his kids. Matt had learned to fly along with Dusty, and obtained the rating of a commercial pilot, but he had never been interested in making a living at it. And neither had Skylar.

But Dusty and Tanner were born to fly. It was in their blood and bones, in their hearts and in their guts—and it had been that way for both of them from the very beginning.

Flying was like that. You either fell in love with it, or you didn't. It was as simple as that.

Dusty's thoughts returned to Tori. She had given up flying after Shawn died. But why?

Was it the same reason she'd given up him?

He'd asked her a dozen times the past few months, but she refused to tell him. Maybe she didn't know the answer herself.

Something was very wrong with Tori, something he couldn't fix by himself. She had to help him fix it, repair it, restore it—and she had to do it soon.

He'd done all he could for her, but there had to be something else . . . something he hadn't thought of yet.

Damn it, there *had* to be some way to get through to that woman!

He'd honestly thought Dakota would do it. Tori was against having another child, but that was because she didn't want to take the chance on another baby dying of crib death. And according to the doctor, sudden infant death syndrome did sometimes run in families.

But with Dakota it was different. The kid was over a year old; there was no need to worry about that now.

Dusty knew taking the responsibility for Dakota was something he should have discussed with Tori two weeks ago when he found out about it, but he had put off telling her because he was afraid she'd take off before Laurie's sister turned the baby over to him.

But this wasn't some sort of trick on his part to get her to stay. He truly believed he could be a father to Dakota. If he didn't believe that, he wouldn't have honored Matt's letter.

Dusty stared up at the sky, his hands in the pockets of his leather flight jacket, his fingers curling into two tight fists. Shawn's face slid through his mind and lingered for a moment ... and Dusty shook his head.

Shawn was gone and there wasn't a damned thing he could do about it. He'd miss him for the rest of his life...miss what they could have had together...what they *should* have had together.

He had lost his son. So why did he have to lose his wife, too?

And worst of all, she expected him to let go gracefully...to stand back and wave goodbye with a big smile on his face.

Like hell. Those two words entered his brain like two flaming knives and stuck there, burning through all the grief and guilt and pain he'd collected this past year.

Chapter 5

"What's wrong?" Tori demanded a week later, looking from Dusty to Tanner, and then back again.

"Sandy quit." Dusty's voice was terse.

"He quit? But why?"

"Jordan Air Guides offered him more money," Dusty stated flatly.

Tori was stunned. "But doesn't he know how much we need him?"

"He knows. And he doesn't give a damn."

She sat down at the desk, her eyes still on Dusty's set expression. "I thought he was our friend."

"Not a very loyal one."

Tori was silent. Loyalty was extremely important to Dusty, ranking up there with trust and guts. And she could feel his anger—he was actually steaming—and those deep green eyes shot off sparks wherever he looked.

"Sandy has a wife and kid—and a second one on the way," Tanner put in. "You can't blame the guy for wanting to get ahead."

"I know that, Tanner! I know that all too bloody well! But now we've got four planes and only two pilots!" Dusty suddenly wheeled around on Tori, and she didn't like the growing light in his green eyes. "Actually, we have three pilots—"

"Forget it."

But he was leaning forward, his palms flat on the surface of the desk, his green eyes intent, glowing, mesmerizing her, as his idea took hold of him and grew. "Tori, you're a commercial pilot. You work without pay. You're perfect for the job."

She looked steadily back at him. "I told you I was leaving. And in case you've forgotten," she added quickly before he could argue with her again, "there's Dakota. Remember her?"

"Eleni's looking after her during the day."

"I'm not flying."

"I mean it, Tori. I need you to fly one of the planes on a full-time basis."

"Are you deaf? I said—"

"I know what you said. But I can't cater to this particular whim of yours. Not now. We have to keep at least three planes in the air just to break even." His dark green eyes were holding her still. "We really need four."

"Then get yourself two more pilots."

"No one wants to work for an ex-con," Tanner said quietly. "You know that."

Tori's attention shifted from one to the other of them. They were ganging up on her. Was this another of Dusty's ploys to get her to stay? she wondered uneasily.

Or was this for real? Just how bad was the company's financial situation? she wondered.

She'd been so wrapped up in her own problems these past several months, she hadn't given much thought to Dusty's. Could it be the rumors were true? That McKay Air Service was in deep financial trouble?

Tori searched Dusty's grim expression. He wasn't kidding, she realized. This air service was all he had . . . and all he had left of his father. . . .

"Just give me until the end of the summer," he was saying.

Until the end of the summer? That was months off—months of seeing Dusty every day, of having him close by every night. . . .

"No," she said firmly. "I'll stay until the first of June, but that's it. After that, I'm leaving."

"But summer is our busiest season," he protested, pushing himself away from the desk. "Damn it, Tori."

"Till the first of June," she repeated, trying not to waver. But he was making this so difficult. He looked like hell, with his bruised eye streaked with every color from pale yellow to deep purple. His dark blond hair was too long, his face too weary, his eyes shadowed with too much pain.

And a small knot of anger twisted in her stomach. Why? she cried out silently. Why couldn't he let her go quietly? Why did he have to keep reaching out for her?

"I told you I'd stay," she said slowly, carefully, each word clearly stated. "But I want a one-way airline ticket to Phoenix as payment for my services. Due the first of June. That's two weeks from now," she added when he didn't answer her. "*And,* I'll only take the mail runs." Mail runs were made every other day. "Because—" she eyed him pointedly "—I've got a baby to take care of, remember?"

"It's a deal," he said, an edge of resentment, like a sharp knife, cutting through the gentle tone he used.

Tori quickly stood up, circled the desk and headed for the door. She had to brush past Dusty to get there, and for a moment she thought he was going to try to stop her hasty departure, but he didn't. He simply stood where he was and let her pass.

Once outside, she breathed a sigh of relief. She had just committed herself to staying here for another two weeks, and she wasn't sure why. To help Dusty out? Or was there another reason?

As she took the path to the log cabin, Tori's thoughts skidded back in time, to the day her parents were visiting her at school and she had introduced Dusty to them. She'd wanted them to like Dusty, to approve of him—but they hadn't. Her father, at least, had made an effort to be polite, to keep his feelings to himself. Her mother hadn't bothered.

"Are you sleeping with him?" she demanded the moment Tori was alone with her.

"Mom, I don't see—"

"No, don't bother denying it. I can see it in your eyes." Marsha Fleming looked reprovingly at her and then added, "A bush pilot? Tori, even for you, this is too much."

"I love him."

"What are you going to do after you graduate? Move in with him? Become his common-law wife? He isn't going to marry you, Tori. Bush pilots aren't the type to settle down. Oh, I can see the attraction," her mother plowed on, totally unaware of Tori's hurt and anger. "He does have a kind of rugged sex appeal. And I can understand how the life of a bush pilot in Alaska could be romanticized by a young girl. But you're wasting time with him, time that could be spent on more worthwhile pursuits, with more worthwhile young men."

Tori was furious. Her mother couldn't see past his long hair and faded jeans to the man he was inside. Sure, he was well built and strong, but he was made of finer stuff. Dusty was gentle and intelligent and he had an inherent quality of decency that filtered through him even on his worst day.

Tori reached the cabin she had once shared with him, and sat down on the porch steps. She'd been eighteen when she met Dusty, and she'd known all about his reputation for being a womanizer. At twenty, he was considered emotionally dangerous and sexually lethal.

So Tori had been wary of his onslaught of attention toward her. For a guy who never dated the same girl longer than a weekend, she found his intent interest alarming. And unsettling.

Until she got to know him.

Tori leaned forward and rested her elbows on her knees, cupping her chin in both hands. Her mother warned her that he'd never marry her, that he'd never settle down, never be faithful to her. But not once in the past eleven years had he ever given her a reason to doubt him.

She smiled as she remembered what Dusty's younger sister Skylar had blurted out to her years ago. "He hasn't looked at another girl. Dusty's a one-woman man since he met you."

Tori felt the tears stinging her eyes. Their relationship had been a storybook romance, even from the beginning, and it had seemed as if nothing could ever touch it, or them.

But something had. Something ugly and horrifying had seeped in between the cracks last year, and their once-passionate marriage had deteriorated into a holding pattern of outward appearances.

Dusty didn't like to keep up appearances—he hated pretense of any kind—and she soon found herself having to endure the painful thrust of his personality into the stronghold of her composure.

He just wouldn't leave it alone, she thought in resentment. Always probing...pushing...stirring things up when all she wanted to do was retreat into herself and rest. And forget.

The front door opened and a woman appeared. Eleni peered at her with a worried expression, and Tori jumped up and quickly took a swipe at a tear that had escaped. "What are you doing, child, sitting out here all by yourself?" she asked in concern.

"Just enjoying the view. How was your day?" Tori said, coming up the steps to slip an arm around the older woman's shoulders. "Did Dakota give you any trouble?"

"She was an absolute angel." A wide grin split the bronzed face of the Eskimo woman. "Just an angel."

Tori held back a sigh, and she found herself wishing that Dakota had been into some mischief, like any normal walking, talking one-year-old.

Why had she agreed to stay here for another two weeks? she wondered uncertainly. The thought of fourteen days with Dakota was more than she could handle right now. Fourteen days of touching the little girl...of holding her...and feeding her. Oh, God, why is Dusty doing this? she groaned inwardly.

Why had he agreed to take this child?

He'd been close to Matt, but to raise his daughter? And what had Matt been thinking of? Dusty didn't know the first thing about raising a little girl.

But, of course, Matt was including her in his daughter's future, too. Yet he'd had no idea of her plans to leave Alaska. And Dusty.

If Shawn hadn't . . . died, she thought painfully, then things would be different. She'd have welcomed the toddler into her home with open arms . . . and an open heart.

But now Dakota was just a distressing reminder of what Tori had lost.

"Eleni, does she seem okay to you?" Tori asked as they went inside the cabin.

"She's missing her mama."

"That's what I was afraid of."

They entered the large kitchen, and Tori immediately went over to the high chair and picked up the baby. Holding her close, breathing in the sweet baby smell of her, Tori rocked her gently in her arms. She could feel Eleni's eyes on her and she looked up. "What?"

"You're that baby's mama now."

"You spend more time with her than I do."

The keen ebony eyes searched Tori's face. "I saw her eyes light up when you came in just now."

"She likes me," Tori said.

"Not half as much as you like her."

"Who wouldn't like a baby as cute as this one?" Tori retorted.

Eleni just smiled and gathered up her things. "I'll see you both in the morning," she said and left by the back door.

Tori stood in the middle of her kitchen, holding the baby and feeling more than a little inadequate. It was Eleni who had taught her to quilt as a way to ward off cabin fever in the winter, a casual hobby that had quickly grown into an obsession. And it was Eleni she'd turned to after Shawn was born, for advice on child care, and for emotional support.

Eleni was a widow, and she had buried two of her children at birth, but she focused her attention on the seven she had left—and her thirteen grandchildren—and never looked back. She faced each morning with courage and a sunny smile on her weathered face.

Tori both envied and admired her.

She quickly turned her attention to getting Dakota fed and bathed—the two things Tori dreaded the most.

She hated this physical contact with the baby. Dakota kept reaching out for her, and Tori couldn't bring herself to pull away. So she suffered the tiny fingers gripping hers, and the way Dakota had of snuggling her head into Tori's chest while she was being bathed—with Tori desperately trying to block all feeling. All memory.

It was an emotional tug-of-war—the needy toddler on one side, Tori's memories of Shawn on the other.

And Tori was losing.

The small dark-haired child had the power to shift Tori's feelings of loss into high gear. And she was scrambling to repair the damage, to rebuild the walls around her.

She was combing the baby's straight black hair when she heard the key in the lock. And she uttered a sigh. Dusty had been over here every night this week, playing with Dakota, and getting in her way.

"I see more of you now than I did when we were married," she greeted him irritably, and he grinned.

"We're still married."

"You know what I mean."

"Yeah." He dropped down next to her on the couch, and held his arms out to the baby. Dakota went to him willingly, her eyes lit up like two bright coals, and he sat there with her on his lap. "Do you think she seems smaller?"

Tori had to smile. "Smaller than what?"

"Smaller than when I first brought her home." His eyes were taking inventory of the toddler. "Thinner. What does she eat?"

"Not much of anything. She picks at her food," Tori said.

"I guess she misses Matt and Laurie," he said softly.

"I suppose so."

"You think she's okay?" The green eyes lifted to meet hers. "She never laughs."

"It takes time, Dusty. She just lost both her parents."

"You think she's depressed?"

"I don't know. Do babies get depressed?" Tori watched Dakota fretfully, wanting to do something, but knowing there was nothing she could do. She had taken Dakota Grace to the doctor, and he said she was healthy and that her appetite would come back once she got used to her new surroundings. But Dakota was so solemn, watching everything with intent interest, but without emotion. "I'm going to take her to a doctor in Fairbanks if she doesn't perk up soon," she added. "She's not happy—"

"She's not supposed to be happy," Dusty said. "Both her parents are dead."

"But she's only a baby. She should be getting into things, laughing and getting ticked off and generally making a nuisance of herself," Tori complained. "But she just sits on the floor and looks around as if she's trying to figure out where the hell she is. And that's not a good way for her to live.''

''What would you have her do?'' He was looking at her, an odd gleam in his eyes, but she barely noticed it. She was too intent on answering his question.

''Dakota has her whole life ahead of her. She should be adjusting to living here with us . . . I mean, living here with you—she has to get used to living without Matt and Laurie, and accept you as her new dad.''

''That's a big adjustment for someone her size to make.''

''But what other choice does she have?'' Tori demanded. ''We can't give her parents back to her, we can't make it all better. All we can do is love her and keep her safe. But she has to learn to embrace the world again, to find joy and happiness, and, damn it, life—'' She broke off and shrugged helplessly, her eyes fixed on the small dark head. ''I feel so sorry for her, and I want to help her so much. But I can't take her hurt away. And it makes me so angry and so frustrated that I can't help her. Do you know what I'm saying?''

''Yeah.''

And something in his low voice made her look at him, into his softening green eyes, and Tori suddenly realized the impact of her words. ''But of course, Dakota's only a baby. With adults it's different,'' she said lamely, and cringed under the steady, deep green gaze.

''Is it? Do you mind telling me how?'' His tone was friendly, conversational, but his eyes . . . there was a combative light in them that alerted Tori.

She got up from the couch, not bothering to answer him, and began straightening up the living room. She could feel his eyes watching her, and she suddenly wanted him to just go. But this was his cabin—it had been built by his father over twenty-five years ago—so he had a right to be here, and he had a right to see Dakota. Dusty was her legal guardian and he was responsible for the child's welfare. She couldn't just throw him out.

But she wanted to. Oh, God, she wanted to kick him out the door.

Tori moved about the room, keeping herself busy and trying not to listen to him as he played with Dakota and rocked her and stroked her dark hair.

Yet she couldn't help but notice the trusting way Dakota snuggled against him. Soon the baby was asleep and Dusty offered to take her into the nursery and put her in her crib.

But then he was back, advancing upon her with purpose in every line of his body, his intentions clear.

He unnerved her with his sexy grin, his long, lean body, his sleepy, seductive green eyes and that husky drawl of his. And Tori steeled herself against him, thinking that her long-ago first impression of him had been right on target—she'd thought he was too good-looking, too self-assured.

Too dangerous.

"Why do you keep stacking and restacking those magazines?" he asked in that slow, delicious voice of his.

He was standing next to her, and Tori fought back her rising panic. "Have you eaten?" she asked.

He shrugged. "I had a sandwich at Mooseheart." His eyes never left her face.

"Would . . . would you like me to fix you something?" She groaned inwardly. She wasn't going to wait on him, do for him, on any level. It was too tempting, too risky.

But fixing Dusty something to eat would give her something to do.

"I'm not hungry," he said and Tori looked at him.

"Well, I am. So if you'll excuse me . . . ?"

But then he was reaching out, and he took her slim hand in his. His hand was calloused, strong and warm around hers. Dusty was trying to look innocent and friendly, but she didn't believe it.

She could feel the warmth in his eyes. It was a tangible thing, reaching out for her, as he let his green eyes drift downward, over her breasts in a slow, deliberate glance. A sudden memory seized Tori and she fought hard against it.

But it was no use.

She had total recall of what it was like to make love with Dusty... the gifted way he kissed... the feel of his long hard fingers, hot and eager, yet so gentle and patient... the gentle sucking, pulling, tugging motions his mouth made on her breasts. Her lower body contracted with a pleasurable ache as she remembered that first time, years ago... remembered the sweet piercing of her flesh, then the strength and depth of his penetration... that first time... and the last time... and all the times in between.

His dark blond hair hung below the collar of his shirt, and tension radiated through his finely muscled body. His long legs were encased in jeans that had seen hard wear, his hips narrow and sexy, his deep green eyes riveted on hers, his watchful gaze leaving her no escape.

The air was charged with heat and need and sexual tension and one move—all it would take was one move, from either of them—and they'd be in each other's arms and making love. Probably in the middle of the living room floor. And for a brief, crazy moment, Tori wanted it...just one more night with him...just one more time.

But her defenses were too strong, too deeply ingrained by now. She couldn't take the chance.

"I'm asking you to leave," she said quietly, the words fairly wrenched out of her, and he smiled, a slow, sweet smile that broke her heart. "Dusty... let go of me."

"Why should I?" he taunted lightly.

She swallowed hard. "Please."

His eyes grew hard and flintlike, yet when it came, his voice was soft and slow. "Do you think it's so damned easy to throw everything away?" he asked her, his fingers tightening around hers, his grip strong and urgent and suddenly begging... needing.... "Do you?"

She shook her head. "No, it's not easy." Her own voice was equally soft.

"Then why are you doing this to me? To us? What did I ever do except fall in love with you?"

"You... you..." But she had no words to fit her emotions, no words to make him understand how much he frightened her.

"What?" he snapped impatiently when she continued to stare helplessly at him.

"Are you trying to start something with me?"

"You're damned right I am." His voice was low and tight and he pulled her forward and into his arms, his mouth touching hers, one kiss leading into another—deep, slow, endless kisses, an open sea with no land in sight, no anchor, nothing to hold on to, nothing to keep her from drowning in the feel of him. His tongue slipped inside her mouth and she started to tremble in reaction, the intimacy of it too unbearably sweet and tempting and much too arousing.

And if she could, she would have crawled inside his skin.

His heart was pounding against hers and his mouth was no longer gentle. She pressed close for just an instant—before sudden panic ripped her out of his arms, and he was too startled to try to hold her.

"Get out." Her voice was low and shaking.

"Like hell."

"Get out!"

"Why?" His hands were on her shoulders, his fingers digging into her. *"Why?"*

"Because I want you to."

"And what *you* want is all that matters, right?"

"I don't want to fight with you, Dusty, please—"

"But I want to fight! If we can't make love, then we can sure as hell fight about it," he snapped. "I want something, some spark, some kind of explanation, something, Tori, that tells me you're still living and breathing in there!"

"You're not being fair—"

"Fair? You call this fair? It's been a year, Tori. Twelve months since Shawn died. And I've tried being patient and I've tried being reasonable and I've tried being a first-class jerk—but nothing works with you. You won't let me touch you or hold you or make love to you or even talk to you. I don't know how or why I got to be the enemy in all this, but you've stuck me in that role and I want to know why."

"You never wanted Shawn." Her words cut through the tense silence between them. "Not really. You didn't want him."

"That's not true," he insisted.

"The hell it isn't."

"The timing was a little off, but—"

"He was an accident, you mean," she said raggedly.

"Tori..." His hands gentled on her shoulders, his fingers caressing, calming, soothing. "I've never given you a reason to think I didn't want him, and you know that, deep inside you know that. I was a good father to him, and you know that, too.'' His voice was low, his patience strained, the words softly spoken. ''This isn't about that. It's about you. It's about you shutting me out of your life. It's about you wanting to face the loss of Shawn all by yourself.''

''It's the only way I can face it.''

''But why? Why can't you let me in? Why can't you let me help you?''

She was shaking her head, her eyes fixed on him, and she had no answers . . . just a terrible yearning to do this on her own.

''Tori, you're scared to death. Anyone can see that. But what are you afraid of?''

''Of love,'' she whispered. ''Any kind of love. But especially your kind.''

He looked as though she had fired a bullet into his heart. He also looked as if he wanted to take her and wring her neck.

Dusty gently caressed her right cheek with his hand, his voice like steel. ''The trouble with you, Tori, is you have no guts. Not when it counts. You can defy your parents by going to school in Alaska, and then staying here after you graduated. And you can assert your independence by going against them and marrying a bush pilot. But when it gets right down to it, when it gets down to things like love and commitment and toughing it out—you're a damned wimp. So maybe you're right. Maybe you don't belong up here with me.'' He turned, grabbed his leather jacket off the couch and headed out the door.

And Tori sank to her knees in the middle of the room, her eyes staring at the closed door. She had to get out of here before Dusty ended up hating her.

Chapter 6

"Three ball in the side pocket," Dusty said, and tapped it lightly, sending the ball home. He circled the pool table in the back of Mooseheart and got into position. "Four ball in the right corner." He missed that one and stepped back, holding his pool cue lightly as he watched Tanner set up for his turn.

As usual, Dusty felt like the world's worst bastard. As usual, he'd only made things worse.

He'd had no right to come down so hard on Tori tonight, he railed inwardly. No right at all. But he'd been angry and frustrated, and he'd wanted her so much that the pain of it was a raw ache in his gut.

Why couldn't she trust him? he wondered. Tori used to have enough strength to let herself be vulnerable with him, to need him, to ask for his help, but ever since Shawn died, it was as if she were desperately building walls to keep herself sane. All she had to do was let him in, talk to him, love him—and let him love her—and they could face anything.

Even the death of their son.

Dusty felt the slow pain as it eased through him, a familiar pain now, low and deep and tucked away inside him, never quite disappearing, but not as sharp and deadly as when it had first made its appearance.

A year ago, Dusty thought a man could actually die from shock and grief. He'd channeled all his energy into Tori, giving her all the strength he had, because the change in her terrified him. He'd buried everything he felt, leaving it inside to fester and grow, until one night, feeling isolated from Tori and very much alone, he'd sat down to write his weekly letter to Tanner, and something erupted inside him. He poured out everything to his kid brother, everything he felt about his son's death, and his fear that Tori wasn't going to survive this.

He hadn't expected a response from Tanner, but he'd gotten one, anyway.

And after that things started to ease up inside him. He'd written to Tanner often, encouraged by his brother's care and concern, and since he'd been released from prison, they'd stayed up talking lots of times until three or four in the morning.

And Tori needed that kind of release, that kind of support.

"You're paying for the coffee." Tanner roused him from his thoughts.

Dusty set his pool cue in its rack and signaled the waitress. They were playing for coffee, one cup per game.

When they were settled at a table, the coffee in front of them, Dusty hunched over his cup and tried to ignore the stabbing loneliness deep inside.

"You have another fight with Tori?"

"How could you tell?"

"You lost," Tanner said. "Three games in a row. And you never lose at pool unless you're having trouble with a female."

Dusty grunted, not bothering to answer him. Tori wasn't just another female—she was the only woman he'd ever been in love with in his life.

"Why don't you fix things up with her?"

His eyes lifted to meet his brother's. "And just how am I supposed to do that?"

"Would you stop answering all my questions with more questions? I don't know *how,*" Tanner said impatiently. "All I know is you're both driving me nuts. You and Tori obviously still love each other. Yet you let her get away with pushing you aside, like you're some stray puppy instead of her husband, and it's crazy to let her do that. Tori doesn't know what she's doing, it's up to you to set her straight."

Dusty laughed. "Oh, yeah, playing the macho caveman will really get me somewhere with her—like headfirst in Norton Sound."

But Tanner was serious. "One thing I learned in prison is that life's too short. And one thing I've learned since I've been home is you and Tori belong together, no matter what."

Dusty was silent, digesting Tanner's observations in slow degrees. He wanted to believe what Tanner was saying, but he wasn't sure anymore. At one time, he'd thought nothing could touch him and Tori, nothing could hurt them, nothing could tear them apart.

Now he wasn't so sure.

"She thinks I never wanted Shawn."

"What?" Tanner looked stunned.

Dusty shrugged and leaned back in his chair. "Her pregnancy was...unplanned. It took me by surprise. I wasn't expecting it, so my reaction wasn't as enthusiastic as it should have been." He paused, his gaze shifting away from Tanner to wander restlessly around the room. "I think that's when a lot of this started. Tori never quite forgave me for not being as excited about the baby as she was."

"Didn't you guys talk about having kids before you were married?"

"Sure. After we built up McKay Air Service, we were going to have at least two. Maybe three. But the timing was off. You were gone, I'd just bought the Cessna 185 and then I was faced with losing Tori as a pilot and breaking in a new one. I guess I reacted to on-the-job stress instead of reacting to the idea of being a father."

"But you both were happy until..." His voice trailed off uncertainly.

"Until Shawn died." Dusty could say the words now without flinching. "And the funny thing is, I was just getting into it, into being a father and actually enjoying it. I was feeling more relaxed and secure about picking him up and holding him—stuff like that." He stopped because flashes of memory were too vivid, too painful, and he reached for his cup of coffee and took a sip.

Tanner was watching him. "I still think you need to do something about Tori. Straighten her out."

"I can tell you've never been married," he grunted, and then regretted his choice of words. Tanner had been engaged at one time—to Kelly Jordan.

Zach Jordan's younger sister.

"Then what about trying another approach?" Tanner suggested.

"Like what?" Dusty asked.

"Stop chasing her. Give her some room, and maybe she'll come around."

"And maybe she won't." But Dusty was intrigued with the idea. He'd been pushing her hard the past couple of months, and so far it had backfired every time.

Maybe it was time to change his tactics.

"Mind if I join you?" a soft female voice asked, breaking into his thoughts. Dusty looked up.

Jenna Bradshaw Jordan was standing at their table, one hand on the empty chair between the two men, her other hand holding a glass of white wine. She was looking at them patiently, expectantly.

"Have a seat." Dusty pulled the chair out for her and she settled herself into it, crossing her legs and sending him a blinding smile.

Dusty glanced at Tanner and noticed his brother was not too happy about this woman's presence. Dusty wasn't too happy about it, either, but what was he supposed to do? There was an empty place at their table, and the room *was* crowded.

And if he were being honest with himself, he'd admit he was in just enough of a bad mood to enjoy spending time with Zach Jordan's wife.

"How come you're on the loose tonight?" Tanner drawled softly.

"I needed some company." She looked at Tanner. "Isn't coming to Mooseheart what one does when one is bored and lonely?"

"Maybe one should try reading a book once in a while—or keep one's husband company," Tanner retorted.

She leaned back in her chair, her fingers sliding up and down the stem of her wineglass, her eyes fastened on

Tanner's face. "Zach's having a boring dinner with his parents, a dinner I chose not to attend."

Dusty's eyes wandered idly over the woman as he listened to this exchange. Jenna was a classic beauty, with long blond hair, big blue eyes, a button nose and a size-four body. He should be attracted to her, but he wasn't. And he never had been, even in high school when she used to come on to him.

Of course, she came on to all the guys, and still did, despite her two-year marriage to Zach.

Dusty took a sip of his coffee and watched her. Jenna Bradshaw Jordan was an enigma. In high school she stole her friends' dates and then wondered aloud why her friends stopped calling her. She'd often dated brothers or cousins or best friends simultaneously, and became visibly upset when they'd exchange words—and sometimes blows—at her parties. And she still flirted outrageously with every male over the age of eight.

She also attended church every Sunday, was the first to volunteer to teach Sunday school or watch the nursery, and was deeply involved in many community activities serving the poor or the homeless or the abused.

The women in Nome tolerated her because of her energy and devotion to her many worthwhile activities, and the men were both attracted to and wary of her.

Except Tanner. Dusty watched his younger brother react to the tiny blonde's presence at their table, but he couldn't decide if Tanner liked or disliked the woman. Tanner had gone to high school with Jenna, had been in many of the same classes, but it struck Dusty that in all these years, he'd never once heard Tanner comment on Jenna Bradshaw Jordan. And Tanner usually commented on everything. Even things he shouldn't.

"I understand Matt left you his daughter to raise," she said, smiling warmly at him, and it took a moment for Dusty to realize the remark was addressed to him. "Her name's Dakota?"

"Dakota Grace."

"Grace was your mother's name, wasn't it?"

"Yeah." Dusty reached for his cup and took a slow, deliberate sip. His mother had died of cancer when he was ten.

"She was a lovely lady. She taught me how to play the piano."

"Mom taught every kid in Nome how to play the piano," Tanner put in dryly, and Dusty looked at him, into his gray eyes, the expression in them unreadable.

But Tanner appeared to be watching Jenna closely, his eyes searching out every gesture, every facial expression, every change of nuance in her mannerisms.

What in hell was wrong with him? Dusty wondered, sensing the growing tension between Zach's wife and his brother.

Dusty took another sip of coffee and set the cup down. He started to get up, deciding to call it a night, when Jenna's hand lightly touched his arm. "Leaving so soon?"

"It's getting late."

"Would you mind walking me home then? I get nervous walking alone at night."

"I'll take you," Tanner offered unexpectedly, and she glanced at him.

"But what would Zach say to that? You two haven't been exactly friends since you killed Kyle."

Tanner's gray eyes glittered dangerously. "So you think I killed him?"

She shrugged. "You were tried and convicted."

"I'll take her," Dusty decided. Jenna was up to her old tricks. Nothing she liked better than stirring things up and causing trouble, and tonight she was acting as if she were out for a little taste of blood.

It was better if it was his blood and not Tanner's.

Dusty walked down the quiet streets of Nome, thinking about Tanner. And about Jenna. He had escorted her home, said good-night at her door and then left. But what he couldn't understand was why she'd chosen their table to sit at, or one of them to take her home.

And Tanner. He didn't understand his brother at all. The guy was edgy and he had a number of mystifying secrets of one kind or another.

Tanner was a fiercely independent person, and privacy was one thing he valued the most. At an early age, he'd drawn a line down the center of himself and wouldn't let anyone step over it, or invade his personal life.

Tanner kept his private life private.

Dusty shook his head. Since he'd been released from prison, that was even more true.

He'd arrived at the two-bedroom cabin he now shared with Tanner and was about to enter, when he glanced next door at the larger one, the one that Tori occupied in solitary grief. Dusty decided to give it one last shot.

The lights were on in the living room and he knocked on the door, thinking that would be the more considerate thing to do. "Who is it?" she asked.

"Dusty."

There was a pause, and then the door opened cautiously. "What do you want?"

"To say I'm sorry—about before." And then, "Tori, what do you say we call a truce?"

"A truce?"

"Yeah. Let's stop fighting and concentrate on getting along. I need you to take care of Dakota, and I need you to fly one of the planes for the next two weeks. At this point, I can't afford to keep making you mad."

Her smile was hesitant. "What do I have to do in return?"

"You can stop treating me like a stranger," he said softly, and gently kissed her cheek. Then he left.

He was on Tanner's front porch before he heard her door close.

The next morning, Dusty set the green and silver SR-9 down on the island of St. Paul—a misty, fogbound breeding ground for fur seals—and helped his two passengers unload their gear. The husband-and-wife team were bird-watchers and photographers, and had quite a lot of paraphernalia.

St. Paul was one of the five Pribilof Islands, located two hundred miles northwest of the Aleutian Islands. During the flight from Nome, the talkative duo had informed him of the 1.1 million seabirds who nested there: thick-billed murres, auklets, kittiwakes and something called a puffin, dispersed among the ducks and owls and sandpipers. But they were mainly interested in the seals.

Every May, the mating seals arrived from faraway Pacific waters, and the island turned into a frenzy of activity as the more than one thousand males roared jealously in pursuit of their mates. And this couple intended to photograph them.

Dusty, by now, had learned more than he ever wanted to know about the mating habits of seals.

He bid them farewell, promised to pick them up at the end of the week and headed for the tiny post office to deliver the mail. He took the time to have a late breakfast, and afterward, on impulse, he bought Tori a pair of jade earrings, and headed back to the plane.

Dusty checked the floatplane before takeoff and then again when it was airborne. The SR-9 climbed in altitude, and Dusty's thoughts drifted to Tori. He wondered how she was doing. She was flying the DO 27 north to Kotzebue, a route she'd taken hundreds of times for McKay Air Service.

But he was worried about her state of mind.

Logic nudged against his concern. Tori was an excellent pilot, and she'd been a commercial pilot for six years. She was perfectly qualified and emotionally equipped to fly for an air service.

So why had she given up flying?

He answered the question that had been pushing into him all morning—because she's hell-bent on giving up all the things that matter to her...all the things she loves....

Like flying.

And like him.

Dusty's green eyes constantly scanned the controls and the view below him. He was flying at an altitude of thirty-five hundred feet, and below him there was nothing but water, and icebergs breaking from the shore and floating beneath him, as if some toddler had thrown a handful of ice cubes into a bucket of water.

He liked this view the best during freeze-up. As winter approached, thin sheets of ice would form on the ocean, and as the temperature dropped, these sheets of ice would slide over one another. From the air they'd appear as delicate as lily pads. As the pads became thicker and thicker, and the days grew colder and colder, the sheets of ice would collide and freeze until they formed a solid deck of ice.

In many places, it was a solid deck of ice all the way to Siberia.

The whole thing was in reverse at spring breakup.

And again his thoughts returned to Tori. Walking along the beach in Nome, freeze-up was especially eerie, and it could be frightening when you'd never heard it before. As the lily pads of ice collided and froze, the pressure caused the ice to scrape and whine. On nights in early winter, one could swear there were howling, moaning monsters in the depths of the Bering Sea. Tori would burrow her face into his shoulder, seeking comfort in his arms.

But last year, she'd stopped seeking comfort—or anything else—in his arms. She didn't want to live without Shawn. She couldn't imagine life without their son.

Or a life with him.

And it was too bad she couldn't imagine a life with him in it, Dusty thought. Or imagine a life with other children like Dakota and maybe, in time, another baby of their own. Tori was just too deep inside herself to see any future for them.

Dusty checked the control panel again and tried to force his thoughts away from Tori, and out of the past.

She didn't want him; she'd made that damn clear.

Maybe it was time for *him* to try to imagine a new life without her in it. That would be a start in the right direction.

Dusty heard a soft sound from behind him, in the direction of the curtained baggage compartment, then something—or someone—suddenly bounced into the seat next to his.

"Isn't this one gorgeous day?" Jenna sent him a blinding smile as she slipped into the seat next to his, and tossed her blond hair off her shoulders. The big cobalt-blue eyes were moving over him happily, and Dusty couldn't stop the coarse expletive that slipped from his mouth.

And then, "What the hell are you doing in my plane?"

"I stowed away in the baggage compartment."

"But—"

"I hid behind one of those crates of groceries while you and Mr. Bird-watcher were unloading their stuff." She crossed her legs and lifted her arms in a luxurious stretch. "I'm in the mood for some fun. How about you, Dusty? What are you in the mood for?"

Chapter 7

Tori paced the small office, her booted feet tapping on the hardwood floor with fury and purpose and a supreme need to shoot and kill the next person who came through that door.

Dusty's plane had just landed, two hours late, and through the window she'd seen the tiny blond woman climb out of the cockpit.

Jenna Bradshaw Jordan.

She paced the office once more, muttering furiously beneath her breath. What was Dusty doing with . . . with Zach's wife? Was he out of his tiny mind?

Or was Dusty looking for her replacement already? she fumed, angry at her own hurt and fury, and scared of it, too. Because anger meant she cared.

And she didn't want to care.

Tanner sat with his feet propped up on the desk, a mug of coffee cradled in his hands, his kind gray eyes watching her every move.

She could feel his gaze, and it looked like pity to her. And why not? Dusty was a man, wasn't he? Long denied female companionship and affection. And sex. Tanner was probably thinking she was getting what she deserved.

Her imagination was roaring along a route she dared not take. But she couldn't help herself. Dusty was a prime target for a woman like Jenna.

Women like Jenna Jordan had a constant need for male attention.

Jenna came in first, her long blond hair windblown and messy, her eyes sleepy and filled with a certain smugness.

Dusty followed her in, looking innocent as hell and twice as sexy—and he stopped cold when he noticed the look in Tori's eyes.

"Tanner, would you take Jenna home, please?" The green eyes never left her face as he spoke quietly to his brother.

"Sure." Tanner was already out of his chair and grabbing his jacket. "Let's go," he urged Jenna.

Jenna leaned toward Dusty and placed a hand on his arm. "I had a real nice time today, Dusty...especially when we had to wait out the bad weather." She yawned. "Now I can go home and sleep like a baby."

"Let's *go*." Tanner took Jenna firmly by the arm and steered her out the door.

Dusty still hadn't taken his eyes off Tori. "Where's Dakota?"

"At home asleep. Eleni's granddaughter is watching her."

He sighed gently. "How was your flight today? Have any trouble?"

"My flight was fine. What about *yours?*" she asked pointedly.

"It was okay. That rainstorm delayed the trip home for a couple hours."

"So Jenna said."

His eyes were fastened on hers. "She stowed away on the plane. I was stuck with her."

"Poor thing," she said sarcastically.

"You bet."

"Zach was over here looking for Jenna. And for you."

He looked uneasy. "Is that why you're . . . ?"

"What?" she asked sharply when he let his question dwindle into thin air.

"I don't know," he said slowly. "Why you're mad, I guess."

"I'm not mad. But don't you think it's a little weird to take another man's wife off on some joyride—especially when that man's looking for some reason to slit your throat? And I don't mean that strictly in the figurative sense, either."

"I wasn't out joyriding," he denied, his temper rising.

"Then what do you call it? Out with some man-hunting female doing God knows what—" She broke off in horror, realizing what that must sound like to him, but she couldn't snatch back the words. It was too late for that.

Dusty was looking at her, an odd, flat light in the dark green depths of his eyes . . . and then the light started to glow.

And then burn.

"You think that Jenna and I . . . ?"

Tori turned abruptly away from him. "No, of course not." She fingered some papers on the desk, and discovered her hands were shaking.

"But you did think it."

"No."

He was already turning her around, forcing her to look at him. And when he spoke, his voice was gentle and disbelieving. "You mean you actually thought that I could get turned on by that...that...bubble-headed little snit?"

"She's...very pretty," Tori said lamely, and he grinned.

"And you're not?" He laughed and angled his body closer to hers. "But I can see I haven't convinced you. So maybe I should just prove to you that my latent desires haven't been slaked." Dusty shoved his fingers up through her hair and cupped her head in his hands, his fingertips firm against her scalp, his thumbs meeting beneath her chin.

And then he kissed her, his mouth on hers as intimate as any physical act. His tongue thrust deep in her mouth...tasting...taunting...and exploring...and was as hot and hungry and erotic as any thrust of his male flesh.

Tori struggled to pull free from her mind all the cold, hard reasons that she couldn't love him anymore, why she couldn't simply let him lock out the rest of the world with his hard body and strong arms and gentle heart.

But she was failing miserably.

She could only think of how good it felt to hold him . . . to feel the pure sexual power of him . . . .

He smelled like rain and leather and sweat and fuel, and she pressed close to him. Yet even while her body invited greater intimacies, yearned for them, a small, insistent inner voice urged caution.

She was about to tell her inner voice to take a hike, when the kiss ended, finally, and she was staring into his eyes wordlessly.

"I brought you a present." His hand dug into the pocket of his leather jacket and he handed her something wrapped in white tissue paper. She could still hear his deep, ragged breathing, and feel his aroused body against her own.

The gift was a pair of jade earrings.

"I bought them as a peace offering, for my having been too bullheaded to take no for an answer." His voice was low, his eyes a hot, burning green, vivid with emotion and the struggle for self-restraint. "But now I guess it's simply a gift."

"Thank you," she said when she found her voice.

He stepped back, away from her. "Would you be willing to have dinner with me?"

"Oh...Dakota—"

"Couldn't Eleni's granddaughter baby-sit long enough for us to get something to eat?"

Tori hesitated, then nodded. "All right. We can stop by the cabin on the way to Mooseheart and ask her."

Dusty watched as Suzi fussed over Tori, making sure her baked salmon was the way she liked it, making sure she had enough sour cream on her baked potato. He realized it had been a long time since Tori had been in here for dinner, and Suzi had always been genuinely fond of his wife.

He was relieved when Suzi finally left them alone. "She misses you," he commented. "I don't think she believes anybody in Nome can survive without her personally feeding them.''

Tori smiled. "I've missed her, too."

He reached for the basket of deep-fried hush puppies. That was a big admission on her part; to miss someone meant you cared, meant you needed them in your life—and Tori needed no one.

Or so she kept telling him this past year.

"How did you like flying again?" he asked her, breaking a hush puppy in half and spreading it with butter.

"It was wonderful," she said slowly, her golden-brown eyes lifting to meet his.

"And you didn't expect it to be?"

"I didn't say that."

"No, but I know how hard it is to accept the fact that flying can get into your blood and your heart and your soul."

"Spoken like a true bush pilot."

He laughed. "I remember my grandfather telling me about the time when he couldn't fly anymore because of his heart condition. I was...I don't know, maybe five or six . . . and he said his life's blood was up in the sky, tangled within the clouds. I didn't know what he meant until I soloed for the first time."

"I wish I could have met your grandfather."

He smiled at her wistful tone. "Pop was a great guy. An original. He was right up there with Eielson in the early 1920s flying those old Jennies that would only cruise at 85 MPH, and only had enough fuel for a four-hour flight." Dusty shook his head. "Can you imagine having to haul cans of fuel and land halfway between stops, pour in fuel and then take off again? There were no fields to land in, and no floats on the planes, so you couldn't land on water." He shook his head again and reached for his cup of black coffee. "Those were the days of the true bush pilots."

"And I bet you just hate missing those glory days."

There was something in her eyes he didn't understand. "Alaska wasn't equipped for airplanes back then," he said.

"And you think it's easy these days?"

"It's not easy, but we have better, faster planes, better safety regulations and we can land on the water. And most pilots aren't like the freewheeling ones in Pop's day."

"And none of that matters when it comes to weather conditions."

"It's better than it used to be. Pop was always talking about how he'd take off sometimes in an open-cockpit biplane and didn't know if his engine would stay warm enough to run."

Tori was silent. After a moment, she asked, "Who's this Eielson you mentioned?"

"Carl Eielson—he was the leader of the pack. After World War I, there was a surplus of Curtiss Jennies, available to anyone for six hundred bucks. And a lot of these planes found their way into Alaska. Eielson took off from Fairbanks in July 1923. And the rest is history."

Tori nodded. "I seem to remember your telling me all this on our first date. But I'd forgotten the name of the pilot."

"I talked about an old bush pilot on our first date?"

"You sure did."

"I must have been crazy."

"I thought you were."

Dusty grinned. They were actually talking in a civilized manner, which had been his intention tonight. To start over with her. To touch on something that had nothing to do with a dead child. Or a dead marriage.

"Those first bush pilots had to make regular runs between the four main cities in the early 1920s—Nome, Fairbanks, Juneau and Anchorage—and they had to do it in those Jennies, year-round, in order to make a living."

"Just like you do." There was something very even in her tone. "To get food and medicine and mail to the people."

"Yeah. I guess." He frowned slightly at the almost sad look in her eyes.

"And now we have tourists to haul out to the bush for their vacations in the wilds," she said.

"That's how my dad built up this air service," he said quietly. "In addition to delivering the necessities of life to all the small, remote villages as well as to the larger, more populated ones, we can appeal to the average businessman who dreams of a rugged, wilderness vacation. Air services have expanded a lot over the years. And it was my dad's dream to keep ours growing and thriving."

"Your father died for his dream."

Dusty grew still. "No, he didn't, baby. He *lived* for it. He lived for flying every day of his life."

Tori was suddenly intent on finishing her dinner, and Dusty watched her for a moment. His father had been dead for ten years. He had crashed in the Endicott Mountains shortly after Dusty's twenty-first birthday— and died instantly.

He'd been fifty-eight years old.

He'd left behind three motherless kids: sixteen-year-old Skylar, eighteen-year-old Tanner, and Dusty—who became the head of the family and his sister's legal guardian.

He'd also left behind a stable air service business that was the McKay family's only source of income.

Dusty shook his head slightly as he thought back to those first years without his dad. Keeping tabs on Tanner and Skylar had not been easy, with both of them being pilots—and teenagers—but somehow they'd made it through.

And except for Tanner's being framed for a murder he didn't commit and sent to prison, he thought they'd survived quite well. But it had been hard at times. And Tori's faith that he could handle the job without alienating his brother and sister completely was the one thing that had helped him the most.

Why didn't she have that kind of faith in him now? he wondered.

And why didn't she have that same kind of faith in herself?

A sudden thought struck him. "Tori, are you afraid to fly? Is that why you're always reluctant to go up anymore?" He'd never thought about that possibility.

But she seemed surprised at the question. "No, I'm not afraid." She picked up her second cup of hot tea and sipped it gingerly. "Why did you ask that?"

"I don't know."

If it wasn't fear of flying, then what was it? Fear of living? Fear of love? Of change?

None of those sounded like Tori. He had married a woman who was fearless and resourceful—no matter what turmoil was around her. She thrived on change and adventure and excitement. She lived life fast and hard and enjoyed every moment of it.

As for her fear of love, well, that was plain crazy, he decided. He didn't care what she'd told him last night. There had to be more to this. But what?

He dropped his head in his hands and massaged his temples. He was bone-tired, but it wasn't a physical weariness; it was an emotional one brought on by too many unanswered questions and too many nights sleeping alone.

"Dusty? Are you all right?"

He looked up and after a moment reached again for his cup of coffee. "Yeah." He drained it quickly and then set it down. Seeing that they were through with their meal, he picked up the check and walked over to the counter to pay Suzi.

He had wanted a pleasant evening with Tori, but they couldn't seem to get past all the differences that stretched between them, differences that were rapidly becoming a deep chasm of hurt and resentment, with questions unanswered and feelings unexplored.

Out on the street, Dusty reached out to take her hand and she let him hold it as they walked. They were both silent, but it wasn't uncomfortable. *Or* companionable.

It was just silence.

"What about a walk along the beach?" he suggested and she turned her head to look at him.

"Dusty..."

"I'm not trying to get you into a romantic mood," he quickly reassured her. "I just want to take a walk with you." And when she continued to look at him uncertainly, "Damn it, Tori, you and I had a lot more in our relationship besides sex."

Her grin was sudden. "I thought you'd forgotten that."

"Well, I haven't," he growled, and led her toward the beach.

They walked along the windswept and wave-battered beach with some semblance of ease and contentment between them, if only for a little while, and his fingers tightened around her hand.

"You know what I was thinking about today?" he asked.

"What?"

"About the first time I brought you out here during freeze-up."

She shivered, her expression rueful. "I'd never heard anything like it in my life." Then she shrugged. "Now I don't even notice."

"That's because you're a true Alaskan now."

"I should hope so," she retorted. "I've lived through eleven years of seven-month winters, forty-below temperatures, winter days with only four hours of twilight and found out that cabin fever was no joke."

He laughed. "Yeah, but think of the summer days with twenty hours of daylight..."

"That's only in June and July."

"...and temperatures in the eighties—"

"Only for an hour or two," she interrupted. "Mostly it's fifty-degree temperatures. Sixty if we're lucky."

"What about the bright blue sky and fluffy white clouds?"

"And bright sun that makes a pair of sunglasses an extremely valuable possession," she said wryly.

"You're looking at it all wrong. We have the sun to dry us off on those countless days when we're soaking wet from the rain, and to guide us through the thick fog that appears out of nowhere."

Tori was laughing. "You don't have to convince me of Alaska's virtues or disadvantages. I've lived here long enough to know them all."

Dusty looked out across the water. It was still light, even at nine-thirty at night. In May they had about seventeen or eighteen hours of daylight, and the sun hovered over the horizon, not even close to setting.

"Is that why you want to leave, Tori? Because you're sick of this place?" The question escaped before he realized it.

"I guess I'm just tired of fighting the elements."

"The elements? Or me?"

The brown eyes lifted to meet his. "What exactly does that mean?"

"It means that I don't believe you. You love it here, you always have," he added quickly. "And you love flying. And the people. And yeah, even the weather. The weather's a challenge, and you've always loved a challenge." He shrugged, not taking his eyes off her. "At least you used to."

"Did you bring me out here just to fight with me?"

"No. I guess...I guess I hoped we could talk about it."

"It?"

"This...wall you've built up between us—" He broke off when she turned away and wandered down the beach, restlessly, nervously. He hesitated then followed her. "Like the one you're putting between us now." He caught up with her and swung her around to face him.

And he was startled to see the tears streaming down both cheeks. She didn't resist as he drew her into his arms, and then she was holding him, pressing into him, kissing him, and his hand moved under her open jacket to cup her breast, his fingers shaping and reshaping her through the denim shirt, her nipple going rigid in his hand.

Then she was trying to pull away from him, shaking her head, the wind whipping her red-gold hair out behind her, and Dusty's control started to slip. She was between him and the sun, and it lit up her hair and skin. His fingers itched to explore every inch of her. His body ached to feel her respond to him just once more.

Then maybe he could let her go.

Maybe.

His hands came up to rest on her shoulders, his fingers digging into the jacket, soothing her, calming her—but it wasn't working.

She looked terrified.

Of him?

His grip eased, although he didn't let go of her. He couldn't. Not yet. Dusty was afraid if he released her now, she'd take off running down the beach, and he couldn't bear the thought of her out here alone and scared.

"Why are you making this so damned hard?" he asked softly, and then became aware of the solid bulge pushing against the zipper of his worn jeans...pushing against her lean, tight body...seeking her warmth and comfort...searching for the kind of heat and release that only she could give him, and Dusty almost laughed. "Why are you making this so difficult?" he repeated, rephrasing the question so he wouldn't appear crude or insensitive.

"Just let me go, Dusty."

"I can't."

"Can't? Or won't?"

"Both."

"Let go of me! Let me go back to the cabin . . . let me go back to Arizona—damn it, *just let me go!*"

"No!" He took a deep, ragged breath and let it out in a rush. "No. Not until you tell me what it's going to take to make it work with us again. Not until you tell me what you want me to do to get you back."

Her brown eyes stared endlessly into his as the silence stretched between them. *I want you to come with me,* the voice inside her head screamed. Her voice. The voice of unreason.

The voice of fear.

I want you to move to Arizona with me . . . I want you to give up the air service . . . to give up flying. . . .

I want you to give up everything for me.

Then maybe I'll feel safe.

But she couldn't say that to him. It wouldn't be fair. So she said the next thought that came to mind. "I've lost everything in this godforsaken place." She said it quietly, just for him, the words wrenched from the depths of her pain and grief.

Dusty released her, only to brush his knuckles gently across her cheek, his eyes searching hers. "You haven't lost me," he said gently. And then, "Tori, Shawn didn't die because we live in Alaska."

"Stop it. I don't want to hear this."

"He died of sudden infant death syndrome. Crib death." Dusty's voice was low. "It would have happened anywhere."

"You don't understand."

"Then make me understand. Talk to me. Open up to me about what you're feeling right now, right this minute—"

She shook her head slightly, her eyes avoiding his. "I . . . I need a steady, dependable life. . . ."

"We have that. Or at least we did, until you decided to give up on us."

"Alaska is not a safe place to live—"

"Alaska is not your enemy, Tori. It's a place, like any other place, with good things and bad," he said wearily.

"I can't stay here, Dusty. I can't," she stated softly, and started down the beach in the direction of the cabin.

And he followed slowly after her.

Chapter 8

Tori restlessly circled the living room, like a caged animal. Dakota was asleep and the cabin was too quiet. And felt too empty. Tonight she had wanted to ask Dusty to choose between her and being a bush pilot in Alaska.

And she'd almost said it. She'd almost played the part of selfish, demanding, unreasonable wife.

But what was wrong with wanting safety and security? They'd been pushing against the odds long enough—that's why Shawn had died.

They'd been wrapped up in loving each other, blindly going about their lives without a thought to the dangers, to the instability of the Fates, simply being happy and in love and trusting things would work out for them.

But things hadn't worked out.

They'd conceived a child from love...and then watched him die.

It wasn't the natural order of things for parents to lose a child. They weren't supposed to outlive their children.

So she wasn't taking any more chances with the natural order of things. She loved Dusty. God help her, she did love him. With all her heart.

But being in love, and being safe and happy, didn't seem to mesh all that well. So she had to guard against it, protect herself from the pain as much as possible.

And that meant a normal life.

Certainly not a life up here in the wilds of coastal Alaska, with Dusty out there flying every day, risking his life and their happiness.

And for what? Because McKay Air Service was his dad's business? Because Dusty was a third-generation bush pilot and therefore bound by tradition?

She circled the room again. But there was more to it than that. Dusty loved to fly. It was part of him, part of who he was, an important part of Dusty's framework—his value system, his strengths...and his weaknesses, too.

She had fallen in love with flying and with Alaska because of Dusty. Seeing this state through his eyes was definitely an experience. And there was no way she could separate Dusty from this place, even in her mind.

Did she really think she could ask him to give up Alaska? To give up flying? To give up his life for her?

The next time she circled the living room, she dropped down on the couch and buried her face in her hands. But it was the only way she could have him. Away from here.

Away from the treacherous mountains and the deep, ice-encrusted sea. Away from the unexpected rainstorms and howling wind that raced down from the mountains and made visibility next to impossible.

Why couldn't Dusty see how dangerous this place was? she wondered. But all he could see was the vast sprawling beauty of the land—the three great mountain ranges, the rugged canyons, broad treeless valleys, the rolling hills and crystal-clear lakes and ice blue glaciers, the waterfalls and the deep-shadowed rain forests.

Tori leaned back and looked around the cabin. Her parents thought the cabin was shabby, and that Nome was a rowdy, disreputable place to live. But she had always liked it here and she loved the cabin. It had a rustic charm, an easy feeling, as if a great deal of living had taken place inside its rooms.

Dusty had spent most of his life in this cabin. His father had built it when Tanner was a baby, when the smaller, two-bedroom cabin was too confining for a growing family.

And after she and Dusty were married, Tori had turned it into hers, the first home of her own she'd ever had. The first one she'd ever been able to be herself in.

That was one of the great things about living in Alaska, she thought reluctantly. There weren't any rules. Not the conventional, stifling, choking rules she'd been forced to grow up with. In Alaska you were free to be creative and inventive and resourceful. In fact, it was expected of you.

Tori jumped up, blocking off those feelings. She didn't want to be inventive and resourceful anymore.

She wanted to be safe.

She headed down the hall toward her bedroom, and stopped in Dakota's room to check on her. The baby was whimpering softly, and Tori bent over the crib, one hand gently stroking the child's cheek so Dakota would know she was there.

The dark eyes opened and Dakota gazed sleepily up at her. Then the little girl slowly smiled and lifted her arms. "Mama," she said happily. "Mama..."

Tori picked her up and held her, choking back the tears as Dakota stared at her in confusion, and then started to whimper uncertainly.

Tori understood the baby's confusion and sense of loss.

She felt that way herself.

Dusty prowled around his bedroom. He didn't understand Tori at all. What did she want from him?

He'd been on shaky ground with her for months, but he hadn't expected her to leave him . . . not like this.

He paused by a window and looked out. The lights were still on next door, and for a brief moment he toyed with the idea of going over there, just to check up on Tori and Dakota. But then he quickly dismissed it as impractical. They'd only get into another fight, and he was sick of fighting with her.

He needed to take action, but what kind? What was he supposed to do now? What *could* he do?

His eyes swept the surrounding area: the hangar where the Curtiss Jenny was kept . . . the tiny office that was little more than a shack . . . the large three-bedroom cabin his dad had built and where he and Tanner and Skylar and Matt had grown to maturity . . . the small two-room cabin that his grandfather had built for his grandmother and finished the morning of their wedding . . . and the one he was living in now, with Tanner. His life was all wrapped up in these buildings, in this parcel of land by the sea.

He pushed impatiently away from the window and whirled around to stare unseeingly at the far wall. Sometimes he thought he understood. Tori was an only child, and she'd never been close to her parents. When she arrived in Fairbanks to attend the university there, Tori had been rather reserved, but equally determined to make her own way through life. And on her own terms.

She'd been afraid to trust him at first, afraid to believe in his love for her. But gradually, over a period of time, he'd managed to convince her his feelings were real and deep and lasting.

But she'd held off marrying him because she wanted to make certain he was ready for that kind of commitment. Dusty knew she'd been afraid of love, of any deep, emotional involvement, and maybe she'd been right.

Losing Shawn had devastated her.

He sighed and shook his head. She wouldn't listen to him, she wouldn't trust him that things would get better if she gave it a chance.

If she gave *him* a chance.

A soft knock on his door made him turn around. "Yeah?"

The door opened and Tanner wandered in, wearing only a pair of jeans and yawning. "I thought I heard you up and about. What's wrong?"

Dusty looked at him. "The usual stuff." He grabbed his jacket and headed out of the room. "I'm going for a walk. Maybe it'll clear my head."

But he doubted it. Outside it was still light, the air crisp, and he headed over to the office and unlocked the door, his hand reaching for the light switch. Maybe he should just do some paperwork since he couldn't sleep.

Dusty was stunned silent. The office had been ransacked—one filing cabinet had been overturned, the drawers turned upside down, spilling files all over the floor, the desk swept clean of papers and several chairs turned on their sides with the cushions slashed.

He took several cautious steps into the room, and then knelt down to retrieve the leather-bound logbook. Every flight had to be logged in, every passenger's destination, along with the date to retrieve them from the bush, had to be recorded. The last several pages were missing, and Dusty glanced helplessly around the room. He had three separate parties that had to be picked up this week at the Gates of the Arctic—a pair of honeymooners in Kobuk Valley, the bird-watchers on the island of St. Paul and four men at the Wood-Tikchik State Park—only he didn't have the exact dates for retrieval in his head.

And he didn't have the slightest idea who had to be picked up next week, or the following one...or even where they were!

All he knew was they'd all be stranded out there if he didn't get those missing pages back.

"How'd they get in here?" Tanner wanted to know the next morning as they tried to make some order out of the mess in the office. "The door was locked."

"They broke the lock on the window. Used a crowbar, it looks like."

"I'd like to use a crowbar on somebody."

"Hey—" Dusty slammed a file drawer shut and whirled on his brother. "You stay away from Jordan."

"Dusty..."

"I mean it, Tanner. You go anywhere near Zach and I swear I'll knock you cold myself. Is that clear?"

The gray eyes registered shock, and Dusty pushed away from the file cabinet to set a chair upright. He stared down at the slashed cushion and started to swear under his breath. And out of the corner of his eye he saw Tanner watching him uncertainly.

"What are we going to do?" Tanner asked him quietly, and Dusty shook his head and sank onto the chair.

"I don't know. Not once have we failed to pick up someone. Maybe not right on schedule because of bad weather or mechanical problems, but we've never flat-out actually *lost* them before!'' He flared up out of the chair and headed for the door.

''Where are you going?''

''To see Caleb.''

Tanner followed him outside. ''It won't do any good. He's Zach's brother.''

''Caleb's a cop, isn't he? It's his job to listen to irate citizens.''

Several blocks down the street, Dusty pushed open the door to the police station and walked over to the front desk. Several police officers were standing around the coffee machine, Caleb Jordan among them. When he saw Dusty, he walked toward him.

''Want some coffee?'' Caleb asked.

''No thanks. What I want is for you to do something about Zach.''

Caleb regarded him silently for a long moment, his blue eyes thoughtful, then gestured toward the hallway. ''Let's find an empty office so we can talk more privately,'' he calmly suggested.

When the door closed behind them, Dusty turned around. ''I want you to go to Zach's house and get back the missing pages from my logbook. If he still has them, I won't press charges for breaking and entering. But if they've been destroyed, I want him arrested.''

Caleb passed him and took a seat behind the desk, setting his cup of coffee down on the solid surface. ''Someone broke into your office?''

''You might say that.''

''And you think it was Zach.''

''I know it was.''

Caleb leaned back in his chair, his eyes searching Dusty's face. ''What's this about your logbook?''

"They took my logbook and ripped out the last several pages." He watched the grim expression enter and linger in Caleb's deep blue eyes.

"Is that all that's missing?"

"That's it."

"So you have tourists scattered all over northwest Alaska, and you have no way of knowing the exact time or place you're scheduled to pick them up."

"You got it," Dusty said grimly.

"I'll see what I can do."

"While you're at it, you can deliver a message for me. You can tell Zach that Tanner's part of this community and he's going to stay part of it. So he'd better adjust to it, and he'd better adjust fast, or I'm going to personally see that he does."

"Is that a threat?"

"You can count on it."

"You're treading on thin ice, Dusty."

"Then keep your brother in line." He whirled and headed for the door, only to pause, his hand on the doorknob, when Caleb spoke again.

"You and I used to be friends—close friends."

Dusty sighed, half turning to face him. "That was a long time ago."

"You were the first friend I had in Alaska." Caleb's voice was quiet. "You and Matt. And I didn't even know Matt had been killed until I heard it through the town grapevine."

Dusty leaned against the closed door. "I'm sorry. I should have told you myself."

Caleb looked at him as if he were about to say something, but didn't know exactly how to phrase it. Finally, he stated flatly, "I don't like what's been happening between our two families. The heat's been turned up to an uncomfortable degree since Tanner got home. And you and I have to find a way to cool it down. Before somebody gets hurt.''

''Then keep Zach on a leash.''

''Dusty—''

''Tanner spent five years in prison. So why can't Zach just back off and leave him alone?''

''Because our kid brother's dead.''

''Nothing will change that, Caleb. Nothing's going to bring Kyle back.''

The blue eyes were bleak. ''Zach and Kyle were close. Too close, I guess. When Kyle died, I guess something snapped inside of Zach. He's changed, Dusty. And he's bitter. He's not the same guy he used to be.'' Caleb sighed and stood up, walking around the desk to face Dusty. ''And he's convinced of Tanner's guilt. Sometimes I think it would be better if Tanner moved away and built a new life for himself somewhere else. This town's too small for the two of them.''

''Then Zach's free to leave. But Tanner's staying here. Get used to it.''

Dusty slammed out of the office and out into the street, debating whether or not he should confront Zach Jordan personally, or give Caleb time to get those missing pages back. He was growing tired of playing by the rules, of controlling his temper, and he wanted the pure satisfaction of slamming his fist into Zach Jordan's face.

''You certainly look mad enough to murder somebody this morning,'' a familiar voice said pleasantly, startling Dusty, and he whirled around.

''Don't you know enough not to sneak up on me?'' he growled at his former college roommate who merely grinned at him.

"I spoke to you twice. You didn't hear me," Joey Arnett replied.

Dusty's grin was slow, grudging. "Sorry. It's been a rough morning."

"What's new in the McKay-Jordan feud?" he asked lightly.

"Someone broke into my office last night and tore out the last several pages of my logbook."

That statement was greeted with a long, low whistle. And then, "Did you report it?"

"I talked to Caleb about it."

"And?"

Dusty shrugged. "And he's going to try to get the missing pages away from Zach."

Joey stood there a moment, his dark eyes narrowing. "Something has to be done about that guy. He's over the top."

Tori opened the door of the office and abruptly halted, her eyes taking in the disheveled room at a glance. "Did we have a hurricane in here?"

"Yeah. Compliments of Zach Jordan." Tanner looked up from the desk, and she read the sheer fury in his gray eyes.

"He did this? But why?"

"I'll give you three guesses—and two don't count."

"Tanner—"

"That's right. And I've had it. I'm outta here."

She suddenly realized he was packing his duffel bag, throwing his Walkman and several of his cassette tapes in on top of what looked to be a pair of his jeans.

"You can't leave."

"Why the hell not?"

"Because it would break Dusty's heart." She watched him in growing horror, recognizing that determined glint in his eyes.

"Why should you care about Dusty's heart? You didn't think about that when you announced you were leaving."

"That's different." She realized Tanner was angry and frustrated, but it still hurt to have him talk this way to her. "You're letting Zach drive you away from your home and your family."

He gave the zipper on his duffel bag a jerk to close it, and set the bag on the floor near the desk. "Things are only going to get worse. Dusty just about split a gut building up this air service and making it pay its own way. Now he's losing money like crazy and it's because of me—"

"Tanner, you can't do this. You just can't. Where will you go? What will you do?"

"It doesn't matter."

"It matters to me."

His grin was unwilling. "I didn't think the McKay brothers were your favorite people these days," he said slowly.

Tears stung her eyes. "You know that's not true."

"No. I don't know that. And I don't think Dusty knows it, either."

Tori was practically beside herself with frustration. She wanted to grab hold of him, to keep him from leaving before Dusty could talk to him. "Does Dusty know what you're planning to do?"

He shrugged. "He knows how I feel."

"You mean you've mentioned leaving to him before?"

"Yeah. Several times."

Tori grew still. "I...I didn't know that." No wonder Dusty had been so rattled lately. "Tanner...Tanner, listen to me." She was kneeling beside his chair, her hands clutching his arm. "No one was hurt. The office can be cleaned up."

"That's not the point. As long as I'm in town, Zach's going to make my life a living hell...and Dusty's... and yours and Dakota's."

"But this is your home," she protested. "You were born and raised here. You can't let them take it away from you. You have to fight back. And we'll be okay, no matter what happens. But I won't have you taking off like this."

"She's right, Tanner."

They were both startled when they heard Dusty's voice. He was standing in the doorway, and Tori hastily got to her feet. "I...I was just trying to—"

"I know what you were trying to do." The forest green eyes landed on hers for an instant, before sliding over to Tanner. "It's the same thing I've been trying to do for weeks—talk some sense into him."

"This place is going under fast," Tanner said hotly. "And after last night, we're going to lose our shirts. Those people won't ever do business with this air service again. Not only that, they'll tell everybody they meet how we screwed up."

Tori was confused. "I don't understand."

"Zach tore out the last several pages in the logbook."

"Oh, my God..." Tori couldn't believe this. She glanced at Dusty for verification and he nodded. "That's a terrible thing, I admit, and it sounds like something he'd do, but I don't see how that could ruin us," she said.

"Tori, without those pages, we don't know when or where to pick up anybody," Dusty said patiently.

Tori looked at him for a full moment. "I keep a duplicate logbook in my desk in the cabin." As they both stared at her blankly, she felt she should defend herself. "I've been telling you guys for years we shouldn't have to depend on just one logbook, in case of fire or something." As they kept staring at her, she added, "I told you I was doing this weeks ago. Doesn't anyone around here ever listen?"

All of a sudden, Dusty was hauling her into his arms, laughing and hugging her, and she was struck by the sheer relief she saw on his tired face.

And she suddenly felt like bursting into tears.

Chapter 9

"Dusty?"

"What?" He kept his green eyes fastened on the front door, waiting, watching, and Tori gave a soft sigh of resignation. Part of him was begging someone to start something, and she only hoped and prayed that Zach had the good sense not to show up at Mooseheart tonight.

"Let's go," she said.

He shook his head. "Not yet."

"I have to get home to Dakota."

"I didn't ask you to stay."

No, he hadn't asked her. But she'd felt compelled to stay here with him, disliking his mood, and hating the grim tension in his eyes. Tanner had left earlier, obviously wanting them to spend some time alone together, but she doubted this was what her brother-in-law had had in mind for the two of them.

Dusty sat at a corner table, a glass of whiskey in front

of him. He sipped at his drink, silent, watchful, his attention never straying far from the barroom door, making a careful mental note of who came in and who left.

And his edgy, nervous behavior was making her decidedly uneasy.

"Dusty, you shouldn't be drinking."

"The only flight we have scheduled is one tomorrow afternoon. Tanner's taking that one."

She watched him as he took yet another wooden match out of the small box on the table and struck it. The flare of the match lit Dusty's face. He looked wary and a little brutal in the flickering light.

"Dusty..." But what could she say to him? This was a side to him she'd never seen before.

But that wasn't entirely true, she thought as a memory hit her. At Tanner's trial, when they'd found his younger brother guilty of involuntary manslaughter, he'd been like this for days afterward.

But she'd been able to reach him then, she'd been able to hold him and comfort him, and he'd opened up to her.

But he was locked away from her now, and she realized she was the one who'd locked him up tight inside that emotional prison he was in.

Could she unlock it?

Should she even try?

He smelled of whiskey and wooden matches and warm male flesh, and the scent was arousing...stirring....

She reached across the table and touched his arm, trying to drag his attention away from the door, but he didn't respond. She glanced briefly at Dusty's impassive features.

"Dusty, tell me what you're feeling."

He blew out the match and tossed it on the pile with the others that littered the table. "I don't feel a thing." He looked at her, and she saw fury and something else—something darker. "Not a thing."

"You've had too much to drink."

He shook his head. "I haven't even started."

She came halfway out of her chair. "I'm going to go find Tanner—" His hand on her arm stopped her.

"What's the matter, baby? I'm too much for you to handle alone?"

"You're not used to drinking," she reminded him. The only time she'd ever seen him drunk was the night they took Tanner off to prison. "And I'm not used to seeing you like this."

"Like what?" Once again his eyes strayed to the door.

She was exasperated. "Dusty..." Was he drunk? She didn't think so. His glass was nearly full. Tori leaned forward, trying to get a better look at him, and finally decided he wasn't drunk on whiskey, he was drunk on rage—sheer, pent-up, thundering, lethal rage.

Someone was trying to destroy what he'd built with years of hard work.

Someone was trying to destroy his family.

His anger was sheathed at the moment, but not for long. If Zach came through that door, there was no telling what Dusty would do. She had to get him out of here.

"Let's go back to the cabin and I'll fix you some dinner," she offered and he turned his head slowly to look at her.

"You must really think I'm in danger of making a fool of myself tonight."

"You can't afford any more trouble."

His green eyes fastened on hers. "If I go home with you, will you let me stay the night?"

She lowered her gaze. "I offered dinner. Nothing else."

"Then I'm not interested."

"You're a piece of work, do you know that?" Tori came out of her chair, her hands pulling him up. "A hot meal and giving Dakota her bath will make you feel one hundred percent better, so move. *Move!*"

A full minute ticked by as he gazed down at her, and then he grinned, slowly, and she felt his hard resistance melting by slow degrees. She guided him toward the door, paid Suzi for their drinks, then pushed him outside.

"This is the no-nonsense lady I used to know and still love," he said as the door closed behind them.

"Shut up."

They were almost to the cabin when he asked, "Why are you so angry with me?"

"I'm not angry. But you're a grown man, supposedly of sound mind, yet you insist on doing everything humanly possible to get your stubborn head battered and that gorgeous body beaten up."

"I'm only protecting what's mine."

"That's your problem. You always think it's your job to protect Tanner and Skylar and me and McKay Air Service, but it isn't."

"Then exactly what is my job?"

"Well, it isn't taking responsibility for the whole damn world!" she shouted.

"I'm not. I'm only taking responsibility for my own small part of it."

She glared at him. "What were you going to do back there? What were you trying to prove? That you're bigger and tougher and dumber than Zach Jordan? You want to prove to the entire town of Nome that *both* the McKay boys have outrageous tempers and aren't afraid to use their fists when the going gets tough? That's exactly how Tanner got sent to prison, remember?" she railed over his protests. "If he hadn't punched out Kyle in Mooseheart that night, if he hadn't threatened to kill him, then they wouldn't have come looking for evidence—and they wouldn't have found that baseball bat."

"That bat was planted in Tanner's plane," Dusty growled.

"I know that, damn it. But there would have been no reason to look for it if Tanner hadn't stirred things up in Mooseheart. You guys can't stop playing macho men long enough to see the danger here. The real danger," she repeated, hitting each of the last three words hard and fierce.

His steps slowed. "The real danger is losing McKay Air Service. Or worse, having Tanner take off so I won't lose it."

Tori shook her head impatiently, wanting to strangle him. "No, the real danger is the man who beat Kyle Jordan to death." Dusty had stopped walking now and was staring at her. "He's out there, Dusty, getting away with murder, getting away with ruining Tanner's life—and probably sitting around somewhere laughing at all of us, at the Jordans and the McKays, watching us suffer, watching us tear one another apart when we used to be more than just neighbors. We were friends."

"But Tori—"

"It's in this person's best interest to keep the heat on Tanner, to keep the feud going." She stood looking at him. "Apparently, no one cares who actually did murder Kyle or why. Everyone's too wrapped up in trying to run Tanner out of town, or McKay Air Service out of business. This guy has a strong motive, Dusty," she said quickly, without giving him a chance to agree with her or not. "And you're playing straight into his hands by continuing the feud."

"Zach's the one—"

"You do your part to keep it going!" she snapped.

He stared at her, started to say something, thought better of it and walked a few feet away, only to turn around and throw up his arms in a gesture of helplessness. "What am I supposed to do? Let Tanner leave?"

"No, of course not."

"Then what? Zach's trying to take everything away from me. Either I hand him Tanner on a silver platter or he's going to run us into the ground! And you're just as bad. Zach's trying to drive Tanner out of town, and you're trying to drive me out of your life!"

She turned in disgust and walked up the steps to the cabin.

"At least I know what's wrong with Zach. But you... you keep me at arm's length without even bothering to explain. We lost our son, Tori. But does that mean we have to lose each other, too? We have a second chance with Dakota—"

He'd been right behind her when she turned, and her hands had lifted automatically to keep a margin of distance between them, her fingers pressing into his leather jacket.

"Are you telling me all we have to do is replace Shawn with Dakota, and then everything will be like before?" she asked softly.

He shook his head. "No, of course not. But Dakota lost both her parents, and she needs us. And whether or not you're willing to admit it, we need her, too."

Tori's eyes filled with tears. "You can't substitute one baby for another."

"We're not substituting one child for another, damn it! But what's wrong with picking up the pieces and going on with our lives? What's so wrong with loving Dakota and raising her as our daughter? This is Matt's little girl, Tori, she's part of him—''

''I'm leaving Alaska,'' she broke in, her tone even, ''and there is nothing you can do to stop me.''

''Isn't there?'' he muttered, and his arms suddenly came up to brace against the solid oak door at her back, caging her to the spot.

''Dusty...'' Her voice trailed off as she gazed up at him, into those deep, clear, beautiful green eyes, and her fingers slowly tightened into two fists, gathering up the smooth, cold leather in her hands.

She felt as though she were drowning. It had always been like this with him—one touch of his hand, a certain look in his eyes, and she didn't have a chance.

His eyes showed the tension of desire—deep and longing and on the edge. They reached out to her, deep into hers, pulling her toward him, glinting with a fierce need and yet they softened with a sudden, nearly desperate yearning.

He missed her; she knew he did. Not just the sex, but the warmth, the closeness after making love, the ... connection.

She knew how he felt, because she felt the same way.

But it was that connection that scared all the life out of her.

Her hands pushed gently at him, but he didn't move. And she saw the eyes blazing a hard green light, briefly, a hurt gaze, just before it was quickly masked.

He stepped away from her. ''You offered to cook me dinner.''

She turned quickly and fumbled for her key. She got it into the lock and turned it, her hands trembling, and then she pushed open the front door.

They found Tanner in the kitchen shoveling strained peaches into Dakota's mouth, laughing and making faces at her. The baby was actually smiling back at him, sweet, slow, shy smiles, but she was smiling.

Tori was delighted. "She looks so happy."

"Why shouldn't she? She loves peaches." Another spoonful was nudged against Dakota's rosebud mouth, but the baby had stopped chewing and swallowing when she saw Dusty and Tori, and her black eyes lit up with pleasure. She made a chirping, baby sound as a greeting, and Tanner seized the moment to gently shove the spoonful of peaches into her open mouth. She looked surprised, then smacked her lips appreciatively, and they laughed.

"Where's Eleni?"

"She had to leave. I told her I'd take care of the kid."

"Looks like you're doing a good job," Dusty commented.

"Tanner, you gave her more than peaches for dinner, didn't you?"

"I gave her the peas and carrots and mashed potato that Eleni cooked. And she ate it all, every bit of it."

"She did?" Tori was impressed. "For that, how about if I fix dinner for both you guys?"

She saw Tanner glance at Dusty, hesitate, and then, as if reading his brother's mind, he accepted the invitation. She picked Dakota up, the baby's face, hands and clothes smeared with carrots and sticky with peaches, and handed her to Dusty. "You can make yourself useful by giving her a bath while I get dinner ready."

Tanner followed him out of the room, leaving her alone with her thoughts, and it was then that Tori gave in to the feelings that were rippling through her.

She buried her face in her hands and held back a groan. She was using Tanner as a wall to hide behind, a defensive tactic to keep from being alone with Dusty tonight.

And she was well aware that both men knew it.

"Tanner, who do you think killed Kyle?" Dusty asked as he sat in the rocking chair and gently dried Dakota's dark hair with a towel.

"I have no idea." Tanner had built a fire in the fireplace while Dusty was giving Dakota her bath, and now he sat down on the hearth.

"You were his best friend."

"Sometimes I feel like I didn't know him at all," Tanner said sadly.

Dusty glanced quickly at him, but the steel gray eyes were cool, remote. Tanner had the smoky eyes of a timber wolf, and the temperament to match. "Tori believes we're playing into the killer's hands."

"Do you think the person who killed Kyle is trying to drive McKay Air Service out of business?" Tanner asked him slowly.

Dusty shrugged. "Could be. No one investigated Kyle's death after you were charged, convicted and sent to prison. So we can only assume the killer is out there wandering around somewhere."

Tanner looked thoughtful as he stared into the flames, his expression tightening, shifting, as if scenes from long ago were playing inside his head.

Dusty knew without a doubt that Tanner was innocent. When Dusty had gone to visit him in jail, he'd asked him straight out if he'd killed Kyle. Tanner had denied it, quietly and with conviction, meeting Dusty's gaze squarely, and Dusty knew he was telling him the truth.

But Dusty was also aware that Tanner knew more about Kyle's death—or Kyle's life—than he was willing to admit.

"But why would the killer want to stir up trouble now?" Tanner asked.

"Suppose you tell me."

Tanner shrugged, and continued to stare into the fire. There was a palpable tension in him, the same tension that had penetrated every conversation they'd had these past five years. And Dusty was sick of his brother's evasive answers.

Prison had hammered out most of Tanner's personality and natural irascibility, leaving in its place a struggling life fighting for his right to reenter society. And Zach Jordan was doing everything possible to try to take that away from him.

With emotional gruffness Dusty stated flatly, "I wish you'd tell me what was going on back then."

Tanner turned suddenly to face him. "But why? It was a long time ago. It's over."

"And the guy who beat Kyle to death used *your* baseball bat to do it." He kept his voice low because of Dakota, but he leveled his dark green gaze on his brother's face. "Don't you want to find out who killed Kyle and get your name cleared?" When Tanner didn't answer, Dusty's gaze narrowed. "Or is it that you already know?"

"I don't know a damned thing." But he couldn't quite meet Dusty's eyes.

"You spent five years in prison for something you didn't do." Dusty's voice was gentle. "The person who killed Kyle knew both of you. He knew you loved baseball and kept the equipment in your plane. And he chose the bat with your initials carved into it, the bat Dad gave you for Christmas the year he died.''

''Dusty—''

''Someone set you up,'' Dusty added tautly. ''He broke into your plane, stole the bat and went after Kyle with malice and forethought.''

''Dusty, knock it off.'' Tanner's steel gray eyes landed on him. Eyes as hard and rigid as the structure beams for a skyscraper.

Dusty knew that look. But it didn't stop him. ''Does this have anything to do with Kelly?'' he asked, and Tanner looked away, a sudden, brutal pain entering the clear gray eyes. Dusty immediately regretted asking the question.

Kelly Jordan was Kyle's twin sister—and Tanner's former fiancée.

Kelly had broken their engagement during Tanner's trial, and moved to Juneau even before a verdict was reached. She hadn't been back to Nome since.

''I'll go and see if Tori needs any help.'' Tanner got to his feet and headed out to the kitchen.

Dusty's sigh was resigned. Kelly was a sore subject for Tanner, and one he never discussed. And Dusty felt guilty for bringing it up tonight, bringing up a painful memory for his brother.

He finished drying Dakota's hair, breathing in the scent of baby powder and baby shampoo, and set the towel to one side. Dakota looked at him with a solemn expression on her little face, as if she knew exactly what he was thinking, and he picked her up from his lap and hugged her.

She wrapped her arms around his neck and laid her cheek against his. Dusty liked the feel of her. The flannel sleeper she was wearing was soft and warm and dry, her slim toddler body was sturdy, and her gentle breathing soothing to him.

Dusty felt the healing had begun—for him, anyway.

Chapter 10

"How do you like that guy?" Dusty said as he dried the last dish and put it away. "He won't give an inch."

Tori wrung out the dishcloth and hung it across the faucet before she responded. "Tanner's a private kind of guy. Don't forget how long it took him to admit to his feelings for Kelly—even to himself. He insisted they were just friends for a long time."

"Kelly. You say her name like she was the love of Tanner's life," he accused.

"Maybe she was."

Dusty made a gesture of impatience. "Have you forgotten what she did? She sent her engagement ring back to him without a word of explanation—"

"I think Tanner's being on trial for her twin's death was explanation enough."

"But she didn't even have the common decency to face him. And she left town without hanging around long enough for the verdict."

"Dusty. . ." Her voice trailed off and she looked away from him.

"What? What did I say?" he demanded when she didn't respond.

"Nothing."

"I suppose you think I'm being too hard on Kelly."

She looked at him. "All I can remember is that day in the courtroom when Kelly burst into tears and rushed out of there," she told him softly.

"How can you stand there and defend her?"

"Because things aren't always black and white. Kelly's brother—her *twin* brother—was brutally beaten to death, and before they could even bury him, her fiancé. . . the guy she's been absolutely crazy about since she was a kid—was hauled off to jail. And her family was more than willing to believe the worst."

"Then you're saying it was okay for Kelly to take the coward's way out?"

"I didn't say that!" she said angrily. "I know she hurt him, but it must have been horrible for her to sit in court listening to the details of Kyle's death and the evidence piling up against Tanner. Can't you understand how hurt and scared and confused she must have been?"

"I thought she loved him," he muttered.

"I'm sure she did."

"Not enough."

Tori pushed herself away from the counter and shook her head. "You're impossible. You think being in love is simple, that love conquers all. But it doesn't. It doesn't always block the pain."

"It can if you let it. If you hold on and trust each other," he said. His low voice had turned gentle, and her brown eyes were suddenly bright with unshed tears.

"We were talking about Tanner...and...and Kelly," she said softly.

"And now we're talking about us. You and me. And what we've lost."

She shook her head, her eyes downcast. "Don't start with me. I'm not in the mood."

"But I am. I'm in the mood for a lot of things."

She moved away from him as if she needed to put essential space between them and began putting the place mats back on the table. Leaning against the sink, he watched her, the heels of his hands resting against the edge of the counter at hip level, and tried to decide what to do next.

The tension in her appeared to be vibrating at a new and higher frequency, so Dusty thought it wise not to pursue this personal conversation.

He wanted time with her, time to gain her trust, before he tried to talk to her again. And if he were to be perfectly honest with himself, talking wasn't what he had in mind, anyway. He kept remembering how it felt to hold her, and memories came crashing in on him—graphic, sensual, compelling memories.

He tried to picture his life without her. To picture this cabin without her. To picture his bed without her. And he couldn't do it.

He couldn't let her leave him.

She turned the lights out in the kitchen and headed for the living room, and he followed her. She turned on every lamp in the room, then settled herself on the couch as if she had forgotten he was there.

Only she hadn't. Her awareness of him was almost tactile. It screamed at him with every movement, the way she tucked her feet under her on the couch, the way she held her quilting hoop as a shield against him, the businesslike way her fingers moved as she added stitches to her quilt, the self-conscious, totally affected way she bent over her work.

The message was painfully clear. Hands off. Violators will be prosecuted to the full extent of the law.

Husbands will be hanged at dawn.

"I thought quilting was supposed to be relaxing," he observed.

Tori promptly stuck the needle into her finger and muttered something he couldn't quite hear. Sucking the pinpoint of blood that had beaded up on her index finger, she glared at him. "It's hard to relax when you... you... *stand there.*"

"Sorry." And then, "Do you mind if I add another log to the fire?"

"It's your house and your fireplace. You're free to do what you want with it. But not with me," she added quickly, firmly, and he grinned, that same grin that once had the power to heal any rift between them.

But not anymore.

When the fire was hot and bright and warm, when he was comfortably settled on the hearth, Tori suddenly tossed her quilting aside and folded her hands in her lap. "Do you enjoy tormenting me?"

"Is that what I'm doing?"

"Yes."

"I don't mean to."

"The fire feels good," she said nervously.

"It's warmer over here."

She actually smiled at him. "Dusty..."

"Sorry. It's a habit."

The silence stretched uneasily between them, each of them lost in their own thoughts. "Okay," Dusty said finally, when he could take it no longer. He sat on the raised hearth, his back to the fire, his knees wide apart and now he propped his elbows on his knees and let his hands dangle. "Whatever Tanner's keeping from us must be terribly important to him," he said, changing the subject.

"He could be protecting someone."

Dusty thought about that for a moment. "But who? Kelly? And what's he protecting her from?"

She shook her head. "Someone killed Kyle and made it look as though Tanner did it," Tori said slowly. "We're certain about that part of it. But what we don't know is *why*. Kyle wasn't the type of person to end up being beaten to death with a baseball bat—"

"And Tanner's not the type to be sent to prison," Dusty added.

"So something happened to the two of them, something Tanner can't—or *won't*—talk about. But we have no idea what it was or why he continues to be secretive about it."

Dusty was silent for a moment. Then he sighed heavily. "There are only two things I'm certain of right now— Tanner's innocence and that he's as stubborn as hell."

She laughed. "Another McKay trait."

His grin was fleeting. "I still believe he knows more than he's telling about Kyle's activities just before he died."

"He certainly acts like it."

Dusty stood up and moved aimlessly around the room, trying to think. He was dead tired. Finding the office torn apart last night hadn't left him in any mood for sleeping, and now his mind and body were paying for it. He should go home and get some sleep, but he couldn't bring himself to leave the cabin, or more to the point, he couldn't bring himself to leave Tori. Not yet.

She was his whole life, his anchor. She grounded him, and his connection to her was fierce. He had wandered casually from girl to girl until he had gazed into Tori's eyes eleven years ago—and he'd been hooked ever since.

Hooked on the sunset color of her hair. Hooked on her smile, her energy and her keen intelligence. She was everything he'd ever hoped to find, and a hell of a lot more.

Dusty stopped by the windows and looked outside. The lights were on in Tanner's cabin, and he held back a groan. No explanation had been offered tonight; his conversation with Tanner had been a waste of time.

And Dusty knew he was facing an implacable will, a will wrought of iron—the same kind of will that had presented itself when Tanner was learning to tie his shoes or catch a ball or fly a kite. It was in his nature to do it alone. He had always steadfastly refused Dusty's help, almost as a point of pride.

In a way, Tori was a lot like Tanner. Strong-willed, stubborn. And a loner.

Neither one would come to him for help.

The baby's abrupt crying made him spin around in surprise. Tori was already off the couch and halfway out of the room. He started to follow, but the cries suddenly ceased, and he could hear the soft murmuring and the creaking of the rocking chair as Tori settled herself in it, so he remained where he was.

Dakota was still having trouble sleeping, and he could relate to that. He knew firsthand what it was like to have dream-filled, restless sleep in which fears took shape and came like wraiths in the night.

He dropped down on the couch and leaned back, his hands folded across his belt buckle, and stared up at the low ceiling of the cabin. He was so tired of worrying about Tori and Tanner and the air service and Dakota.

He yawned and closed his eyes for a moment, and his heart shifted and seemed to move imperceptibly with an unbearable ache for what might have been . . . if Tanner hadn't been sent to prison . . . if Matt and Laurie hadn't died . . . if his own son had lived. . . .

The creaking of the rocking chair and the low rise and fall of Tori's gentle voice lulled him into that soft, dark, falling void just before sleep. A place where light and laughter prevailed. The only place where Tori lived these days.

Tori closed the door to the nursery and entered the living room, only to stop when she saw Dusty sound asleep on her couch. He was stretched out on his back, one foot still on the floor, and her first impulse was to wake him up and throw him out.

But then she relented and got a quilt out of the closet, muttering to herself. "I'm not running a hotel here."

She covered him with the quilt and stood for a moment, listening to his gentle breathing. She not only listened to it, she could actually feel his breathing, and Tori hugged herself, suddenly cold as ice. With every breath he took in this cabin, he was breathing life back into her, and she couldn't afford the luxury of taking it in.

She sat down on the hearth, her eyes wandering over him against her will. His dark blond hair glinted gold in the firelight, and as he stretched and groaned softly in his sleep, he reminded her of a tawny cat, sleek and lean and restless, always thinking, wanting, needing. . . .

He had too much life in him. Too much passion. For flying. For Alaska. For his family. For the air service.

For her.

He was easy to love. Too easy.

Her eyes landed on his face and lingered there a moment, before drifting once again down the length of him, noting with admiration the long legs and narrow hips and washboard belly. She closed her heart to the slow warmth spreading through her.

She loved this man, loved him too much to stick around and see his body splattered against the base of a mountain one day.

She loved him too much to ever bring another child of his into this world where danger lurked around every corner.

She sat there on the hearth hugging her knees for a long time that night.

Tori dragged herself out of bed and stumbled down the hall to the nursery. Dakota was sitting up in her crib, crying and rubbing her fists into her eyes.

"Mama."

Dakota was getting much too attached to her. Half the time, Tori didn't know if Dakota was calling for her own dead mother, or for her.

Please, God, please, please let her be calling for her own mama. Not me. Please not me.

Tori scooped her up in her arms and settled down in the rocking chair beside the crib. Dakota was warm and dry and sleepy, and she clung to Tori as if she'd never let her go.

"Mama."

"I'm not your mama, sweetheart," Tori said gently. "I'm not. I'm *not.*"

"Mama."

Tori shifted them both into a more comfortable position, her arms cradling Dakota close to her, her eyes raking over the baby's face. "Shawn would be just about

Here are your BIG WIN Game Tickets potentially worth from $100.00 to $1,000,000.00 each. Scratch off the PINK STRIP on each of your Sweepstakes tickets to see what you could win and mail your entry right away. (SEE BACK OF BOOK FOR DETAILS!)

This could be your lucky day—GOOD LUCK!

TICKET 1
Scratch PINK STRIP to reveal potential value of cash prize if the sweepstakes number on this ticket is a winning number. Return all game tickets intact.
LUCKY NUMBER
4J 220350

TICKET 2
Scratch PINK STRIP to reveal potential value of cash prize if the sweepstakes number on this ticket is a winning number. Return all game tickets intact.
LUCKY NUMBER
2T 111668

TICKET 3
Scratch PINK STRIP to reveal potential value of cash prize if the sweepstakes number on this ticket is a winning number. Return all game tickets intact.
LUCKY NUMBER
9S 235724

TICKET 4
Scratch PINK STRIP to reveal potential value of cash prize if the sweepstakes number on this ticket is a winning number. Return all game tickets intact.
LUCKY NUMBER
7M 095673

TICKET 5
Scratch PINK STRIP to reveal number of books you will receive. These books, part of a sampling program to introduce romance readers to the benefits of the Reader Service, are free.
FREE BOOKS
AUTHORIZATION CODE
130107-742

TICKET 6
All gifts are free. No purchase required. Scratch PINK STRIP to reveal free gift, our thanks to readers for trying our books.
FREE GIFT
AUTHORIZATION CODE
130107-742

YES! Enter my Lucky Numbers in The Million Dollar Sweepstakes (III) and when winners are selected, tell me if I've won any prize. If the PINK STRIP is scratched off on ticket #5, I will also receive four FREE Silhouette Intimate Moments® novels along with the FREE GIFT on ticket #6, as explained on the back and on the opposite page.   245 CIS AQYD (U-SIL-IM-10/94)

NAME _____

ADDRESS _____ APT. _____

CITY _____ STATE _____ ZIP CODE _____

Book offer limited to one per household and not valid to current Silhouette Intimate Moments® subscribers. All orders subject to approval.

© 1991 HARLEQUIN ENTERPRISES LIMITED.   PRINTED IN U.S.A.

FOLD AND DETACH ALONG THIS DOTTED LINE—RETURN ALL GAME TICKETS INTACT.

THE SILHOUETTE READER SERVICE™: HERE'S HOW IT WORKS

Accepting free books places you under no obligation to buy anything. You may keep the books and gift and return the shipping statement marked "cancel". If you do not cancel, about a month later we will send you 6 additional novels, and bill you just $2.89 each plus 25¢ delivery and applicable sales tax, if any.* That's the complete price, and—compared to cover prices of $3.50 each—quite a bargain! You may cancel at any time, but if you choose to continue, every month we'll send you 6 more books, which you may either purchase at the discount price. . .or return at our expense and cancel your subscription.

* Terms and prices subject to change without notice. Sales tax applicable in N.Y.

BUSINESS REPLY MAIL
FIRST CLASS MAIL   PERMIT NO. 717   BUFFALO, NY

POSTAGE WILL BE PAID BY ADDRESSEE

SILHOUETTE READER SERVICE
3010 WALDEN AVE
PO BOX 1867
BUFFALO NY 14240-9952

NO POSTAGE
NECESSARY
IF MAILED
IN THE
UNITED STATES

your age now, if he'd lived. He'd be almost thirteen months old.''

''Mama.'' Dakota smiled up at her, the fingers of one hand wrapped tightly around Tori's thumb.

Tori gently smoothed back the straight, Indian-black hair. ''Shawn's hair was dark blond, like his daddy's. And his eyes were green. Also like his daddy's.'' Her fingers slowed and she glanced toward the windows. It was light outside, but it was the middle of the night. This was springtime in Alaska, and nineteen hours of daylight now.

She remembered many nights like this a year ago, rocking her infant son back to sleep after his two o'clock bottle. She'd been filled with peace and contentment back then. Her life had been so full.

But now her life was empty.

Why was God doing this to her? she wondered. Why had he taken Shawn from her, only to send her this beautiful Indian baby to take his place?

If she did accept Dakota as her daughter, if she allowed herself to love this baby, wouldn't God just take her away, too?

Tori shook her head as if to clear it, and stood up. Dakota was asleep now, and she carefully lowered her into the crib and lifted the side into place. Covering her with a soft blanket and even softer quilt, Tori patted her for several seconds before backing quietly away from the crib.

The light streaming in from the windows seemed brighter than usual, and she hesitated momentarily, then decided to investigate. But even before she reached the windows, she knew something was wrong.

''Oh, no,'' she breathed as she stared out the window. The hangar was on fire, bright orange-red flames shooting up from one side. She could see the four planes were outside and a safe distance away but the beloved Jenny, the plane that had been Dusty's grandfather's, was inside the hangar.

The hangar and the plane exploded the instant fire hit fuel.

Chapter 11

Tori watched the neighbors and fire fighters battle the fire. There wasn't much left of the hangar—or the plane—but the fire was almost out, thanks to the "deck gun" on the fire engine, and the experienced members of the volunteer fire department.

Dusty and Tanner had managed to get the other planes to safety before the fire could destroy them, too, but this looked to be a deliberate and malicious act of sabotage.

The general opinion seemed to be that things could have been worse. No one had been injured, the three cabins and the office had come out of it without a scratch and their four working planes had survived.

Tori gazed up at the fire-illuminated, smoke-filled sky. Yes, things could have been worse, she silently agreed. But she only hoped and prayed no one would express that particular opinion to Dusty right now. Or to Tanner. The Curtiss Jenny had meant everything to the two of them.

It had been all they'd had left of their grandfather.

Both the McKay brothers were with the fire fighters spread out on the perimeter, waiting to put out any pockets of fire if the need arose. The deck gun was still pumping gallons of water onto the section that was still blazing, the smoke and fire bathing the men and fire trucks in an eerie glow.

It had been an arduous battle for the fire fighters to keep the flames from spreading to the cabins. Eleni had taken Dakota to her house for the night, and now Tori sat down on the front steps of the cabin and watched the scene playing out before her in a kind of detached numbness.

Several women milled around near her, friends, neighbors, wives of the fire fighters and curious onlookers drawn to the fire.

Tori glanced over at Zach Jordan, also standing with the fire fighters. He had fought the fire as diligently as the others, and she frowned, watching him.

"Are you all right, Tori?" She looked up, into the gentle deep blue eyes of Caleb Jordan, and she nodded.

"What about you?"

"One hell of a fire," he said.

She nodded. He looked exhausted, his face and clothing blackened by soot. "I'm just thankful no one was hurt."

She had danced with him at her wedding, she remembered. A wedding that seemed a long time ago. A lifetime ago. For both of them.

She felt a sudden tension in the group near her, and her attention was drawn back to the fire as a new and different kind of disaster erupted. Dusty and Zach were in the middle of a heated argument, and Tori rose from the porch steps just in time to see Dusty slam his fist into Zach's jaw.

Caleb rushed forward and Tori followed. When they reached them, Tanner and some of the fire fighters were trying to separate them, and Zach was shouting, "I didn't do it, Dusty! I swear I didn't—"

Tanner had Dusty's hands pinned up between his shoulder blades, trying to restrain him, but Dusty was trying to land a kick at Zach's groin area when Caleb pushed between them.

"Stay outta this, Caleb," Dusty growled, trying his best to go over him in order to reach Zach.

"I didn't set the fire!" Zach insisted.

"Zach, back off—just leave him alone," Caleb warned.

"Leave him alone?" Zach was incredulous. "He jumped me—"

"Back off, Zach!" Caleb had one hand flat against Dusty's chest, the index finger of his other hand aimed at his brother.

"I didn't do it."

"The hell you didn't." Dusty was still kicking and straining against those trying to hold him, and he let loose with a string of oaths in rapid succession as Tanner finally managed to half drag, half carry him over to the front steps of the cabin.

"I didn't do it." Zach stood there, his face bleeding, and he didn't take his eyes off Dusty as he watched him wrestle free of Tanner and throw himself down on the top step. Zach's eyes moved to Caleb, then to some of the faces of the people who were staring at him accusingly, and then his gaze landed on Tori. "I didn't do it," he said softly. "I didn't set the fire. I didn't."

She stared into the dark blue eyes for just a moment, and she found herself starting to believe him. Almost. She turned away quickly and headed for the cabin.

Dusty was sitting on the top step, his feet braced wide apart, and he was bent double, his fingers plowing through his dark blond hair as he continued to vent his rage with a string of vile expletives.

Tanner stood there, one hand on Dusty's shoulder, for comfort or restraint—Tori wasn't sure which—and his eyes met hers as she joined them.

"Are you through?" Tanner asked him when he finally ran down.

Dusty nodded, his breathing ragged. "Yeah." Dusty looked up, his gaze skidding past Tori to the wreckage behind her. "Pop's plane. The one he used to start McKay Air Service over sixty years ago." He lowered his head wearily and held it in both hands.

"It was only a chunk of metal." But Tanner's voice was too low. Too quiet.

"Who did this, Tanner?" His head shot up, green eyes blazing. "And don't give me attitude—just say it, straight out. Who did it?"

"I don't know."

Dusty came off the step like a rocket. "And I say you're lying."

Tori stepped in front of him. "That's enough. Tanner, go home and get cleaned up, and get some sleep," she said over her shoulder, her hands pushing at Dusty. "And you—inside. Right now. Before this goes any farther."

She held firm while Dusty glared angrily at Tanner, and then he turned, with only slight pressure from Tori, and went inside the cabin. Tori quickly shut and bolted the door. When she turned around, Dusty was there, waiting for her, his expression grim, his eyes a bright, hot, burning, freezing green that tore at her insides.

He'd had enough—too much—and Tori's sigh was soft, resigned. She reached out for him, reached out to offer whatever comfort she could, knowing it wouldn't be enough, knowing he'd only want more....

He held her tightly, crushing her against him, and her face was buried into his shoulder. He smelled of smoke and ashes. And then his hands were going up through her tangled hair, hauling her up so he could look into her eyes. His breathing was shallow, ragged, and his eyes flared at the same instant she felt his surging arousal straining against the confines of his jeans. His fingertips pressed into her head, his thumbs gently caressing her earlobes, her cheeks, the underside of her chin, and he never took his eyes off hers.

"I keeping thinking what if the fire had spread to the cabins," he said. "What if I'd lost you or Dakota or Tanner—"

"But you didn't."

"It was an act of God that I didn't, that you're all safe." Reaction was setting in, she could feel it. Feel the sharp fear... the blind fury... the trembling need... the growing hunger. It all came together inside him, spreading through him as the flames had spread through the hangar... spreading, churning, boiling and then bursting into a white-hot fire.

He pulled her roughly into his arms and held on to her in a choking embrace, his hands wandering through her hair and down her back, stroking, smoothing, his fingers restless and impatient as he drew her close against him.

She wasn't certain, at that moment, whether fury or passion was driving him, and she had a brief moment of fear. She'd never seen him so out of control before... never seen him this... driven... before.

He was kissing her eyelids and cheek and throat, his fingers brushing against the open collar of her denim shirt, his mouth following the same path his hand took, and her fear evaporated beneath his exquisitely gentle touch. He was gripped by deep emotion, but he'd never hurt her, she knew that. She'd always known that, even from the beginning. Their first time, years ago, had been wildly passionate, yet gentle. Very gentle. And painless, even though Dusty was the first man she'd ever been with.

The only man she'd ever been with.

This was like the first time, she was thinking as he kissed her, the kiss deepening and lengthening and threatening her resolve. A kiss like their first one when she was eighteen and determined not to fall in love with him.

But she'd fallen in love, anyway.

She loved the way he kissed her. As though he'd never let her go. As if she were the most exciting, desirable, most beautiful woman on the face of the earth.

She loved the steady strength of his heartbeat, his supporting arm around her, while his free hand worked its way through her clothing to find her left breast. His fingers molded and shaped and reshaped her breast even as he deepened the kiss. A low moan escaped from her, from somewhere deep inside her that she'd boarded up against him.

Still kissing her, each kiss more prolonged, more hungry, more satisfying than the last, Dusty guided her down the hallway toward their bedroom, their clothes coming off easily and discarded at random along the way.

She heard his jeans hit the floor, his metal belt buckle making a clinking sound on the tile floor, and she realized they were in the bathroom. The water in the shower was running and he guided her in, and closed the glass door behind them.

Her body was turning warm and fluid from his onslaught of passion, the warm-hot water rushing over them, washing off the stench of smoke and ashes. Her senses were being battered by him...by the tough-tender way he kept kissing her...by his hot, exploring fingers...and by the love words, the sensual words he used freely.

Tori felt battered by his emotions, by his hunger and his need for her.

He was closing in on her, tearing down her defenses, and Tori felt her walls crumbling, crashing down around her, and she felt herself breaking apart.

The rushing water made the same sound as the fire had made outside...that same sound that drowned out all sense of time or reality...that swept all thought and reason aside....

She touched him everywhere, her hands slick with soap, the water steaming, her fingers touching, seeking, exploring—her hands expressing what words could not.

She couldn't get enough of him—enough of his hands or mouth or body.

It had been so long. Too long.

She was vaguely aware of the water being turned off, of him reaching for a towel, of them stepping out of the shower stall. And the rush of feeling she experienced when she looked into his passion-drugged green eyes made everything else seem faraway and long ago.

They never made it to the bed they'd once shared. He dropped the towel and lowered her onto it, and covered her body with his.

She was feeling too much...she was feeling his hands...feeling the pulsing of his body.

Feeling . . . him.

His mouth touched down on hers as he moved within her, each slow thrust making her body arch up to meet him, her hunger growing, that relentless ebb and flow of desire washing over her body.

And she felt Dusty, slippery-wet from the shower, tremble in her arms. He was moving inside her, faster, harder, his driving strength taking them both over the edge . . . spinning them into a world of shattering, blinding light and sending them floating through space, fused together through wind and fire and rain and then into the soft, warm sunlight.

She floated back to earth.

She opened her eyes and Dusty was looking at her, a slow burning wonder in his eyes. "I love you," he said, and Tori squeezed her eyes tightly shut, one tear escaping and trickling down her cheek. "Tori?"

A sob broke free . . . and then another.

"It shouldn't have happened." She spoke the first thing that came into her mind.

He was still inside her, still hot and hard and only temporarily sated, and she was telling him it shouldn't have happened. He wasn't surprised at her reaction; he just hadn't counted on having to deal with it this soon.

"Tori—"

"It shouldn't have happened," she broke in, her voice soft with confusion. She turned her head away from him. "It shouldn't have happened," she repeated fretfully.

"Why not?" His finger gently forced her to look at him. There was such misery, such brutal pain in her eyes, that it took him a moment to concentrate on her answer.

"Because it makes it so hard to leave you."

"Then don't go."

"I have to."

Dusty held her for a moment, easing himself out of her and then onto his side, his arms tightening around her. "I love you, Tori. I can't stop loving you because I no longer fit in with your plans. I fell in love with you the moment I saw you—you know that—and I don't know how to let go. I wish I could," he added truthfully, his voice gentle. "I really wish I could."

"I'm sorry."

"I know. I am, too. I'm sorry you're afraid. I'm sorry I'm not enough anymore."

"You're enough," she said quickly. "You're too much. That's the problem."

He didn't want to argue about it. He was tired of arguing with her. He didn't know how to make her feel safe; it had to come from within her. It couldn't come from him.

"Dusty, I love you."

"Yeah." He kissed her cheek and got up. In the bedroom he rummaged through the dresser and closet until he found some clothes. Most of his stuff was still here. He'd left it, thinking he'd move back in with her at some point, but now it looked as though he'd be moving back in . . . but not with her.

He put on a pair of jeans and fastened them, then slipped on his shirt. Buttoning it and tucking it in, he left the bedroom. They'd left a trail of clothing through the cabin, and he gathered up his stuff and tossed it in a heap near the front door. He pulled on his boots and then looked up as Tori entered the living room.

She was wearing the long black velour robe he'd given her for Christmas one year, her red-gold hair brushed out and tumbling past her shoulders. She looked a little flushed from the heat of the shower—and the heat of their lovemaking—but her lips were pale, and her eyes were too big for her face.

"It's nearly dawn," he said. "I'd better go."

"No." She moved toward him. "Don't. Stay here." She was trembling, and when her hands reached out to touch him, he discovered they were ice-cold. "Make love to me again." Her voice was low, but very clear and decisive. "Once more."

"Oh, God, Tori." He grabbed her around the waist, his mouth taking hers roughly, and then the kiss grew gentle, even as his hands were opening the robe and shoving it off her shoulders.

It fell to the floor, and she stood there before him in all her naked beauty. He picked her up in his arms, carried her into the bedroom and placed her on the bed. "You're driving me crazy...flat out of my mind," he stated tightly, evenly. He was on the bed, kissing her again, and she wrapped herself around him. "But I want you. I can't deny that."

Dusty woke up to an empty bed and an empty cabin. But Tori had left a note for him in the kitchen.

It read:

I'm taking the mail run. Dakota will stay at Eleni's today. I made coffee, and there are bagels and cream cheese in the fridge.

Dusty stood there wearing a pair of jeans and nothing else, and sighed heavily. He'd wanted to talk to her, to apologize for last night, and to get an explanation for her abrupt turnaround as he was leaving the cabin.

The first time had been hot and hungry and urgent, and a little rough and he felt he owed her an apology for letting it happen. No, for causing it to happen, after she'd made herself quite clear on the subject.

And the second time...Dusty poured himself some strong, hot coffee, toasted himself a bagel, spread cream cheese on it and sat at the table trying to think. The second time they'd made love had been slow and just as hot as the first time, but with a difference.

She'd been caught up in the passion the first time...but the second time she'd been saying goodbye to him.

He tossed back his cup of coffee, and poured himself another cup. He needed the caffeine this morning to get himself in gear. He had things to do and places to go.

And people to see.

He had to put Tori in a private corner of his mind for the time being and leave her there. Because if he thought too much about last night, about how good she'd felt in his arms, how it felt to touch her and taste her and feel her again, then he was going to...to...to what?

His patience and understanding were stretched tautly and wearing thin. It was as if some invisible leash was the only thing holding him back, and he couldn't trust himself around her any longer. He was afraid of what he might do or say to her. .

He ate the last bite of his bagel and drained his second cup of coffee. He'd already done everything he could possibly do to get her to listen to reason. And he was running out of ideas.

All he ever seemed to accomplish was to make things worse.

He stood up and poured himself a third cup of coffee and turned off the coffee machine. He had to put this problem with Tori aside for the moment and concentrate on other things.

The fire, for one. He had insurance, of course, so he could rebuild the hangar. The money wouldn't cover the emotional value—or the loss—of his grandfather's Jenny, but that couldn't be helped.

This morning reminded him of another morning, ten years ago, the morning after his father had crashed his SR-9 into the mountains and died. Dusty had sat here in this very kitchen and planned what to do, how to keep things going, how to keep Tanner and Skylar on an even keel, how to keep their lives intact.

He'd been determined to move forward, to build up the air service, to preserve his father's dream. And this morning he was equally determined to go forward—and save McKay Air Service.

And get the Jordans off his back once and for all.

But first he had a few choice things to say to his one and only kid brother.

He finished getting dressed—and downing his third cup of coffee—and headed out the door.

Dusty found Tanner out by the hangar, surveying the wreckage. "I'm sorry I blew up at you last night."

"Forget it." He smiled but it didn't quite reach his eyes. They were the dark gray of thunderclouds this morning. "I have."

Dusty stood there, all too aware of the uneasy silence between them. "I'm going to put a question to you and I want you to be straight with me."

"Shoot." But he avoided looking directly at Dusty.

"Do you know who started the fire?" When Tanner didn't immediately come forth with an answer, Dusty pressed, "How much does it have to do with Kyle's death? What were you two up to before he died? What did you fight with him about?"

"I thought you said one question."

"They're related. Now answer them, Tanner, every blasted one of them, or I'm going to be the one facing prison, because I'm going to beat you to a bloody pulp if I don't get some answers and get them soon." His voice was low and pleasant, but there was a determined gleam in his eyes that Tanner couldn't possibly miss.

"I believe you mean it." Tanner's eyes searched his brother's face.

"Tanner, do you remember that time you let Skylar talk you into taking her to Fairbanks to go shopping, and you lost her? Do you remember how mad I got? Well, I'm twice as mad as I was then. I'm also older and about to tangle with a tough ex-con, but I still think I can take you. That's how ticked off I am," he warned softly, and Tanner grew still. "Tell me why you had the fight with Kyle the night he died."

"I can't."

"Can't? Or won't?"

The gray eyes darted to his. "Let it go, Dusty."

"Someone deliberately set fire to this hangar last night."

"We don't know that for sure."

"The hell we don't. Do you think it started by itself? Tanner, this thing is out of control. We're no longer talking about a few shoves in a bar, or some hot verbal exchanges with Zach and his friends. We're talking about breaking and entering, property damage, and now it's arson. We're lucky the wind didn't shift and spread the fire to the cabins. We'd be homeless this morning if that had happened. Or worse." Dusty watched his brother's lips tighten, his expression laced with tension. "What was Kyle into?" he asked bluntly.

"He was sleeping with Jenna."

Dusty digested this by slow degrees. And then, "Jenna? His brother's *wife?*"

"She wasn't Zach's wife back then."

"No, she was just his girlfriend since tenth grade. Lord, Tanner—"

"Kyle was in love with her." Tanner's sigh was soft, distracted. "I tried talking to him about it. I tried reminding him how jealous and possessive Zach is, especially where Jenna's concerned..."

"Obviously with good reason," Dusty put in.

"...but he wouldn't listen. He told me to stay out of his personal life."

"You were jumpy as hell for months before Kyle was killed. Was that the reason? Because of Kyle and Jenna?"

Tanner picked his way carefully through the wreckage of the hangar, trying his best to avoid Dusty's level gaze. And Dusty waited patiently for him to answer his question.

Finally, after several minutes had ticked by, Dusty said quietly, "Did Zach kill Kyle?"

Tanner shook his head. "No."

"You sound pretty confident it wasn't Zach who bashed Kyle's head in with your baseball bat. Why is that?" Dusty asked, his eyes leveling in on his brother.

Tanner's steel gray eyes looked into Dusty's. "Zach wouldn't hurt Kyle—no matter what."

"Zach's trying to run you out of town," Dusty said after a moment.

Tanner's grin was fleeting. "He said he didn't start the fire."

"Do you believe him?"

"I believe Zach took Kyle's death hard. I believe he was able to keep it together until I got out of prison and came home. I believe the very sight of me causes more pain inside Zach than anyone can possibly imagine."

"Why?" Dusty frowned.

"Because Kyle, Kelly, Zach and I were the Four Musketeers. Always together. Always close. Seeing one of us brings back memories of the others." He paused for a heartbeat. "That was the explanation Kelly gave for breaking our engagement. In the letter, she said it hurt too much being around me. I expect Zach feels that way, too."

Was that the way Tori felt about him? Dusty wondered uncomfortably. That the very sight of him brought back too many memories of Shawn, and it hurt her to be around him?

Was it as simple, and as complicated, as that?

He dragged his attention back to Tanner. "But you're innocent—"

"Yeah," he cut in, and the words splintered painfully through Dusty, "I'm innocent, but what difference does it make? Even if I hadn't been convicted of Kyle's murder, I doubt if Kelly would have married me. I'm too painful a reminder of Kyle."

Dusty didn't know what to say. He had stormed out here to demand answers; now he wasn't certain he should even be asking the questions. Tanner's feelings about Kyle and Kelly and Zach were too deep, too private.

Dusty's thoughts drifted back to Tori. Why couldn't he show her the same consideration he showed Tanner? Why couldn't he respect her right to grieve in private? To handle Shawn's death the way she wanted to handle it?

Why couldn't he?

"There is no evidence that Zach started the fire," Caleb said patiently.

"But there is evidence the fire was not accidental." Dusty leaned back in his chair and watched Caleb glance down at the papers he had on his desk.

"According to this report from the chief of the fire department, the fire at the hangar was started with gasoline-soaked rags and a cigarette lighter." There was a pause. "Whoever started the fire made certain you would know it was intentional. They left everything in the open for us to find. It seems like it was meant to be a warning."

"A warning? What kind of warning?" Tanner asked from the window, and Caleb glanced at him.

"Who else would benefit by causing trouble for McKay Air Service?"

"Zach's the only one I know of," Tanner answered.

Caleb's sigh was heavy. "I talked to Zach. He swears he had nothing to do with the fire."

"What about breaking into my office and stealing pages from the logbook?" Dusty asked sharply.

"He denies that, too."

"What do you expect him to say? Yeah, bro, I did it? You're a cop. Of course he'd deny it. He'd deny his dark hair, blue eyes and Scottish heritage if he thought it'd do him any good."

Caleb appeared to ignore the outburst. "Let's forget about Zach and the feud and Tanner and everything else for a moment. Is it possible you guys have an enemy you don't know about? Someone who is deliberately trying to put McKay Air Service out of business?"

They both stared at him blankly. And then Tanner said slowly, his eyes fixed on Caleb's face. "The only person I can think of is the person who killed Kyle."

Dusty watched Caleb's face, watched the conflicting emotions of shock, doubt and consternation move over his features as he stared back at Tanner.

"Do you know who it is?" Caleb finally asked.

"No, I don't."

"Then why—"

"Maybe he thinks I know."

And then Tanner moved forward, leaned across Caleb's desk and placed his hands on the surface. "I know you think I killed your brother, but I didn't." His voice was low and soft and fierce with emotion. "I had nothing to do with Kyle's death. I loved him. He was my brother, too, Caleb—*inside,* where it counts, he was my brother, too. And his killer is out there walking around, free as a bird." He paused, and when he spoke again his voice was softer still. "I know you don't believe that, but the evidence was stacked against me. I was set up. Framed for something I didn't do. And I know it's hard to believe what I'm saying, but what if I'm telling you the truth? What if you're wrong, Caleb? What if your family's wrong about me?"

Dusty watched the struggle going on inside Caleb. "Then who killed him?" Caleb asked, the words wrenched out of him.

"I know that I didn't. And I know the bloody baseball bat was planted in my plane in order to make it look as if I did."

Caleb's eyes searched Tanner's face for an instant. And then he stood up, circled his desk and closed his office door. When he turned to face them, his expression grave, Dusty saw he had come to a rather painful decision.

"Why?" he demanded. "Why were you set up?"

"Caleb—"

"I want you to tell me what you know about Kyle's activities the last year of his life."

Tanner, who was now sitting on the edge of Caleb's desk, looked stunned. He glanced uneasily at Dusty then back at Caleb before he slid off the desk and wandered over to the window.

"I already know about Kyle's affair with Jenna."

Tanner whirled. "But how . . . ?"

"It doesn't matter how. What does matter is that I know Kyle had a lot going on in his life before he died. And an affair with Zach's girlfriend was just the tip of the iceberg, wasn't it, Tanner?"

"He was scared, Caleb. He was scared out of his mind." Tanner's voice was gentle. "He didn't want to harm any of us. He just wanted to get out, but he didn't know how."

"Get out of what?" Caleb demanded, his expression tight. "Tanner, damn it, come back here!"

But Tanner was already out of the office, and Caleb stared wordlessly at Dusty.

Chapter 12

Alaska. There was nothing like it in the whole world.

Tori peered out of her floatplane at an ice floe adrift in the Bering Sea. In March, nearly the entire Bering Sea north of Nunivak Island was covered with one to ten feet of ice. But in May, the flat masses of floating ice drifted through the cold gray-blue waters like large chunks of frozen vanilla ice cream dusted with powdered sugar.

Alaska. The last frontier. And it took rugged individualists to settle here. Alaska was more than twice the size of Texas, spanning four time zones, and its coastline was over six thousand miles.

The state was so big that it was subdivided into six distinct regions: Southeast, Southcentral, the Interior, the Arctic, the Southwest and the Northwest—the area where Tori lived and worked.

When she'd first arrived here eleven years ago, she thought she'd died and gone to heaven. It seemed to her that one could do anything here, and so much needed to be done. There was a place for anyone who had the skills and the desire to do something.

And it was certainly a challenge to get things done.

It was true the environment in winter was hostile, Tori thought ruefully, but that added to the challenge. She had to be concerned about such basic things as warmth and food and shelter, to match herself against the environment. It was healthy, and it made her feel good about herself.

She liked Fairbanks and Anchorage and Juneau, but she loved the rural areas of Alaska. Two hundred thousand people, half of Alaska's entire population, lived in Anchorage, and she and Dusty had spent a week there for a honeymoon. It had been wonderful, but she preferred being in Nome, where she counted, where she *mattered*. Because she was a bush pilot.

Distances between the cities and towns were huge and there weren't many roads, so airplanes were still the principal means of transportation and communication. McKay Air Service delivered mail, supplies and people to remote villages, villages ranging in size from about fifty people to six hundred. Alaskan bush pilots were similar to the pony express riders of early America, braving land and weather to get through, and she was part of it, thanks to Dusty.

At the thought of him, Tori's heart started to ache. She'd been attracted to Dusty from the beginning because of who he was—this cocky, self-assured bush pilot from Nome, Alaska.

And now she wanted him to be someone he could never be in a million years—someone safe to love.

An Alaskan bush pilot had to know everything—his plane, the terrain, the people. He had to be at the top of his capabilities at all times. He had to watch for and do things no other pilots ever had to do because of the sheer danger.

The weather changed by the minute—going from crystal clear to zero visibility in minutes. There were squall lines that could turn your flight in any direction. And if the pilot didn't know the area well, he could easily get lost or disoriented, which was why Tori took the short runs, the familiar runs servicing the villages along Norton Sound and Kotzebue Sound, with Dusty and Tanner taking the longer, more difficult runs.

Both men had been born and raised here, and they'd been flying since they were old enough to handle a plane—and their dad had taught them well.

But she still worried.

Everything was flat here. No landmarks except a few lakes that were bigger or shaped differently than the others. And pilots and planes got lost on the coast because of the extreme changes in the terrain.

And mountains came out of nowhere. Flying in extreme weather it was easy to lose contact with reference points and just fly into a mountain—as Dusty's father had done ten years ago and crashed and burned.

She hadn't been afraid until last year, she thought miserably. She had trusted Dusty and never worried about him.

And she had loved flying, loved it in the wintertime when the whole scenery changed, especially the first snowfall of the season. The animals hadn't changed colors yet and she could pick them out against their snowy background. The bison herds, not native to Alaska, which were brought here over twenty years ago and numbered more than three hundred. And the bears, deer, mountain sheep and goats and the reindeer in the far north. And musk oxen on Nunivak. And the birds of prey, including bald eagles, who were endangered in other states, but had a population of thirty thousand in Alaska.

There was much to enjoy in this vast winter wonderland of ice and snow and northern lights. She had a preference for snowy owls, sea lions, the bull moose and walruses.

Tori's thoughts nudged and pushed against each other at random, circling and avoiding the subject of Dusty. Or more to the point—avoiding the subject of last night.

We made love.

That one thought sizzled through her brain, causing her emotions to short-circuit.

They'd made love. Not just once—but twice.

Now what? She owed Dusty an explanation, but what could she say? She couldn't go back to her standard routine, not now, not after last night. He'd never believe she didn't want him touching her. He'd never believe that again.

Her walls had crumbled down around her, and she was feeling naked and exposed as the liar she was.

Tori tried desperately to grab on to her thoughts, to keep them contained, to steer her thoughts to a more comfortable, and less painful, topic. She decided to think about flying.

She was a pilot—and what had Dusty said about pilots? Pilots were aggressive, and the desire to improve flying competency is common among them.

That's why pilots constantly tried to further their ratings. They weren't content with a private pilot certificate. They had to strive to become an instrument pilot— to meet the demanding, ultimate challenge of flight by reference to instruments instead of external vision. Because you weren't truly a member of the pilot fraternity until you had your instrument rating.

Dusty was eighteen when he'd obtained his, and then went on to acquire his commercial pilot certificate a year later. And he was a certified flight instructor by the time she met him.

Dusty was aggressive, all right, she thought.

Being a pilot demands the ability to make decisions. She could almost hear his voice in her head. *And flying is discipline—self-discipline as well as conformity to flight practices and procedures.*

And maturity is what a pilot needs to make decisions and obtain self-discipline—especially bush pilots.

She'd heard it all before.

And at one time, Dusty thought she'd possessed these qualities. All of them.

It was hard to tell what he thought of her now. She didn't even know what she thought of herself.

Tori's sigh was barely audible. She had none of those qualities. And maybe she never had. If she did, she'd lost them somewhere along the way.

She couldn't even make a decision and stick to it. And self-discipline? If she'd had any self-discipline, she wouldn't have ended up in bed with Dusty, now, would she?

Maybe all pilots were crazy. One would have to be to land on water or a frozen sea or take off on a fifteen-hundred-foot strip of land. A commercial pilot put his or her life at risk day after day after day.

But it wasn't her life she was worried about. It was Dusty's. *Oh, God, what was she doing to him?* She didn't know if that thought was a question or a prayer.

She was ruining his life. She knew that much. She couldn't bring herself to actually pack up and leave, yet she couldn't make the commitment to stay.

A few minutes later she was landing the floatplane in Hamilton, at the mouth of the Yukon River on Norton Sound, when the engine suddenly spat black smoke and quit. Fighting down panic, Tori dead-sticked it into the wind and it started up, and she drew in a sigh of relief. She safely landed the plane and jumped out of the cockpit. The SR-9 had been mostly hers until Tanner was released from prison, so she was familiar with it, and she did a quick inspection of everything that could possibly have caused the problem. But she found nothing.

It was getting late in the day, so she hurried into the tiny, mostly Indian, village of less than three hundred people, and gave the mail and several packages to the postmaster there. She was back at the plane in less than twenty minutes, threw her sack of outgoing mail onto the rear seat and made a preflight inspection just to be certain she hadn't missed anything before.

Minutes later, she took off, the engine working fine, and she made three more stops without any more trouble, before Koyuk, her last stop of the day. She was an hour's flight from home, and it had been a busy day, with the villages along Kotzebue Sound this morning, and Norton Sound and the lower Yukon this afternoon.

She was landing the SR-9 when once again the Wright engine started spilling smoke and quit.

And this time it wouldn't start up again, no matter what she did. She had a rough landing, but she made it down safely and bumped and skipped her way to a stop.

When it appeared to be dead in the water, Tori got on the radio, contacted Dusty at the office, got someone to pull her to shore and then delivered her mail and packages. She bought a cup of coffee and took it back to the plane with her, where she sat on the bank of Norton Sound and sipped it.

The sun was still high in the sky and she was reminded, once again, what it was like in Alaska during late spring and summer. It was a great deal lighter now than it had been at this same time two weeks ago. All these daylight hours in summer had a way of making up for the constant twilight of winter.

She saw Dusty's approach in his own SR-9 and she stood up, holding the paper cup of coffee in both her hands. Her heart was thundering beneath her rib cage and she was finding it difficult to breathe all of a sudden. She watched him land the plane and jump out of the cockpit—and her heart nearly fluttered to a stop.

She was amazed and embarrassed, she realized, at the depth and width of the gulf that had grown between them this past year. As she watched him walk toward her in faded jeans and leather jacket, his long blond hair giving him a wild, rugged look, it was as though she were watching a stranger approach her.

"Are you okay?" he was asking even before he'd reached her.

"I'm fine." Her eyes slid over him and she became acutely aware of him as a third-generation bush pilot, blending in with his surroundings as if he belonged here. A tidal wave of sexual desire flooded through her.

And not especially desire for Dusty—the man she'd loved since she was a teenager...the *boy* she'd fallen in love with as a young girl...the kind and gentle and loving person she'd been married to for the past five years— but sheer, blunt, physical desire for the man approaching her now.

"Are you sure you're okay?" The forest green eyes touched down on her face, and she nodded without saying anything.

What could she say? If Dusty had been a total stranger, she'd still be willing to go anywhere with him. And do anything he asked her to do.

He started asking her questions about the plane and she answered them automatically, feeling strangely light-headed and disoriented. Then she watched as he turned away and started his own inspection of the dead engine.

She heard his low savage oath, ground out of him with fury, and then another one came sliding out of his mouth as he jumped off the floatplane and landed on the shore.

"What is it? What's wrong?" she asked.

"There are pinholes in the carburetor float," he said, wiping his hands on a rag. "When you dropped the flaps and changed the pitch for a landing, the float filled with gas and sank, flooding the engine. You've been flying all day with it like that," he stated evenly, cleaning the last bit of grease and oil off his fingers.

Tori didn't understand. "Pinholes? In the float?"

The green eyes leveled into hers. "Punctures. A deliberate act of sabotage."

"Dusty…oh, no, you don't think— Oh, my God…." Horror roared through her as she clapped a hand over her mouth, her eyes fixed on Dusty's face.

"Everybody in northwest Alaska knows the red and silver SR-9 belongs to Tanner," he said evenly, shoving the rag into the pocket of his jacket. "Puncture a few holes in the float and just sit back and wait for him to glide into the side of a mountain or into the sea—sort of like playing Russian roulette in the sky."

Tori didn't like the way he looked. He was taking this too calmly. There were usually two stages to Dusty's an-

ger—a flash of temper and then this deadly inner stillness.

The stillness inside him was the worst.

"What are we going to do?" she asked.

"I don't know." He glanced past her for a moment, at
some place behind her left shoulder, and she thought she
heard him sigh. He was struggling to get a grip on his
emotions and she waited patiently for him to say or do
something. And then, "There's nothing we can do about
it now. I'm hungry and tired and I'm sure you are, too.
We'll deal with this tomorrow."

He started for the planes and she followed him. They
took the mail sack and packages out of one plane and put
them in the other, and then Dusty locked it up for the
night and they both got in the green and silver SR-9.

Tori's thoughts were subdued. She had no idea Zach
Jordan was capable of this. But who else could have done
it?

The person who killed Kyle?

Her attention was suddenly drawn to Dusty as he took
off and circled to the south instead of heading west toward Nome.

"Dusty, where are we going?"

"Into Unalakleet for a hot dinner. I'm starving. I
haven't had anything to eat since breakfast."

"But we're only an hour from home."

"And a half hour from Unalakleet."

Tori didn't say anything but she was suddenly suspi-
cious of his motives. Her earlier attack of raw desire had
faded in the face of cold reality, and she was instantly on
guard.

After a moment, she said, "But Dakota—"

"Tanner's taking care of her. And Eleni's down the
street if he has any trouble."

It all sounded perfectly reasonable. He was hungry, the baby was being well taken care of, so why did she feel this sense of forboding?

She had expected him to head for Nome and for Zach's house for a confrontation.

She didn't want him to do that, of course. It was better for him to cool off first, but she also didn't want to have dinner alone with him in Unalakleet.

She was trapped.

Unalakleet had an airport like Nome, so Dusty had the SR-9 fueled up before he and Tori had dinner. The town only had a population of six hundred, but the small family-operated Bear's Paw Restaurant served stuffed salmon and fried shrimp that even put Suzi's cooking at Mooseheart to shame.

"I should have known," Tori commented when the waitress set two plates of salmon and shrimp in front of them.

"Do you remember the first time we ate here?"

Tori reached for her glass of iced tea. "I remember." It had been the night they first made love.

Dusty's hand slid across the table and grasped her left hand in his. "You were so scared, I almost lost my nerve."

"I wasn't scared."

"The hell you weren't." His grin was gentle. "I was, too."

Tori took a sip of her tea and set the glass down. The warmth of Dusty's fingers sank into her hand. "That night seems so long ago." Her eyes lifted to meet his and she found him studying her intently.

"Ten years."

Tori was silent. They'd spent the weekend in Nome with his family, and then headed back to school. They'd stopped here, and over a dinner of salmon and shrimp, Tori had summoned up the courage to tell him it was time to take the next step in their relationship.

Dusty had waited months, not rushing her, making no demands, and she'd never forget the startled look on his face when she finally told him it was okay for them to make love.

They ate silently for several minutes. This was so difficult, she sighed. It was hard to be this close, yet maintain a polite distance from him. How was she going to stay in Nome another week and a half? she wondered miserably.

"Do you think Zach punctured holes in the float?" she asked to break the silence.

"I don't know."

Tori was surprised at his answer. "I thought Zach was your number-one enemy these days."

"Zach's the kind of guy to punch your lights out if you cross him. I'm having a hard time seeing him as sneaky."

"Then you don't think it was Zach."

"I didn't say that."

"But..."

"I don't know what to think. Zach's the only one with reason to drive Tanner out of town, but I don't think he'd want to kill him."

"It could have been anybody," she said. "Tanner's plane was sitting out there in the open while everyone was occupied with the fire last night. It would have been easy for someone to sabotage the plane and get away without being noticed."

Dusty shook his head. "But who would want to kill Tanner? And why?"

"Tanner's the only one who can answer that," she said.

Tori resumed eating her dinner. There was nothing more to say on the subject, not really. They couldn't solve this problem tonight. They couldn't solve any problem in one night—not Tanner's, and certainly not the one in their marriage.

Her thoughts skidded uncomfortably back to last night. She wanted to know what he was thinking, but was afraid to ask. He sat there, preoccupied with his meal, and with the fire and the punctured float. Yet at times he seemed to be stalling, weighing his words before he approached the subject uppermost on his mind.

She wasn't surprised when he ordered coffee and sweet rolls for dessert. When the waitress set them on the table and left, he leaned forward in his chair and looked directly into her eyes. "I'd like to talk to you." His voice was low and quiet and reasonable, and she steeled herself for what was coming.

"Go ahead." But she broke her sweet roll in half to give her hands something to do.

"I'd like to apologize for last night."

She kept her eyes on her plate. He was apologizing? That was a switch. And totally unexpected.

"Did I hurt you?"

Tori looked up and grinned. "No, Dusty, of course not."

"I was a little out of it."

"A little?"

"A lot." His grin was fleeting, a little rueful. "Everything's getting to me lately. Tanner. The air service. The break-in. The fire." His green eyes dimmed. "And you."

She slid her hand across the table and touched his arm. "That's why I have to leave."

His sigh was heavy, thoughtful, and he seemed not to have heard her. "I've been thinking all day about us. You never really wanted to get married, did you?"

Tori was stunned. "Do you think I have a problem with being married?"

"I think you have a problem with emotional involvement. And it's tough to stay married without staying involved."

"Then you're saying I'm an emotional lightweight."

"I'm saying you're scared."

"Of you?"

"Me. Dakota. Living in general."

Tori sat back in her chair and stared at him in disbelief. "I made a decision when I was twelve years old not to be like my parents. I didn't want to live in the suburbs, and grow complacent and dull by the time I was forty. I didn't want to get to the point where I needed to have an affair in order to have excitement in my life. I *chose* this unconventional life-style to combat that."

"That was your first mistake."

"Why was it a mistake?"

"Because you expected too much. Alaska isn't some grand, exciting vacation place. Not when you have to live and work here. I told you that from the beginning. Do you remember that? When you wanted to stay? You were raised with every possible advantage, and I was afraid you were caught up in some romantic ideal of what life was supposed to be like."

"So you tried your best to scare me off."

"And you tried like hell to prove you could take it."

She smiled at him. "And up until last year, you thought I'd done pretty well."

Dusty's expression was grave. "Shawn didn't die because we live in Alaska," he told her gently.

"I know that."

"Do you?"

She was about to answer him quickly, but something probing in his gaze made her stop and think. *Did* she know that? Truthfully, was she able to say Shawn would have died in some safe, quiet suburban neighborhood, and actually mean it?

"Okay, so you made your point. But that doesn't mean I never wanted to get married," she said defensively.

"You made me wait two years after you graduated from college."

"Dusty..."

"You said it was because of me, because I had enough to worry about without adding a wife. You said all the right things. You reminded me how lots of people wait to get married these days... but do you know what I think, Tori?"

"It looks as though you're going to tell me."

"You were scared."

"You say that as if it's some great revelation," she accused.

"I think it is. To me, anyway. I grew up believing in marriage. If I learned one thing from my parents, it was the belief that two people could spend their entire lives together without driving each other nuts. That was their gift to me." He paused. "But you grew up with the belief that marriage and commitment and emotional involvement equals pain."

Tori glanced away, and then dragged her gaze unwillingly back to his. "I was twelve years old when I found out my father cheated on my mother. I was eighteen when I found out he'd been having affairs with women since before I was born."

He nodded. "So you ran away."

"I didn't run—"

"You ran to Alaska. When you get hurt, you run." She was shaking her head vehemently in denial. "Then Shawn dies and you run away again—from me."

"Stop it. Please." Her voice was small.

"I can't." He sounded sorry. He *looked* sorry. But he didn't stop. "This is too important. To both of us. Tori, you act as if you're the only one involved here, the only one who hurts. But Shawn was my son, too. Maybe I didn't carry him inside my body for nine months, but that doesn't mean he was any less mine."

Her throat ached. She didn't want to cry in front of him. She didn't. "I know you loved him," she said softly, tears blurring her vision.

"But living the rest of our lives without each other won't bring him back."

She remained silent, unable to speak, unable to see him clearly. But the sound of his voice, the way his fingers closed around hers, was vaguely reassuring.

"Why didn't you to talk to me when Shawn died?" she asked, her words cutting across the silence in the plane, and Dusty glanced briefly at her, before turning his attention back to the control panel. "You acted so strong and self-contained—even at the funeral."

"I didn't want to add to what you were already going through."

He could feel her eyes on his face. "You went about business as usual. You went back to work. You took care of me. But you never expressed any grief over losing your own child," she said.

"You were in shock, Tori. How could I expect you to deal with what I was feeling?"

"How did you deal with it?"

He sighed. "I started writing to Tanner. About you, at first. And then later about Shawn. It helped getting things down on paper."

"I wasn't there for you, was I?"

She sounded so miserable, and so guilty, that he reached out to hold her hand for a moment. "It's okay, Tori. I understood."

The silence in the plane lengthened and deepened, and then she said in a low voice, "I haven't been much of a wife this past year, have I?"

"It's been a rough year. For both of us."

Her sigh was soft and she turned in her seat to face him. "I didn't think you wanted Shawn. I didn't think you cared that he had died. I took your strength and your ability to get on with your life as some ridiculous proof that you had never loved him the way I did. I'm sorry."

"Maybe I should have been more open with you about what I was feeling."

"Maybe. But I don't know if I could have responded. All I know is these past twelve months I've felt as though I've been living in some dark, airless cave."

Dusty remained silent, nearly holding his breath. She was talking to him, opening up to him—just a little, but it was a definite start.

She'd already talked to him more tonight than she had the entire past year.

They landed a few minutes later, took care of the plane, locked the mail in the safe and then headed for the cabin. Tanner and Dakota were sprawled on the floor watching television when they entered the living room.

"Tanner, she should be in bed," Tori chided, bending down to scoop the child into her arms.

"I was lonely."

Dusty waited until she had left the room with the baby before he turned off the television set, and dropped down on the couch.

"What happened to my plane?" Tanner asked.

Before Dusty was finished explaining about the punctured carburetor float, Tanner was sitting up, staring at him. "Tori could have been—" He broke off, only to mutter something beneath his breath. And then, "Damn!"

"It was deliberate. There's no doubt in my mind someone wants you out of the way." Dusty's green eyes drilled into his brother's gray ones. "I want you to stay on the ground for the next few days—and out of sight."

Tanner uttered a flat obscenity.

"I don't want to hear it," Dusty snapped.

"Do you want Tori to go up in my place? Next time she might not be so damned lucky. This is my problem and I'll handle it—"

"It's *our* problem," Dusty interrupted tightly, but Tanner was shaking his head.

"Not this time. I want you out of it. You and Tori and Dakota aren't involved any longer—as of right now." He scrambled to his feet and grabbed his jacket. He put it on and stood there, zipping it up, his gray eyes hardening into steel.

Dusty came off the couch and followed him to the door. "Tanner, you're not—"

"Leaving?" His grin was crooked, a little rueful. "No, I'm not going anywhere. I'm going to do what I should have done five years ago." He yanked open the door, only to have Dusty lay a hand on his shoulder.

"What's that?"

The gray eyes looked into his. "I'm going to find out who killed Kyle."

He left, slamming the door behind him, and Dusty stared at the closed door as several seconds ticked by. Then he turned and found Tori standing in the doorway of the nursery.

"You heard?"

She walked toward him. "Yes, I heard. And it's time, Dusty. It's time Tanner cleared his name."

"If he starts digging for the truth…" His voice trailed off. He was unable to put this last thought into words.

"If he starts digging for the truth," she said, "he'll eventually find it. Which means Kyle's assailant will try his best to stop him first."

Dusty looked into her warm brown eyes and she gazed steadily back at him, comforting him, supporting him the way she used to do.

"Are you going after him?" she asked.

Dusty shook his head. "He has to do this alone. He spent five years in prison without me there to help him. I guess he can handle this by himself."

Her grin was gentle. "I know how much courage that took not to run after him."

He leaned against the door, watching her expression. "I remember my dad telling me once that the hardest thing to do is to sit back and let the other person make his or her own decisions."

She waited a moment and then she said gently, "Tanner's not your responsibility anymore. You're not his father. You have to let him go."

And it looked as if he'd have to let Tori go, too.

"Good night, Tori."

She looked into his eyes and tried to smile. "Good night. And don't worry about Tanner," she added quickly as he turned toward the cabin door.

But he wasn't worried about Tanner. He was worried about how he was going to get through the next fifty years without Tori in his life.

Chapter 13

Tori paused in the kitchen doorway and watched Dusty wrestle with getting oatmeal into Dakota's mouth. He was serious about it. Dakota was equally serious about thwarting every effort he made, and Tori laughed.

He looked up. "Are you sure this stuff's good for her? She hates it."

"You and Tanner keep making the same mistake."

"What's that?"

"She's old enough to feed herself."

Dusty's expression was blank. "She is?"

"Of course."

He held out the spoon for Dakota to take and she stared at it for a moment, then at him, and then reached for it, wrapping her tiny fist around the handle. But she took her other hand, dumped it into the cereal bowl and shoveled the oatmeal into her mouth.

"Like that, huh?"

"Like that." Tori came into the room.

"I guess that's why you're the mommy." Dusty walked to the sink to wash his hands.

"I'm not her mother."

"You're the only one she's got."

Tori grew still. "Don't," she said after a moment, and he turned to look at her, wiping his hands on a towel.

"Don't what?"

"Don't try to appeal to my maternal instincts. My guilt button," she added flatly. "I know this child needs a mother. But there is nothing I can do about it."

He continued to wipe his hands, not looking at her. "Dakota's an orphan," Dusty stated calmly. "She's all alone except for you and me and Tanner."

"Dusty..."

"It's the truth."

"She's not my responsibility." God, she sounded cold. She couldn't believe those words had come out of her mouth. But it was true. Dakota Grace wasn't her flesh-and-blood child.

So what? the tiny voice inside her demanded, and Tori was startled. *She's a beautiful baby girl, isn't she?* the voice insisted.

She's a child who needs you desperately.

Why the hell can't you put aside your fear and respond to her? the voice demanded, sounding too much like Dusty.

He was doing this, she railed inwardly. He was exposing her to this helpless, delicate, needy little child, and expecting her to come through with something she no longer had inside.

Because she'd lost her heart and soul and will to live. Shawn had taken those things with him when he died.

Tori's gaze drifted over to Dakota, and lingered there for a moment. Dakota saw her and her dark eyes lit up, and she wiggled in delight, flashing a warm, sweet grin in Tori's direction.

"Mama."

Tori cringed, hoping Dusty hadn't heard the toddler. But he must have, because he turned and stood watching them, his green eyes moving from the baby up to Tori's face.

"Out of the mouths of babes."

"Dakota's only a year old," she snapped. "She doesn't have the slightest idea what she's saying."

Dusty's grin was slow. "Want to bet on it?" His tone was light, but his eyes . . .

"Mama!" Dakota cried, as if on cue, holding her arms out beseechingly toward Tori. "Mama!"

Tori quickly crossed the room and picked her up, her heart pounding, her hands shaking, and she pointedly ignored Dusty.

"Are you ready to go?" He kept his tone carefully neutral, and Tori nodded, burying her face briefly into Dakota's dark hair, breathing in the clean baby scent of her.

They were going to Fairbanks this morning. Dakota had a doctor's appointment, and after they'd taken off and were heading east, Dusty asked, "Tell me again why we have to take her to see this Dr. Morris."

"She was Dakota's pediatrician."

"She was?" He glanced at her. "How do you know that?"

"I found a piece of paper in the diaper bag with her name and telephone number on it, along with a list of the foods Dakota dislikes. Evidently, Laurie's sister must have written it down for us. For you," she corrected herself hastily.

He returned his attention to the front of the plane. "Can't we have her medical records sent to a doctor in Nome?"

"I'm going to do that. But first I'd like Dr. Morris to check Dakota out and to give me—us—her opinion on Dakota's general health. Just to make certain there's nothing physically wrong with her."

"Is she sick?"

"No, Dusty, but she still isn't eating all that well. Or sleeping." Tori settled back in her seat. "It would ease my mind to have Dakota's own doctor examine her before we take her to one in Nome."

"I wish Matt and Laurie had left us better instructions on the care and feeding of their kid," he complained, and she had to agree.

"Maybe we'll find something to help us at their house."

Dusty was the executor of Matt's estate as well as Dakota's guardian, and the trip to Fairbanks was mainly to settle the estate. The house had been sold, and three hours later they were standing on Matt and Laurie's front porch, reluctant to go in.

"The last time I was here was after the funeral," Tori said softly. And the time before that was nearly two years ago, soon after she had discovered she was pregnant. They'd spent the weekend with Matt and Laurie, and the four of them had discussed, in depth, the responsibilities of parenthood.

And now, Matt and Laurie were both dead. And so was Shawn.

And little Dakota Grace was an orphan.

She hung back, her arms cradling Dakota protectively, as Dusty unlocked the front door. The house was empty, except for boxes of personal belongings stacked up in the living room, and they wandered idly through the rooms, looking around.

"This is all that's left of their life together?" Tori said when they were back in the living room, and Dusty glanced at her. Their eyes met and held, and Tori felt terrible. "An empty house and...and a few boxes?"

"Laurie's sister took some of the things back home with her," Dusty explained. "The rest of it was given to charity."

Tori's eyes wandered around the room, and then landed once again on Dusty's face. "When did you do all this?"

"Laurie's sister did most of it. I stopped here one day last week, and she had me go through Matt's things—and I took what I wanted." He shrugged. "Matt's Goldpanners' baseball cap for Tanner, some pictures and Matt's knife collection. Those boxes—" he indicated the ones stacked up by the front door "—have the rest of Dakota's clothes, her toys and a few things belonging to Matt and Laurie that Dakota will want one day. Photo albums, their wedding rings—" He broke off, glanced at Dakota crawling around on the floor and walked over to the front windows.

Tori followed him, one hand reaching out to touch his arm. "I feel like we let Matt down the past couple of years. We let him slip out of our lives," she said quietly, and he turned his head to look at her, the green eyes moving over her face.

Dusty's grin was fleeting. "I'm not sure what you mean."

"We lost touch with him, especially the last couple of years. We were all so damned busy, and then...then Shawn died and I..." She couldn't finish the sentence.

His eyes searched her face. "They understood."

But she shook her head. "I kept you away from Matt."

"I had lunch with him every time I took the Nome-Fairbanks run. And so did Tanner."

She turned away from the patient, gentle look in his eyes. This house was getting to her, making her think, making her feel—and she didn't want to feel.

She had a vague memory of Matt and Laurie being in the cabin after Shawn died, of them being at the funeral, but that was all. Looking back, it seemed unreal... hazy images, low voices, muted sounds... it was all encased in a deep mist of shrouded emotion.

And it had been like that for the past year. Tori's eyes fastened on the toddler. Until Dakota had burst into her life and started breaking down the walls of Tori's self-imposed isolation.

She whirled on Dusty. "Are we through here? We... we're going to be late if we don't hurry."

Dusty sent her a curious glance, but he nodded. They took the boxes to the plane and loaded them inside, stopped by the lawyer's office to deliver Matt's house key and sign some papers regarding the estate and then found their way to the pediatrician's office near the university.

Tori couldn't shake the guilt that had exploded through her upon entering Matt and Laurie's house. She had dutifully attended their funeral five weeks ago with Dusty and Tanner, but that was the extent of it.

She had made no effort to comfort Dusty, to talk to him, to help him through the ordeal of losing his foster brother—because Matt's death hadn't seemed real to her.

But it did now.

They wandered through Alaskaland, the forty-four-acre park on the Chena River, near downtown Fairbanks, pushing Dakota in her stroller, enjoying the sunny day. The complex featured a gold-rush town, a native Indian village, art gallery, theater, civic center and Mining Valley—an outdoor museum of mining artifacts situated around an indoor-outdoor salmon-bake restaurant.

Dusty's mind skidded along thoughts he would be better off not thinking. This entire day had such a family feel to it: the pediatrician, and then lunch at the Pump House Restaurant and Bar on the Chena River, and now Alaskaland, where tourists and residents took their kids for a day or an afternoon of family fun.

They paused by the newly restored *Denali,* a plush rail car in which President Harding had traveled when he came north in 1923 to hammer the gold spike on the Alaska Railroad, and Dusty noticed that Dakota was sound asleep.

"She looks comfortable," was his brief comment, and Tori smiled at him.

"All this fresh air and sunshine."

"Do you feel better?"

"Better?" She looked confused.

"Dr. Morris said Dakota was a very healthy and normal one-year-old, and that she'd bounce back to her old self in no time. That should make you feel better. You're doing an excellent job of taking care of her," he added. "Dr. Morris said that, too."

She looked at him. "But why didn't you tell Dr. Morris that *you* were her legal guardian, and I was simply Dakota's temporary caretaker?"

He shrugged. "There was no point in it. We'll never see her again. Dakota's next checkup will be with a pediatrician in Nome."

Tori was making this extremely difficult. She'd been nervous and on edge for the past five days, her mood introspective for the most part, her temper flaring at odd moments during the day.

A war was going on inside her, and all Dusty could do was to be patient—and pray.

They rode the Crooked Creek and Whiskey Island Railroad, a small train that circled the forty-four-acre park, and then had an early dinner in Alaskaland's Mining Valley.

It felt good to get away from Nome for the day, to get away from the problems he was having with Tanner and the air service. Those problems had occupied him so much the past couple of weeks, Dusty needed this time alone with Tori to concentrate on her.

He wanted to deal with her in a rational, reasonable way—the same way he had been brought up to deal with all of life's problems. But somehow, logic eluded him where Tori was concerned.

"We'd better be going," he said reluctantly and she nodded, rising to lift Dakota out of her high chair. As they left the outdoor dining area, she surprised him by sliding her hand into his.

"I'm sorry about Matt," she said abruptly. "I was so wrapped up in my own problems, I completely forgot what you must have gone through when he was killed."

They walked along in silence for a moment or two as Dusty tried to think of something to say that would not only reassure her, but keep her from withdrawing even more from him.

That was another habit she had invented the past few days—short bursts of emotion and then she'd back off, hastily building up another wall, carefully keeping her feelings in check, as if she were afraid that once some feeling leaked out, it would be followed by a tidal wave.

Which, in his opinion, would be the best thing for both of them.

"Matt was your brother in every sense of the word. You grew up with him," she continued. "You loved him. And then he was killed and you were alone."

"No one's ever really alone," he told her carefully. "Except by choice."

He could feel her eyes staring up at him, raking curiously over his face. "But I wasn't there for you."

"I had Tanner." He gave a short laugh. "Somehow over the past few years I guess I started seeing him as a person, instead of my kid brother. We got through Matt's death together." He placed a slight emphasis on the last word.

She was still staring at him. He could feel the intensity of her gaze. And then she looked away from him. "Anyway, I'm sorry."

Dusty forced himself to release her hand. "You did nothing to be sorry for," he said quietly, and stopped walking to bend down and retrieve Dakota's toy bear that she had just hurled onto the pathway. Tucking the stuffed bear back in the stroller, he glanced up at Tori, then straightened.

Already he could feel the chill of pain and isolation that surrounded her. Tori was lost somewhere beneath the tautness of a tension that never seemed to leave her. He didn't know how to bring her back to him.

The darkness of panic was slowly piling up in the corners of his mind, and Dusty moved forward, pushing the stroller without seeing where he was going, as he tried in vain to stay calm.

She was leaving in a few days. That was the deal he had agreed to. June first. He had agreed to buy her a plane ticket to Arizona, and to let her walk out of his life without trying to stop her.

June first.

He had five days.

Thirty minutes later, they were flying over the northern side of the three major peaks of the Alaska Mountain Range, called the "three sisters" because, on a clear day, they were so similar to one another. In reality, they were Mount Hayes, Mount Hess and Mount Deborah, and one could always look out a dorm window at the University of Alaska-Fairbanks and view the peaks in the distance. That had been one advantage of going to college in this town, Dusty was thinking as they circled Fairbanks before heading west.

The other advantage was meeting Tori.

The flight home was uneventful, and Dusty used the time to sift through his scattered thoughts. Up here, he was in a world of his own making, safe and isolated from the problems of the world below. A tight cocoon of peace and security. He had the skills to pilot this plane, the experience to handle whatever came up and he knew no fear.

But he was at a complete loss as to how to keep Tori here in Alaska with him, and his fear of losing her, once embedded deep within him, hidden, dormant, was now coming alive. Full-blown and vivid. Ugly and relentless in its power to destroy him.

He'd never felt anything like this in his life. He'd given everything he had to Tori, left himself wide open, and it hurt. It hurt like hell, and then some.

Is this what she's afraid of feeling? he wondered, and the thought was a splash of cold reality.

His thoughts chased one another around in his head. Love hurt. There was no doubt in his mind that it didn't. To totally commit oneself to another took an act of trust that no sane person would ever attempt.

Your entire life hung in the balance—based upon the decisions, justified or not, of another person.

It cost something to love another human being completely, without reservation or restraint. It meant putting yourself second to the needs of the other, to care more about her than you did about yourself.

His sister Skylar hated this life, even though she'd been born and raised here. Well, not exactly hated it, but she'd made her feelings quite clear on the subject. She wasn't about to marry a bush pilot and live out her life in the wilds of Alaska like their mother had done. Skylar had taken off for college in Florida and had only returned for an occasional visit, content to live in a modern, civilized city like Miami for the rest of her life.

So how could he expect someone like Tori to be satisfied with a small cabin, very little money and all the disadvantages of life in Alaska?

It was too much to ask of any woman, much less someone as sensitive as Tori.

Dusty stared outside at the sunny evening. Maybe he'd been not exactly selfish, but self-absorbed all these years, trying to make her fit into a life-style that didn't suit her.

But he was stuck here. He'd always been stuck. By birth, and by blood.

Tori came out of the bedroom wearing her bathrobe, and Dusty sat on the hearth, waiting for her. Dakota had fallen asleep the moment her head had hit the pillow, and the nursery door was tightly closed.

"I thought you'd gone home," she said with a touch of irritation in her voice.

"This is my home."

Her gaze shifted from his. "You know what I mean."

"Yeah."

She turned away from him and picked up a magazine, flipping idly through it.

"We need to talk," he said definitely, but she shook her head, not bothering to turn around. "Okay. *I'll* talk. You listen."

"Dusty, please . . . can't we just—"

"Just what? Go on pretending? Pretending you're not going to leave in a few days?" His tone softened. "I know that your feelings for me have changed this past year."

She looked into his eyes, startled by his words, and then she looked away. "I don't know what you mean."

"Yes, you do." He kept his voice low, his tone even. "You know exactly what I mean."

She remained silent for several minutes, refusing to look at him. Then her eyes darted back to his and slid away once again. Her fingers made idle swipes at the few tears that had escaped down her cheeks. She walked to the hearth and seated herself reluctantly next to him. "What are you getting at?"

"I think there's more to it than what you've told me. I think it's more than fear of being close."

She stared at him for a full moment. And then she started to rise. "I'm going to bed. I'm tired, and it's been a long day."

He caught her hand, stopping her. "It's been a long year."

"Dusty..." She stood there, her face expressionless, remote, her eyes fixed on their entwined fingers in order to avoid looking at him.

"Dakota's one chink in your armor, isn't she?" And then, "I see the way you care about her. The way you love her," he added gently, and her eyes darted up to meet his furiously.

"I don't love her!"

The vehement denial surprised Tori as much as Dusty. *But I don't love her,* the tiny voice of unreason insisted. *I don't. I can't.*

I won't let myself love another human being again. Not as long as I live.

Especially not a child.

Dusty took aim and fired. "And me? Are you saying you don't love me, either?" His words were softly spoken, but the arrow hit its mark, an arrow fired by necessity, out of desperation.

It pierced her protective walls.

She actually cringed. But she stood there, her eyes riveted to his, and she looked like a trapped, wounded animal. "I love you. You know that," she said in a tiny voice, but he shook his head.

"I don't know that at all."

"I'm sorry, Dusty. I'm sorry." She started to pull away, but his fingers tightened around hers.

"I guess I'll always have your undying love to keep me company, is that it?" His watchful gaze gave her no escape. "But undying, romantic, elusive, fleeting, distant love—the kind that will haunt me forever—isn't going to cut it in the real world. There's no substance to it. For either of us," he added, his voice tight and roughening with every syllable.

"What do you want me to do?"

"I want you to be honest with me. And with yourself. I want you to fight—"

"Fight against what?" She looked confused. "This isn't a war, Dusty...."

"It sure as hell feels like it."

"We lost our son. He died. Fighting won't bring him back. Nothing will. Nothing will change, one way or another, no matter what I do."

"Damn you, Tori."

"What? *What?*"

"Nothing." She didn't get it at all. And he was beginning to think she never would.

He released her hand and got to his feet. For a moment, he stood there, his eyes touching hers, and time stopped. His world shattered into glittering, painful fragments.

He bent his head and gently kissed her cheek. Then he picked up his jacket and quietly left the cabin.

Tori took her coffee and sweet roll to a table in the corner of Mooseheart, and sat there reading the newspaper. Normally, she'd go home after her last flight, but not today.

She wanted to start weaning Dakota away from her, and the best way to do that was to make herself scarce. She was leaving in two days, and she told herself it was for the best.

"Hey, beautiful, mind if I join you?"

Tori jumped, startled at the interruption, but she looked up with a smile as Joey Arnett slid into the chair across from hers. He set his glass of beer down, propped his elbows on the table and peered at her thoughtfully.

"That sweet roll will spoil your dinner."

She passed it to him. "Be my guest."

"Thanks." He took a bite, chewed, swallowed and said, "I haven't seen you since the night of the fire. How are things going?"

She shrugged and took a sip of her coffee. People would find out soon enough she was leaving; she wasn't going to advertise the fact beforehand. Loyalty to Dusty kept her silent, although, in a way, she'd like to talk to someone about it. Someone objective. Someone with no ax to grind.

Someone like Joey.

She set her coffee cup down and looked at him, her eyes raking over him with an intensity that made him pause in the act of taking another bite of sweet roll. "Why are you looking at me like that?"

She smiled. "Like what?"

"Like I'm an insect under a microscope." He put the sweet roll on the table, not taking his eyes off hers. "Are you okay?"

"I was just thinking—"

"Uh-oh."

Tori laughed and made a face. "You're practically my best friend up here in Alaska," she told him, and he looked into her eyes.

Joey nodded once, not taking his eyes off her, even as he reached for his bottle of beer. He took a sip, grimaced and took another one.

"What's wrong?"

"A sweet roll and beer. That's what's wrong."

Tori slid both hands around her coffee cup, feeling the heat sink slowly into her, and it was comforting. She'd felt so cold inside for months.

For twelve months.

Cold and dead. It was a residual feeling, the last traces of Shawn . . . the lingering reminder of his brief existence in this world.

"Tori?" Joey's hand slid across the table until his fingers touched her arm lightly. "Is something wrong?"

She shook herself mentally and managed a brief, hollow smile. His blue eyes were kind and he looked concerned, but she realized he wasn't her best friend in Alaska. Dusty was.

She wanted someone to talk to, someone to tell her she was doing the right thing. She wanted reassurance that leaving Dusty was not a mistake.

Oh, God, she wanted a guarantee.

She'd never needed one before, and the very idea disturbed something very basic inside her. Something essential in her.

A guarantee went against the grain of Tori's DNA pattern, and she cringed inside. Had she turned into a sissy? Is that what Shawn's death had done to her? No one had ever dared call her a sissy. She'd always prided herself on taking it on the chin, without complaint, and come back with both fists flying. She was a born fighter.

Fighter. The word shot into her, ripping out a large piece of her inner wall. That's what Dusty had meant a few nights ago, she thought.

But damn it, she wasn't a sissy. She wasn't. She was still strong. It took strength to leave here, didn't it? To leave Dusty? But deep inside, she knew what she was searching for. She wanted a guarantee that leaving Dusty wouldn't break his heart.

Or hers.

She wanted a guarantee that Dakota wouldn't be emotionally damaged for life by being abandoned for the second time in a little over a month.

Tori took a sip of her coffee, cradling the cup in both hands, aware that she was beginning to tremble in reaction. She was not the sort of person who got scared of things or became immobilized by fear. She was a woman of action. She took charge. *She* was the one people came to with their problems.

She was a loner—self-sufficient, organized, independent. And stubborn.

But she wasn't a sissy.

The word made her cringe, and her mind skidded back in time, as a long-forgotten memory took hold.

She was eight years old and trying desperately to ride the red bicycle her father had bought her as a special surprise.

A boy's bicycle—without training wheels.

He'd been patient at first, and then irritated that she wasn't heavy enough to keep the large bike upright. The neighbors were watching and she kept falling off, embarrassing him.

"Tori, it's easy," he had coaxed. "Just get on it and ride. That's all there is to it." Tears of frustration ran down her face and he grimaced. "You don't want the neighbors to think you're a sissy, do you? Do you?" He bent down and wiped her tears away, patted her on the head, and straightened. "Now, let's try it again," he had said evenly. "And again—until you get it right."

Two hours later, battered and bruised, she finally succeeded in riding the bike to the end of the block, but she had felt no thrill of accomplishment—only the sting of her father's disapproval that she had cried.

He abhorred weakness in any form—especially tears or emotion—and Tori learned early that she had to be tough in order to gain his love. She had to be the son he had always wanted, instead of herself.

"Tori?"

She glanced up, startled by the sound. She'd nearly forgotten about Joey. He was sitting there watching her, and she set her cup down with a clatter.

"Can I help?" His voice was gentle, his eyes kind, but she shook her head.

"Afraid not." She couldn't confide in another man, not even Joey.

Dusty was the only one who could help her, and what she really wanted from him was a guarantee that nothing bad would ever happen to her again.

"How's Dusty?"

She shrugged. "Okay." She twisted her wedding ring around on her finger, not looking at him.

"He seemed a little tense last time I saw him."

"He has a lot on his mind."

"Tori, you have to let it go."

Her eyes met his. He was leaning back in his chair, his eyes serious, and Tori noticed how his eyes were the same color as the stonewashed jeans he was wearing.

"Let what go?"

"The baby."

She didn't flinch. She held his gaze. "What makes you think I haven't?"

"You haven't been the same since Shawn died."

That statement nearly sent her into a state of shock. "What...what do you mean?"

"Everyone in town's noticed it. And everyone's noticed the tension between you and Dusty." He paused for a heartbeat. "It's hard to hide it from people who care—and remember."

"Remember?"

"How it used to be between you two."

Tori didn't like this at all. The whole town knew something was wrong between her and Dusty? And that something was wrong with her?

"You guys had this . . . magic between you that most people would give anything to have a shot at—even briefly." There was a ragged edge to his voice, a tightness in the eyes that Tori didn't miss. "I hope you can work it out." He took another swallow of beer, his gaze sliding away from hers.

Before Tori could form any sort of reply, Joey tipped back his chair, balancing on the back legs, and sat there holding his beer bottle on one knee. "What's Tanner been up to lately?" he asked casually and she shrugged.

"Not much."

"I've noticed he spends a lot of time in bars. Is he turning to alcohol to solve his problems now?"

Tori looked at him quickly. "What are you talking about?" And then, incredulously, "Are you saying Tanner has a drinking problem?"

"I'm saying he spends a lot of time in bars."

"But Joey, he's a pilot. He wouldn't jeopardize the air service or his passengers like that—"

"Hey, look, I'm a little concerned, okay?" He sat up, his chair moving forward with a thud, and he set his beer bottle on the table. "I wouldn't have brought it up, except I thought maybe you could talk to him about it. I know it's been hard for him, coming back here, but I'd hate to see him become involved in anything that would be dangerous to his health."

Tori stared at him in disbelief, unable to understand this at all. She hadn't seen Tanner for . . . let's see, four or five days, at least. He'd been busy and she'd been preoccupied with her own problems, but . . .

"I didn't mean to upset you." Joey's voice broke into her thoughts. "And I'm probably making too big a deal out of it, but I thought you should know."

She nodded, distracted by the feeling in the pit of her stomach. Something was wrong here, but she couldn't put her finger on what it was.

"I'm glad you told me," she responded automatically, wondering if their problems would ever end.

He stood up, bent, and, to her surprise, kissed her on the cheek. "I have to go. I've got a date," he said as he straightened, and she smiled at him.

"When are you going to settle down and marry that girl?" she teased.

"What do you mean?" He frowned.

"Kathy. You've been involved with her off and on since before Dusty and I were married."

He merely grinned and left.

Tori stared into her cup of coffee. Something was bothering her about her conversation with Joey, but she didn't know what it was. She knew it wasn't his comment about Tanner having a drinking problem, because that was simply ridiculous.

But what was it? Some passing remark he'd made...

Suddenly, Tanner dropped down in the seat Joey had vacated, and placed a steaming cup of coffee in front of him. She watched him add two spoonfuls of sugar, and he sat stirring it in silence.

She studied his face. He looked tired, as though the very act of stirring the coffee took more energy than he could muster. He looked like Dusty, she noticed not for the first time. He had the same tall, lean body, the same shade of honey-blond hair, the same lean, angular face. Only Tanner had always had this hollow, hungry look about him—even as a teenager. And prison had only deepened the look.

And his eyes ... they were gray instead of green. And while Dusty's were as quiet and deep as the shadows of a forest, Tanner had these young-old eyes, as if he'd been to hell and back.

She watched him glance up, his gaze idly moving around the room, and then she saw him stiffen. Tori turned and looked toward the door, and groaned inwardly. Zach had just entered Mooseheart.

"Tanner—"

"It's okay, Tori," he said softly, without taking his eyes off Zach.

The other man had spotted them, and to Tori's shock and dismay, he headed straight toward them. When he reached their table, his deep blue gaze slid from one to the other of them, and then he asked, "Do you mind if I join you?"

Tori hesitated, and then said, "Have a seat." She ignored the darting look Tanner sent her, and kept her gaze carefully on Zach's face.

He looked subdued, his body laced with tension as he took the chair next to Tori's, propped his elbows on the table and buried his head briefly in his hands. Tori heard the sharp intake of his breath, and then he exhaled slowly and looked at Tanner.

"Why are you roaming the bars and asking questions?" Zach said.

"Because I want to find out why Kyle died."

Zach sat there looking at him, his expression unreadable. And then he said slowly, "What have you come up with?"

Tanner and Tori exchanged glances. They expected most anything from Zach these days—but not this. Certainly not this.

"Nothing." Tanner answered his question, and then added flatly, "Yet." He waited patiently, his eyes never leaving Zach's.

Zach sat there a full moment, his blue gaze tangling with gray, then he sank back in his chair and shook his head slightly. "I don't understand any of this." His voice was so low it was hard to hear him.

"I didn't kill your brother." Tanner's voice was equally low.

And for the first time, Zach actually looked uncertain. "Then who did?"

"That's what I'm trying to find out."

They watched as Zach struggled to digest what must have been for him an impossible concept. Then he said bluntly, "All the evidence pointed to you."

"I was set up."

"Why?"

Tanner hesitated. "I'm not sure."

"That's bull." And then, "But I wish to hell I knew what was going on. All I know for sure is that I didn't break into your office, start that fire—or mess with your plane." The blue eyes shot over to Tori. "Do you honestly believe I'd do something like that? I'm a bush pilot, for God's sake." His gaze landed once again on Tanner. "I wanted you out of town, but I never wanted you dead. Oh, hell, my sister thought the sun rose and set just for you." Tori watched Tanner flinch at these words. "So why would I go that far? I just...I just..." His voice trailed off into silence.

After a moment, Tanner stated gently, softly, "It's tough, huh, being accused of something you didn't do."

Zach looked at him quickly, stood and left without another word.

Tori let out the breath she was holding in a long, shuddering sigh. "Wow, that was intense. Oh, God..." She discovered her hands were shaking.

"Yeah." Tanner was staring after Zach, a thoughtful look in his steel gray eyes.

"Do you believe him?"

He shrugged. "I don't know."

"I remember the night of the fire. Zach said he didn't do it, and I... I almost believed him." And then, "The fire! That's it!"

"What's it?" He turned his gaze on her.

"Something Joey said earlier. He asked how things were going, and he said he hadn't seen me since the night of the fire. But I don't remember seeing him at all that night."

"I saw him."

She frowned at the flat, even tone and his suddenly closed expression. But she shrugged it off and continued, "Isn't that strange? But there were so many people out there that night. I guess I just forgot."

"When did you talk to him?" Tanner asked.

"Who?"

"Joey."

"A minute or two before you got here. Why?"

"What did you talk about?"

"Nothing much." She wasn't about to tell him Joey's concerns about Tanner's "drinking problem." It was Dusty's place to do that. It wasn't hers. "I was kidding him about Kathy—"

"Kathy?"

She laughed. "The girl he's been dating forever. You know—"

"Kathy Kirkpatrick?"

"That's right."

Tanner was already on his feet. He bent and hugged her quickly. "I'd better shove off. I have places to go and things to do," he added lightly.

"But you didn't drink your—coffee," she added to herself. Tanner was already across the room and out the door.

She started up the steps to the cabin when she heard a baby laugh out loud, and she paused, looking toward Norton Sound. Dusty had the baby on the beach. He was swinging her around and around, and Tori was amazed at the change in the toddler. She was laughing, and her little cheeks were as pink as her jacket and tennis shoes— but it was from the excitement and sheer joy the child felt, instead of the wind blowing across the water.

Tori could see that at a glance.

Dusty had been taking Dakota with him the past few evenings, and evidently a romp on the beach was part of their routine, for the moment he tried to set her down, Dakota held her arms up, her body language screaming out for him to swing her around again.

She watched as Dusty scooped the child up in his arms and ran up the beach, and she smiled at the baby's sounds of delight.

She started toward them, and Dusty stopped and waited for her, but she was surprised when he didn't seem particularly happy to see her.

He wasn't unhappy, but the expression in his dark green eyes was neutral.

The hood on Dakota's jacket had slipped down, exposing her dark head and little ears, and Tori's hands itched to reach up and fix it, but she restrained herself.

Dakota wasn't her responsibility; she was Dusty's.

She told herself that over and over again.

Tori fell into step beside Dusty and they walked up the beach. She tried to ignore the way Dakota's dark eyes lit up when she saw her and the quiet mood Dusty was in.

He'd been like this for the past several days. Quiet. Distant. Cool.

"It's almost dinnertime," she said brightly. "What if I fix dinner—"

"No, thanks," he cut her off. "Dakota and I have a date for dinner. Suzi's fixing her a special dessert."

He didn't ask her to join them at Mooseheart, and Tori walked beside him in bemused silence. She glanced up at him from time to time, but he seemed totally preoccupied with Dakota.

And Dakota was totally absorbed with him—her new daddy. Tori felt shut out...disconnected...set aside and cut loose to go her own way.

That's what you wanted, her little voice said ruefully. *You wanted Dusty to stop pushing for something you no longer have to give him.*

You wanted him to stop involving you in Dakota's life.

You wanted it to be just the two of them. And now it looks as though you've gotten what you wanted.

Tori stared straight ahead, and blinked back the tears that threatened to overtake her. But what rocked her to her very soul was that Dusty didn't even notice.

Tori put the cleaning supplies in the pantry and turned to survey the kitchen. It sparkled. She had scrubbed and waxed the tile floor, and polished all the appliances until they glowed.

Everything was clean and in order.

She wanted to wean Dakota away from her, but to be alone in this cabin without Dakota's sweet, sunny smiles and warm hugs was more than she could bear. She felt hot tears stinging her eyes—tears she refused to shed, refused to acknowledge.

She didn't miss Dakota! She didn't.

She was surprised and horrified at the depth of pain inside her at Dakota's absence. It cut through her like a knife, reminding her of the pain and emptiness of Shawn's death.

Tori sank wearily to a kitchen chair, and the tears escaped and splashed on her hand. Maybe she was a sissy. Maybe she'd always been and just hadn't known it.

She heard the cabin door open, and she jumped up, wiping her tears away with her fingers. She turned with a smile as Dusty filled the doorway.

"Did Dakota like her dessert?"

Dusty made no move to hand the baby to her. "She had two helpings. It was chocolate pudding."

Dakota Grace was dozing against Dusty's shoulder, breathing in the scent of his leather flight jacket, and Tori had to steel herself not to reach out and take the baby out of his arms.

Finally, she could stand it no longer. "Do...do you want me to put her to bed?"

"I'll do it." He disappeared into the nursery with the baby, and a few minutes later he came out, closing the door gently behind him.

Tori was sitting on the edge of the couch, waiting for him and feeling useless and deprived. Dusty had stopped talking to her.

He never mentioned the fact that she was leaving this week. And he wasn't trying to stop her from going.

He was going on with his life without her in it—and was adjusting to his loss quite well. Too well, she thought in dismay.

Could he turn his feelings off so easily?

Dusty stood in the living room near the outside door, and shoved his hands into the pockets of his jacket. "She's sound asleep. She shouldn't give you any trouble tonight," he said politely, leaving Tori with the feeling that he was talking to his daughter's baby-sitter.

A virtual stranger.

A woman he didn't know—and one he didn't care to know.

"Do... do you want to sit down?" she asked him hesitantly, and the dark green eyes touched down on hers.

"Why?"

"Why?" Why was he acting this way? she wondered uncertainly. What was he up to? "It's a social thing—sitting down in someone's house. Why don't you give it a try?" she suggested pleasantly.

"I'm in no mood for your games."

"Dusty—"

"If you have something to say to me, then say it."

Brown eyes collided with green. "We have to make plans. I'm leaving in—"

"What kind of plans?"

"About Dakota. Who's going to look after her when I'm gone?"

"Eleni said she would until I can hire someone."

"You talked to Eleni?" Tori said in surprise.

"I talked to her this afternoon."

"She's going to take care of her during the day?"

"That's what she said."

"What about at night?"

He shrugged, his eyes never leaving hers. The expression in their green depths unnerved her. "I'll take care of her. We'll be just fine."

"She has bad dreams—"

"I said I'll take care of her." There was a look in his eyes that silenced Tori, and several minutes ticked by.

"Dusty, I know you're angry," she said finally, hesitantly, and watched him turn away.

"I'm not angry, baby. I've just had enough. You won," he said, jerking open the cabin door. "You got what you wanted. You're free to go anywhere you damn well please."

The door closed behind him, and she was alone.

Chapter 14

Dusty wandered along the beach just before dawn, thinking about Tori. She was leaving day after tomorrow, and nothing short of an act of God could stop her now. He was barely hanging on, barely able to keep his mouth shut and his temper from flaring whenever he looked at her.

But he couldn't fight this. He didn't know how.

This was was like boxing shadows. Her fear was all-consuming, an insidious enemy traveling the corridors of her mind, deeply ingrained into the very mesh of her personality.

She was slipping away from him and he couldn't hold on much longer.

Dusty walked slowly, his gaze idly taking in the morning sky. It was gray with fog and mist, the kind of morning where it wasn't actually raining, but one would be soaked after only a few minutes outside. Darker clouds were gathering in the west, a warning of the storm approaching, and all flights were canceled until this afternoon. Dusty shoved his hands deeper into the pockets of his jacket, and shivered.

The weather suited his mood perfectly.

He was putting distance between them, when all he wanted was to reach out and hold on. He wanted to be honest with her, and he wanted her to be honest with him.

But did he really want complete honesty between them? The thought skidded around inside him, thudding into the darker, more shadowed regions of his mind... the regions where wraithlike monsters of guilt loomed and lived and breathed and tormented him. The regions where he'd built up his own walls to block out all the details of his son's death.

Dusty trudged along the beach, feeling cold and wet and miserable—and very much alone. His life with Tori was just about over now and it all looked so damned hopeless this morning.

He was so deep in his own misery that he didn't see Tanner standing at the edge of the ice-encrusted sea, until he nearly bumped into him. Tanner stood with a mug of hot coffee in one hand, the thumb of his other hand hooked through a belt loop in his jeans.

"You're up early."

"So are you." Tanner glanced at him briefly.

"Can I have some of that?"

Tanner passed him the mug of coffee, and he took a sip, flinching at the unfamiliar taste of sugar and coffee. He passed it back to him.

"What are you doing out here so early?" Dusty asked.

"Thinking."

"About what?"

"My life, mostly." He paused. "Or what's left of it."

Dusty remained silent. He wasn't sure how to respond. Something in Tanner's expression warned him not to push for answers; that he wasn't in a talking mood.

So it surprised him a moment later when Tanner stated flatly, "I thought it'd be different when I got out, when I got home."

"Different how?" he prodded when it looked as if Tanner wasn't going to continue.

"I thought I could start over." He kept his gaze pinned on something out in Norton Sound, something only Tanner could see. "I thought I could put the past behind me, I thought they'd let me forget." He gave a slight shake of his head. "I was a fool to think it'd be that easy."

"It should have been."

But Tanner was shaking his head in vehement denial. And then he looked at him. "I thought I could handle it. I thought I could keep things under control. But I didn't do such a great job of it five years ago, and I'm not doing such a great job of it now."

Dusty felt a sense of dread snaking its way down his spine. "What do you mean?"

"I don't know where to start." His attention was once again drawn to the sea.

Dusty took a deep, ragged breath and let it out slowly as he braced himself for whatever was coming. "Why don't you start at the beginning?"

There was a slight hesitation, and then, "This has to stay between us."

"Okay."

"I mean it, Dusty. No one else can know about this. I want your word."

The gray eyes drilled into his, and Dusty nodded. "You got it."

Tanner took a sip of coffee and stared out at the sea, as though gathering his thoughts. After a moment or two, he said, "It started about six months before Kyle died. I found out he was running drugs."

"Drugs!" The word slid out of Dusty's mouth without his even realizing it.

"I leaned on him hard when I found out about it. I threatened to turn him in if he didn't clean up his act." He paused. "Kyle thought a little extra spending money would entice Jenna away from Zach."

"What did Kyle do when you threatened to turn him in?"

"He seemed relieved. He'd only done it a couple of times, and running drugs wasn't exactly his style. He wanted out. I think he just needed a good hard shove."

"So what happened?"

"Kyle had a partner. And his partner started using Kelly to keep him in line."

"What exactly do you mean by using Kelly?"

"He threatened to kill her if Kyle didn't do what he was told."

"Tanner—"

Tanner was thoroughly agitated now. "That was the way this guy held on to Kyle. You know how close Kyle was to Kelly. They were twins. He couldn't let anything happen to his own sister—"

"He threatened Kelly's life?" Dusty was having a hard time with this, but suddenly everything tumbled into place. Tanner's strange behavior... his evasive answers these past five years...

It was all beginning to make sense.

It was because of Kelly Jordan. She was the secret Tanner had been protecting.

Kelly—the woman Tanner had been in love with all these years. The woman he'd been engaged to at the time of Kyle's death.

"Who was Kyle's partner?"

"I don't know. I never met him." The steel gray eyes locked on his. "I swear. I don't know who he is. Kyle was afraid it would put me in danger if I knew, and we already had Kelly to worry about."

"How do you know Kyle was telling you the truth? How do you know he even had a partner? Maybe the whole thing was a scam to get you off his back—"

"Because Kelly was being harassed at school. Phone calls, weird letters, and twice she was followed back to her dorm. At first she brushed it off as a college prank," he continued before Dusty could react, "but one afternoon, she was downtown in Fairbanks and she was nearly hit by a speeding car. And the next day, someone broke into her room at the dorm, and left a dozen red roses on her bed. Kelly thought it was odd that these things were happening to her, but she wasn't overly concerned about it."

"But you and Kyle took it as a warning."

"It was the only way we could take it."

"Did the incidents stop?"

"As soon as Kyle agreed to transport drugs in his plane."

"So they were back in business." Dusty's tone was grim.

Tanner drained his cup and tossed it on the half-frozen ground at his feet. He was bent under the weight of memories and Dusty was acutely aware of the amount of hurt and frustration and sheer bewilderment that was embedded deep within his brother.

"I didn't know what to do," he told Dusty. "I wanted to wring Kyle's neck for putting Kelly in danger, but I had to back him up. I couldn't go to the police—not with this guy out there threatening her life. So I kept my mouth shut, and things drifted along."

"But then Kelly graduated from college."

Tanner nodded. "I thought I could protect her here in Nome. This isn't like Fairbanks, with all those people and all those college students. I thought she'd be safe." His sigh was heavy. "I guess I was hoping it would go away by itself."

"What happened when Kelly came home?"

"Kyle's partner decided to expand." Something in his low, tight voice made Dusty feel sick inside. "And he made me an offer."

"Tanner…"

"Kyle was the go-between. Kyle's partner wanted his identity to stay buried, so all I had were messages from Kyle. But it came down to this—in exchange for my services, I could marry Kelly and live without fear of losing her." Tanner looked at Dusty and his voice hardened. "As long as I was using McKay Air Service to run drugs for him."

"Tanner… damn it." A tidal wave of feeling washed over Dusty.

"I lost it then. I wasn't about to fall into that trap, so I sent a message to him through Kyle, and told him what he could do with his offer." Dusty saw the fire in his brother's eyes, the harsh edge of control. "That's what Kyle and I fought about the night he died. We'd been arguing about it for a couple of weeks. He wanted me to run drugs in order to keep Kelly safe—"

"Didn't it occur to Kyle that this guy would use Kelly to keep you both running drugs for him until the end of time?" Dusty broke in bitterly.

"He understood that. But we both agreed we had to keep Kelly safe at all costs."

Dusty grew still, suddenly afraid to ask the question that was splintering through him.

"We had two choices," Tanner continued. "We could do as his partner wanted . . . or we could get Kelly out of town." This last part came out softly, painfully, and Dusty looked closely at his brother.

And the truth was in the steel gray eyes that were staring mercilessly back at him.

"You deliberately drove Kelly away," he accused.

"I had no choice."

"But Tanner—" Dusty broke off, the magnitude of what he'd just heard sinking slowly into him.

"Kelly's safety depended on it."

"But—"

"Kelly didn't leave me because she thought I killed her brother. At least, that wasn't the only reason," he said evenly. "She left me because she believed I no longer loved her."

"Okay, wait a minute." This was coming too fast for Dusty. "Let's back up a little. Did Kyle's partner kill him?"

"I think so."

"Why?"

"Someone planted drugs in my plane. I think Kyle knew about the plant, and tried to stop him." The fire of his conviction was in his eyes, burning through him as if to seal a covenant as he said between clenched teeth, "His partner killed him—and then framed me for the murder."

Dusty's thoughts spun in his mind. "When did you find out someone had planted drugs in your plane?" Dusty asked sharply.

"I had a date with Kelly that night, but I'd left something for her in the plane. I went back to get it, and that's when I saw the cocaine—several kilos of it."

"What did you do with it?"

Tanner looked at him. He seemed relieved that this was finally out in the open. "I tossed it into the sea. That's why I took a walk along the beach. That's why I never showed up for my date with Kelly."

"And why you had no alibi for your whereabouts at the time Kyle died."

"His partner timed it perfectly."

"And you have no idea who Kyle's partner was?"

He pondered his answer for several seconds before saying, "I suspected someone, but it turns out I was wrong."

"What makes you think you were wrong?"

"Because the guy has an alibi," he said tiredly, as though it didn't matter any longer. He rubbed his fingers dejectedly into his eye sockets, which were shadowed with fatigue. "It was sort of a crazy idea, anyway. This person wouldn't be involved with drugs."

"Yesterday I would have said the same thing about Kyle."

They fell silent then, each lost in his own thoughts. Dusty's thoughts were grim. Tanner had been railroaded into prison in order to keep Kelly alive, and she had turned around and believed the worst about him.

Where was the justice in this? Where was his reward? He'd lost five years of his life—and he'd lost Kelly, as well.

It was such a waste.

* * *

Tori prowled the cabin like a caged animal. She glanced at the rain-slashed windows and held back a sigh. The storm was fierce and relentless—and so were her emotions.

She should be packing up her things for the move back home, but somehow she couldn't. Not now. Not yet. And Tori felt her throat tighten. *Home.* Where was her home, anyway? It certainly wasn't in Arizona. Not anymore. She'd left there at eighteen and hadn't been back, even for a visit. And she suddenly asked herself why.

But she already knew the answer. Deep inside, buried somewhere behind all her protective walls, she knew.

She'd met Dusty her first week of school, and from the moment she saw him, she knew she'd found a home. A real one.

In his life.

And in his heart.

She'd felt safe and protected with him. Secure. Wrapped up like a cocoon. Encased in warmth, yet allowed to breathe.

To be free.

Dusty and Alaska were one and the same. They both exemplified true strength and courage—and space. Space in which to grow and explore one's boundaries without fear. Space in which to discover one's true self.

And yet she was afraid now, terrified, her confidence shredded and scattered like so many snowflakes. Somehow she'd reached the point where fear had demolished her feelings toward Dusty, and left her life in shreds.

He was everything she was not—strong and tough. She pushed her way through life with a kind of hollow bravado, empty and cowardly. And when the chips were down, she'd wanted out. Out of Alaska. Out of the land of the living. Out of Dusty's life.

And she'd nearly destroyed them both in the process.

But what about Dusty? she thought miserably. Was she too late? Had she pushed him too hard? Had she finally succeeded in driving him away?

Tori paused by the front windows and watched the rainstorm outside, startled at these last questions that were thundering through her.

What was she thinking? It sounded to her as if she'd changed her mind about leaving. And she hadn't.

Had she?

Tori circled the living room slowly. Had she? Dakota was spending the day with Eleni so Tori could pack, but instead of packing, she was wandering around the cabin feeling miserable.

Was it a mistake to leave?

Or to stay?

She stood there, her brown eyes searching the cabin as she tore apart what were the shattered remains of her life—and slowly started to rebuild. She wanted her ducks all in a row again, and it was up to her to put them there.

Dakota, for one. She was a gift that Tori had very nearly thrown away.

Tori smiled at the thought of the little girl who had tumbled unexpectedly into her heart, shoved Shawn over and found room for herself. Tori felt something shift inside her, and she knew it was her heart opening slowly to allow the toddler room to grow.

She picked up a stuffed brown bear and hugged it to her, breathing in the scent of Dakota. The bear was one of Dakota's favorite toys.

Her troubled gaze landed on a small photograph of Dusty.

Would he be able to forgive her and give her another chance? she wondered in mounting panic. Would he let her stay in Alaska with him?

Would he take her back? If she asked him...if she told him how much she loved him, would he take her back?

She was still terrified at the thought of reentering the land of the living. That meant pain and doubt and uncertainty. It also meant joy and warmth and laughter. Most of the time.

And with Dusty it meant love—all of the time.

She needed to talk to Dusty. She had so many things she wanted to say to him....

She turned when she heard the key in the lock, and Dusty entered the cabin with the wind and the rain. He slammed the door shut and raked his hand through his wet hair. Tori ran to get him a towel.

He was soaked, the water running off his jacket and down his face, but all Tori wanted to do at that moment was to throw herself into his arms and tell him she loved him. And that she wasn't going to leave.

She restrained herself with an effort. "Let me take your jacket."

He shook his head and handed her the towel. "It's okay. Where's Dakota?"

"At Eleni's." He smelled like rain and leather and freshly washed denim and she had a sudden, sharp desire to spend the day snuggling with him in front of a hot, roaring fire.

It was raining, they only had two short flights later that afternoon, and Tanner could take both of those. And they had the cabin to themselves.

"Why?"

Tori had to drag her attention back to their conversation. "I...I wanted her out of the cabin while I was packing, but—"

"I see." His detached gaze skidded across her face. "I stopped by to give you this." He unzipped his leather jacket enough for him to slide his hand into the inside pocket, and he produced a slim folder.

"What is it?"

"Your plane ticket to Phoenix."

Tori felt as if he'd slapped her across the face. She was stunned, disoriented. Dusty had come over here early in the morning, during a thunderstorm, to bring her a plane ticket?

What perfect timing.

Why couldn't he have waited until she'd asked him for it? Why the rush? Why did he have to personally deliver it to her? Was he in that big of a rush to get her out of here?

She realized she was staring blankly at his outstretched hand, at the ticket he held, and she lifted her head slowly until her eyes met his.

God, he looked cold. Unapproachable. Distant. Was it so easy for him? It looked easy. It always had. To lose a father, a mother, a son—and now a wife. Nothing ever touched him. Nothing ever stopped him. He just plowed through life, always moving forward—and never looking back.

"It's what you wanted." His low voice broke into her whirling thoughts. "Your flight leaves at ten a.m., day after tomorrow."

She leveled her steady gaze into his, and nodded once. Then she turned around, saying over her shoulder, "Leave the ticket on the desk. I have to finish packing."

It was time she made the break, she was thinking as she entered the bedroom and closed the door behind her. Past time. And it was for his own good. And hers. In time he'd find someone else to love, someone else to marry and to be a mother to Dakota....

Tori suddenly put her hands over her face, hiding herself away. She tried to picture Dusty with another woman, but she couldn't. He'd belonged to her for too many years.

Somehow she had to find the strength to leave him... and Alaska... and Dakota. It wasn't her choice any longer. It was his. She'd pushed him too far, driven him too hard and now he was letting her go.

He was letting her walk out of his life.

She darted toward the closet and hauled down a suitcase from the top shelf. Placing it on the bed, she opened it and began tossing things inside.

It was time she packed, she'd been putting it off for too long. Her fear was piled into huge drifts around her, sheltering her, isolating her and confusing her. Tori pulled out a dresser drawer with a vengeance and carried it to the bed. She packed with new resolve, and a new strength of purpose.

Dusty had always had this maddening way about him, she railed inwardly. All things accommodated, all things fitted into his life in nice, neat little packages.

But Shawn's death didn't fit. There was no place in Dusty's life for their son's death. It was all a blank to him.

And now *she* was a blank to him. Because she didn't fit as easily as she used to.

Tori tilted the dresser drawer upside down and spilled the contents out on the bed. Then she hurled the empty drawer across the room, and watched it smash into the cabin wall. And she stood there, both satisfied and horrified, at what she had done.

The bedroom door opened and she turned, only to tingle with annoyance at the sight of Dusty standing in the doorway.

"Get out," she said in a low, flat voice, devoid of emotion. "I mean it, Dusty. Get out. Now."

He shook his head. "Do you think I object to a temper tantrum?" he asked. "It's about time you had one."

"I am not having a temper tantrum!" He laughed, and she tried fiercely to regain her dignity. "I dropped the damn drawer."

"Oh, yeah. Right. From the sound of it, you must have been up on the roof when you dropped it."

He was enjoying this, she thought furiously. And she turned away. "I'm packing my things. Do you want to help?" she said with bright malice, and there was a tiny silence.

And then he said in a conversational tone, "Do you know what I was thinking just now?"

"I can't wait to find out." She rolled up a T-shirt and stuffed it into the suitcase.

"I was thinking how we never used to argue. About anything." She looked up quickly and saw him leaning casually against the doorjamb, and scanning the room—and her—with keen and critical green eyes. Tori turned back to the suitcase, steeling herself for what was coming. "Until a few months ago. We've always been perfectly in tune with each other."

"It's hard to remember a time when I wasn't arguing with you," she snapped.

The timbre of Dusty's voice changed. "You and I don't know how to fight. We're not used to it. We lack the skills—and the guts—for a real fight."

"A real fight?" Tori was startled out of her annoyance. She turned around to face him. "Are you inviting me outside for a fistfight? Or a duel at sundown?"

"I want you to be honest with me."

Impatiently, she turned away. "Oh, Dusty, leave me alone."

"Not until you talk to me."

"I have no intention of talking to you."

"Have you ever thrown anything before?" When she glared back at him in surprise, he continued. "Or put your fist through a wall? Or screamed at someone? Or even beat someone over the head with a pillow?"

Tori was now openly staring at the man who was resting diagonally in the doorway. "You mean, have I ever behaved in an uncivilized way?"

"Yeah. Uncivilized." Several seconds ticked by. "Human."

There was something in his eyes...some glint she couldn't fathom. She started to answer and then caught herself. What was he up to now?

Whatever it was, she wanted no part of it.

"Tori, have you ever lost complete control—even once?"

She looked coolly at him then. "No."

"Why not?"

She shrugged, and he eased himself off the doorjamb, and came toward her.

"Why not?"

"Because it's pointless."

"It's pointless?"

She nodded. "Of course. To make a fool of oneself is pointless. And immature."

His green eyes snared hers. "That's the most ridiculous thing I've ever heard anyone utter in my entire life."

"I knew you'd say that," she hooted. "You and your legendary McKay temper."

He was standing too close. Much too close. "Tanner's the one with the legendary McKay temper—legacy from my dad. But you know what, Tori? At least with Tanner, I've always known where I stood, as difficult as that may be at times. I can't say the same about you."

Tori's attention was fixed on the pair of socks in her hand. "Is this payback time?" she asked him quietly. "I'm leaving, so you insult me?"

"I'm not trying to insult you. I'm trying to get at the truth."

"The truth? What truth?"

"About us. About you and me." Dusty's voice was soft, his gaze level. "I wanted to marry you after my father was killed, but you said no. You had to finish college first, and I had Tanner and Skylar to look after. It all sounded so reasonable and mature."

"Dusty—"

"I wanted to get married after you graduated, but again, the answer was no. Only I never got a reason I could live with." He paused. "In fact, I never got a reason, period."

She threw the socks into the suitcase and turned to face him, hands on hips. "Why are you bringing this up now?"

"Because I figure you owe me an explanation."

"What difference could it possibly make?"

"I want to know if these past five years have been a lie."

Tori stared up at him in disbelief. "How can you ask me such a thing?" she whispered when she found her voice.

"It's a simple question, Tori. And one you should be able to answer."

"It's a stupid question."

"The hell it is."

"Dusty..."

"You had me wait an additional two years after you graduated. Why?"

"I don't know!" she snapped.

"Good. Now we're getting somewhere."

"Why are you doing this? Why are you asking me all these questions?"

"Because you're leaving, and I want reasons. And I want all of them this time. Not just the ones you think I want to hear," he stated calmly. "Because, you see, Tori, I'm not buying all this newfound fear inside you. I think it was there all along, just waiting for a convenient excuse to get between us and rip apart our lives."

"Shawn's death was not a convenient excuse," she said through gritted teeth.

"No?"

"No!" Tori was so angry she was shaking. And the urge to strike out, to hit him, to *hurt* him, was suddenly more than she could bear. She wrung her hands to keep from slapping him.

"Then why did you put me off for so long?"

"Because you were known for your one-night stands and I didn't want to be another notch on your belt."

"Yeah. I know." He said it softly, but there was something grim and determined in him that should have warned her to watch her step.

But she didn't. He had started this, and she meant to finish it, once and for all.

"You'd already slept with half the girls in school before I even got there."

"Not that many."

"Then you fell in love with me. How was I supposed to know you meant it? It took time, Dusty, lots of time...for me to learn to trust you...."

"And you finally did."

"Yes."

"But you made your first mistake when you left me alone with Shawn that day."

Tori backed up a step, her eyes staring into his, and she shook her head. His face was like carved ivory—and just as unreadable.

"Why don't you do us both a favor and just admit it?"

She shook her head vehemently, and backed up another step. "I...I don't know what you're talking about."

"The hell you don't."

"Dusty—" It came out as a whimper.

"Say it."

"Dusty..."

He crossed the distance between them and grabbed her. Giving her a shake, he said roughly, "You blame me for Shawn's death. You've always blamed me. Only you refuse to admit it. To yourself. And certainly not to me. You think I didn't take care of him. You think I could have prevented his death. And that's the real reason that you couldn't stand me touching you all those months."

A bubble of intense rage burst in her head. The memories rushed in, sweeping aside everything she had carefully constructed to keep them out, and her rage and anguish were boundless. *"I thought you'd take care of him! But you fell asleep on the couch and let him die!"*

Then she gazed blankly up at him, realized what she'd said, and started to cry, clapping a hand over her mouth in horror. Then the cries of frustration changed swiftly into screams of grief. And rage.

Dusty felt dark resignation chill him as if seeking to turn him to ice. He reached out for her, reached past the rage, ignored the screams and held her tightly.

It was done. It was out in the open now—for better or for worse.

But he'd had no choice.

She screamed and vented her rage—rage that soon crumbled... and then she was sobbing wildly, and begging him to forgive her.

"I didn't mean it...I didn't..."

"Yes, you did," he said softly, his arms tightening around her.

For twelve months, she'd held all this inside and felt guilty about it. Dusty guided her over to the bed, slid the suitcase onto the floor and pulled the covers down with one hand. She was shivering violently now, hugging herself and trembling, and Dusty got her into bed and pulled the covers over her.

He stretched out beside her and she turned immediately toward him, to bury her face into his shoulder. She was crying in earnest now, with fresh emotion every few minutes.

She hadn't cried at all when Shawn died. Not even at the funeral. Just about everyone in Nome had attended the church service, and there hadn't been a dry eye in the place.

Except for Tori.

He shook his head slightly, unable to understand how she'd managed to keep it together for so long.

Dusty watched the storm raging outside. The rain was coming down in sheets, hitting the windows with a vengeance, and he watched for a long time. Tori cried until she was exhausted, and then her soft, gentle breathing told him she was asleep.

He was having a hard time with his own memories crashing in on him. He'd blocked out the details of that day so thoroughly that it took some time to retrieve them. But once the memories filtered through, it was as if someone had taken a huge searchlight and aimed it at the darkest, most painful, private part of him.

He'd been recovering from a bad cold and the flu. He'd been too sick to fly, but not sick enough to stay in bed. Tori had always taken all his flights while he was sick, and that particular day was no different. Except their baby-sitter had a worse cold than Dusty, and he'd insisted that he was well enough to take care of one small infant all by himself.

It had been a normal day. Dusty had fed and bathed his ten-week-old son, and put him down for his afternoon nap. Then he'd plopped down on the couch, turned on the television and settled down to watch an old movie.

And halfway through the movie he'd dozed off.

Dusty stared out at the rain as he remembered. He'd been off medication. He hadn't so much as taken an aspirin that day. He'd simply drifted off to sleep.

When he woke up, the movie was going off, and he got up, turned off the television and headed for the kitchen to make himself a pot of coffee. At the last minute, he went into the nursery—and discovered his son was dead.

The doctor called it sudden infant death syndrome—crib death. The cessation of breathing, during sleep, of a seemingly healthy infant under the age of five months. Sometimes it could be traced to a chronic oxygen deficiency—but usually the baby simply dies in his or her sleep, without any prior warning.

According to the medical examiner, Shawn had been dead about thirty-five minutes when Dusty found him.

Dusty had closed his mind long ago to the details of that day. They were too painful to think about. To talk about. But that day had driven a wedge between him and Tori…a wedge that threatened to permanently split them apart if they didn't deal with it.

The doctor had assured both Dusty and Tori that Shawn hadn't made a sound, that there was no way Dusty could have known the baby was in trouble. And he was quick to point out that Shawn would have, in all probability, died anyway. If not that afternoon, then maybe that night or the next, when they were both sound asleep.

It had been just a matter of time.

But Dusty was still unable to absolve himself of the guilt. In his head he knew he wasn't to blame. But in his heart …

Tori moved closer in her sleep and his attention was suddenly distracted by her. She was a bundle of red-gold hair, yellow sweater and stonewashed jeans in a tangle of sheets and quilt. A flash of lust—full-blown and prodding—seized him.

He had taken such a chance today. He'd pushed, and he'd pushed hard, to get at the truth. But to what end? He had managed to break down her walls—but her walls were the only protection she had.

That *he* had.

And Dusty had to wonder if he hadn't contributed to the building of those walls. Getting at the truth could be worse than hiding behind walls of denial. Getting at the truth meant the kind of honest feelings their relationship might not be able to withstand.

"How long have I been asleep?"

He glanced at her, startled to realize her eyes were open. "About an hour," he answered, stroking her hair back from her face. She looked exhausted, and her thick eyelashes fluttered sleepily against her cheeks.

"Is the storm over?"

"Yeah," he said softly, "it's over."

But she didn't hear him. She was already asleep, and Dusty drew her close to him again. He stared up at the ceiling for a long time, content just to hold her. For however long she'd let him.

Chapter 15

Dusty hopped out of the cockpit of his SR-9 and slung the mailbag over his shoulder. He was halfway to the office when he turned and watched Tanner come in for a landing. The storm had cleansed the air and the sky was a cloudless, vivid blue this afternoon. Tanner landed his plane and jumped out, and Dusty waited for his brother to join him.

Tanner didn't waste any time. "I have something to tell you," he said, and pulled him toward the office.

"I have to take care of the mail—"

"That can wait. This is important."

It was then that Dusty noticed the expression in his brother's gray eyes, and he allowed himself to be hustled into the office.

"What's this about?" Dusty dumped the mail sack on the desk and turned to face Tanner.

"Do you remember I told you Kyle's partner had an alibi?"

"I remember."

"I checked out his alibi again today." Tanner looked elated. "I'd talked to this girl yesterday. They were dating at the time of Kyle's death, and I thought—"

"Who was dating?"

"The girl and Kyle's partner. Anyway, she told me he was with her the night Kyle died—the entire night."

"You just walked right up to a stranger and asked her a question like that?"

Tanner looked startled, and then he shot him a hesitant grin. "She's not a stranger. I went to school with her, and we're still friends. She remembered that night clearly because it was the night the two of them became engaged, and they woke up the next morning to the news that Kyle was dead—and I'd been arrested. That blew my theory on who Kyle's partner was—"

"Because he was with her the night Kyle died."

"Right. But this morning, after I left you, I decided to try again. To see if I could get some line on this guy. I was thinking maybe she'd lied, or simply forgotten the details of that night." He looked suddenly grim. "I thought it was worth a try. But Dusty, when I got there, she was in bad shape."

"What happened to her?" But he was afraid he already knew the answer.

"The guy beat her up because she talked to me."

Dusty stared blankly at him, digesting this in slow degrees. "Did she say that?"

He nodded. "He totally lost it, accusing her of conspiring with me against him. With very little prodding I got the truth out of her. The night Kyle died, they had this big fight and he left about eight. He showed up at two the next morning with flowers and an engagement ring."

"Which means he had more than enough time to kill Kyle, plant the evidence in your plane and get back to her." Dusty picked up the mailbag and started for the door. "I'll drop this off at the post office, and then we'll go and see Caleb—"

"No, we can't, Dusty. Not yet."

Dusty turned around. "Why not? You've been carrying this around inside you for five years. It's time—"

"Kyle's partner was Joey Arnett."

Dusty stared at him in disbelief. *Joey?* He was Dusty's friend. He'd lived with the guy. He'd shared a room at college with him for two years.

"Then you're talking about Kathy."

Tanner nodded again. "They've been engaged at least a half dozen times. I guess she's lucky he always had cold feet when it came to marriage," he added dryly.

"How is she?" he asked as he tried to collect his jumbled, whirling thoughts.

"She was beaten up pretty badly. I took her to the hospital and the doc said she'd be okay."

"Tanner, we have to go to the police," Dusty stated flatly. "We have no choice," he added before Tanner could form a reply.

He watched as his brother struggled with the consequences of this decision, and patiently waited for him to make up his mind. And in the end, he did exactly as Dusty thought—or hoped—he would do.

He decided to let go of this one-man crusade and accept help when it was offered to him.

Dusty watched the resignation enter the gray eyes, and then Tanner walked out of McKay Air Service and started down the street toward the police station. Dusty followed him.

* * *

Tori awoke without knowing exactly what had awakened her. She stretched like a cat in the large bed, her head turning to face the window. Sunlight drifted through the window and across the quilt.

That was it, she thought sleepily. The storm was over.

A loud knocking on the cabin door caused her to bolt upright in bed. What in the—? She slung back the covers, threw her legs over the bed and raced to the front door.

"Tori? Are you home?" She heard a familiar voice call out, and she opened the door to find Eleni standing there with Dakota. The baby reached eagerly for her and Tori took her out of Eleni's arms. "I have to rush off. My daughter and her whole family are coming for dinner."

She backed swiftly away, barely giving Tori a chance to thank her. But at the bottom of the steps she turned and said, "I'm trying a recipe I copied out of one of your cookbooks." She smiled and waved, and headed toward her house.

Tori closed the cabin door and padded into the kitchen in her yellow socks. She yawned widely and then laughed as Dakota tried to stick her fingers into Tori's mouth.

"What have you been up to, sweet thing? Did you like your visit with Eleni?"

She settled Dakota into her high chair, handed her a spoon to play with and turned to make herself a cup of tea. She felt groggy and disoriented, but strangely at peace, as if a huge weight had been lifted off her. The cabin was quiet, almost eerily so, she noticed as she added water to the kettle and set it on the back of the stove. A few minutes later, she carried her cup of hot, sweetened tea to the table and sat down. It was then that she saw the note. She picked it up and read:

I took the afternoon flight. There was no need to wake you, and you needed to sleep. Home at the usual time, more or less.

Dusty

She nervously stirred her cup of tea, the events of the morning clicking into place. She abandoned her steaming cup of tea and suddenly, wearily, buried her face in her hands and shook her head.

Oh, God, what had she done? And why had he left before she could explain?

Explain what? a tiny voice inside her mind demanded, and she slowly raised her head. How could she possibly explain her behavior this past year? She didn't understand it herself. Except that she'd been devastated over Shawn's death.

So devastated that she'd turned on the most important person in her life. The only person who had ever deeply and truly loved her. The only person she'd allowed to get close since she was a small child.

Dusty. The only man she would ever love.

Tori took a cautious sip of her hot tea. She had never blamed Dusty for Shawn's death. She'd blamed herself.

All her life she'd railed against the traditional woman's role, fighting like hell to be better, stronger, more gutsy than any man—fighting desperately to prove her worth to her father. And being a bush pilot in Alaska was proof positive that she had succeeded in doing something even her father's son would probably be unable to do.

She hadn't wanted to give up being a bush pilot. Even for her own children. And she'd secretly sworn to herself that a baby wouldn't hamper her in any way, that she could work and still be a mother—and be excellent at both.

Shawn's birth had only deepened her happiness. It had in no way diminished it, and she'd savored those ten weeks she'd spent with her small son. But when Dusty got sick, when the cold and flu had left him weak and incapable of taking his flights, she'd jumped at the chance of taking them for him.

It was as if she'd been set free, at least for a few hours every day. Free of endless diapers and feedings and the sheer work involved in caring for a newborn baby. She had missed flying, and was eagerly looking forward to going back to work when Shawn was three months old. And if Dusty's getting sick had pushed her back into being a pilot sooner than she'd originally planned, then she'd been more than happy to do what needed to be done. She'd been secretly thrilled—and had felt guilty about being thrilled.

But then Shawn died and the guilt flooded in, unrelenting in its power to wipe out all reason and intellect. And sanity.

She should have been there. She should have been in the cabin when Shawn died.

And not because she could have prevented his death. And not because she felt Dusty had neglected their son.

But she felt she should have been with Shawn when he died, because, to a mother, there simply wasn't a more important place to be.

She cringed and felt a shudder go through her as she remembered Dusty's words from this morning: *"You blamed me for his death. And that's the real reason you couldn't stand me touching you all those months."*

That part simply wasn't true.

Tori stared hard at the toddler in the high chair, happily banging her spoon against the wooden surface. The truth was, she stated clearly, honestly to herself, that she'd been afraid of getting pregnant again.

She didn't want another child to love, and possibly lose. And she'd been willing to do anything to achieve that false sense of security.

Even ruin her own marriage.

And it was a false sense of security. Because being alone wasn't being secure—it was clinging to fear. And fear had a way of wiping out all the joy and wonder of life.

It wiped out all the good things about having a baby in the house. And it wiped out the deep-down, gut-wrenching trust she had built up with Dusty over the years.

Was it too late for them? she wondered, her thoughts subdued. She'd hurt him terribly—not just this morning, but every single day this past year.

Where was he? Why wasn't he here?

They'd only had two scheduled flights for today, and Tanner could have made both. So why wasn't he here?

But she knew why. Either someone had dropped by the office unexpectedly, hiring him for a quick hop out to one of the villages, or, more than likely, Dusty had taken one of the flights in order to give himself time to think.

Dusty was predictable. When he was hurting or confused or wrestling with a problem, he always headed for his plane and took to the skies. It calmed him and gave him strength. It was a release, a soaring of spirit.

And she'd wanted to take it away from him.

Tori sipped her tea impatiently, willing Dusty to return soon. She had so much she wanted to say to him . . . so much she needed to explain. . . .

A knock on the cabin door made her jump, and she laughed. She ran to the door, flinging it open after a brief glance out the window told her it was Joey Arnett.

"Am I disturbing you?"

"Of course not." She pulled him into the cabin. "I was just having a cup of tea. Want some?"

"Sure."

He followed her to the kitchen, and Tori took a cup and saucer out of the cabinet, set them on the counter, dropped a tea bag into the cup and reached for the kettle of hot water. Turning, she asked, "Do you take milk or lemon with—"

She broke off in horror. Joey was holding Dakota, cradling her against him with his left hand. In his right hand was a gun, held at hip level, and it was trained on Tori.

Dusty paced the room, wondering how Tanner could stand there by the window so patiently. He'd spilled his guts to Caleb, holding nothing back this time, and Dusty was proud of him. He had a rather remarkable kid brother, he thought, watching Tanner stare out into the street.

Tanner had gone through hell these past five years, keeping this all inside, and coping with prison. But he'd come through it with a quiet dignity that Dusty didn't believe he could have managed if he'd been in Tanner's shoes.

Caleb opened the door and popped his head in. "I finished talking to the sheriff and we're going to pay a visit to Kathy Kirkpatrick."

"What about Joey?" Tanner asked from the window.

Caleb's expression was sober. "We'll bring him in for questioning."

"He isn't here?"

"He's already left for the day. We'll drop by his house after we talk to Kathy. In the meantime, you two go home and forget about this. And if you guys happen to run across him before we do, give us a call. But stay clear of him."

Out on the street, Tanner watched in silence as the sheriff and Caleb drove off. Then he turned to Dusty. "What now?"

Dusty slapped him on the back affectionately, concerned at the expression on his brother's face. He looked drained, spent, battered—as if the past five years had suddenly caught up with him. "Come on, I'll buy you a beer. Or a cup of coffee," he added with a grin, remembering the flight schedule for tomorrow. They both had flights for eight tomorrow morning.

They had to think about hiring another pilot to take Tori's place, he thought dismally as they walked into Mooseheart.

Tori. Just the thought of her made him cringe.

Somewhere up in the sky this afternoon, he'd decided to let her go without putting up a fight. He owed her that much. If she wanted to go, he wasn't going to stand in her way.

It was with a heavy heart that he carried his cup of coffee over to the table by the window.

"Oh, man, what a day," Tanner groaned, leaning back in his seat.

"Why do you suppose Joey freaked out like that? Burning the hangar, rigging your plane to crash, beating up Kathy—it doesn't make a lot of sense."

He shrugged. "I don't know. It's not like I knew he was Kyle's partner or anything. I was just asking questions all over town to see what I could come up with. I didn't know if Kyle's partner had ever lived in Nome, or if he had, if he was still here. But I had to start somewhere."

Dusty was curious about one thing. "What made you suspect Joey?"

"I didn't. Not at first. But the night of the fire, I saw him hanging around my plane. He wasn't doing anything, but that in itself seemed odd. Guys were running all over the place trying to put out the fire, and he was just standing there." Tanner dumped two spoonfuls of sugar into his coffee and stirred it. "After Tori went down in my plane, I couldn't get Joey out of my head. I started remembering things...."

"Like what?"

"I remembered that Kyle wasn't exactly comfortable around Joey—not enough to notice, but it was there. If you bothered to look for it."

Dusty shook his head. "Now all we need is the proof. Which won't be easy. Five years is a long time—"

"At least Caleb can bring him in for assault and battery, if nothing else," Tanner broke in. "Kathy wants to press charges." He paused and his gaze locked on Dusty's. "This isn't the first time he's beaten her."

Tori's eyes snapped from the gun to his face. Joey's expression was unreadable. "W-what are you doing?"

"I'm sorry, Tori. I truly am. But I need a hostage and you're it."

"Joey—"

"Just move toward the front door. Slowly."

Her hand still hovered near the kettle. The kettle that was nearly full of hot water. Hot enough to burn him. Distract him so that she could get away. For a brief, wild moment she considered throwing the kettle at his head, but one look at Dakota made her quickly change her mind. The baby was too close, much too close to him. Whatever she used to hurt Joey would hurt Dakota, as well.

Tori ran her hands nervously down the sides of her jeans, trying to think. She had to find a way out of this.

She'd taken classes in self-defense. Fight or flee—those were usually the only two options. And fight only if the guy was manhandling you.

But he was manhandling her daughter! Holding her like a shield, hiding behind a one-year-old child! If it came down to it, would he actually harm a baby?

Tori looked into the cold, pale blue eyes and suppressed a shudder. She didn't know what he was capable of, but she knew she couldn't take the chance of finding out.

She couldn't fight—and she couldn't run. Not when he had her baby.

"Leave Dakota here and I'll go with you." She spoke calmly, softly, so she wouldn't frighten Dakota Grace. She was surprised she could even speak at all. "Just . . . leave her in her high chair and I'll willingly go with you."

She stopped talking when she saw him shake his head slowly back and forth, his eyes never leaving hers. He gestured toward the door with his gun, and Tori moved away from the counter.

"W-where are we going?"

"To Anchorage. You're going to fly us there."

"Why?" Again he gestured toward the doorway and Tori moved toward it, keeping her back to the door and her eyes on his face. "Why do you have to go anywhere? This is your home—"

He laughed, and the unpleasant sound cut through the dense silence in the cabin. "Not anymore. Tanner took care of that. He's at the sheriff's office now, with Dusty. But, of course, you already knew that."

She started to deny it, and then a thought struck her, nearly blinding her with its clarity, a thought so unbelievable despite the hard evidence pointed directly at her.

She stopped walking, her hands clutching each side of the doorway for support.

"You're the one," she whispered, feeling the reality claw at her throat, nearly choking off her air.

He flashed her a nasty grin. "The one?" His tone was slightly mocking.

She continued to stare at him. And out of nowhere something else clicked into place. That comment he'd made yesterday about some danger to Tanner's health. She thought he was talking about Tanner's "drinking problem," but that hadn't been it at all.

He'd been warning her to get Tanner to back off.

There was a terrible silence and then Tori said quietly, "You killed Kyle Jordan." And watched his icy gaze flatten and go dead.

"I had to."

"Why? *Why*, Joey? Why did you have to kill him?"

"It was an accident." His gaze shifted nervously.

"An accident? You smashed him in the head with a baseball bat! With *Tanner's* baseball bat!"

"I had to stop him from warning Tanner. I didn't want to kill him. I just...wanted to stop him." The words came out soft and slow, and for a moment it was as if her friend Joey was standing there—instead of this stranger with a gun.

"Why was he trying to warn Tanner?" she asked. If she kept him talking long enough, if she could distract him, then maybe...

"I put drugs in Tanner's plane."

Tori was horrified. Drugs! Oh, God, that was it! Kyle must have been involved with drugs! And that's why he was dead.

"Why would you do that to Tanner?"

He laughed. "Because he wouldn't come and play with me."

Tori frowned. "He wouldn't...?"

"Money, sweetheart. It all comes down to money. I needed Tanner and his plane to run a few errands for me. But he refused."

"So you set him up."

He shrugged. "He refused to play."

"And you killed Kyle."

"That was self-defense."

"And made it look as though Tanner had killed his best friend."

"It worked, didn't it?"

"And then you became a cop."

"I had to clean up my act and become a solid citizen. Kyle was dead and Tanner was in jail—so playtime was over." His gaze hardened. "Now turn around and start walking toward the front door. And don't stop until I tell you to."

She turned around and walked through the doorway, saying over her shoulder, "How did you get into dealing drugs?"

"Shut up!" His voice was low and furious.

Maybe she could talk him out of this. Maybe there was a chance she could get him to release her. She'd known him for years. He was her friend.

She had to talk him out of this! She couldn't get in a plane with him. If she did, then she'd never get Dakota out alive. They'd both be killed.

Every instinct inside her was screaming out how useless it was to talk to Joey. He was desperate and desperate men did crazy things. He wouldn't listen to her. She knew he wouldn't.

But she had to try.

He had nothing else to lose. But she did. She had her baby's life to protect.

"Joey, you don't have to do it this way. Explain to the police what happened. Tell him Kyle's death was an accident—"

"And how do I explain setting Tanner up to take the fall?"

"You made a mistake—"

"One mistake?" His laugh was more like a grunt of self-contempt. "Count them, Tori—see how many I've made."

"Then don't make another one. Let us go." They were nearing the door, and once outside there was a chance they'd be seen. And then what? If anyone tried to rescue them, Dakota could be harmed. And she had to be protected at all costs. "Please, Joey, think about what you're doing. Do you know what the penalty is for kidnapping?"

"It's no use, sweetheart. So shut up."

They had reached the door and she stopped, fighting down her rising panic. "What are you going to do with us in Anchorage?"

"I'll let you go."

She didn't believe him. He couldn't let them go. Tori knew too much. This conversation had sealed her fate, even if he'd originally planned to release her. Which she doubted. And Dakota— Oh, God, what would he do to her baby daughter?

"Open the door."

"Joey, please . . . leave Dakota here."

"Open the door!"

She grew still. Would he shoot her if she refused to leave this cabin...if she refused to board a plane and fly him to Anchorage? She turned to face him, lifting her chin slightly in defiance.

She was nearly choking on fear and frustration, but she simply couldn't let this man take her baby outside where God only knows what could happen to her.

"No," she said.

"Open the damn door!"

"You won't shoot me, Joey. You're not a killer. You said Kyle's death was an accident. And besides, if you shoot me, who would fly the plane?"

She saw him start to waver, and then, abruptly, his face changed. Hardened. His blue eyes glazed over. And when he spoke, his voice was low and deadly. "Open the door or I'm going to shoot Dakota instead of you."

He paused to drop a tender kiss on top of the baby's jet-black hair, his eyes never leaving Tori's.

Madness raced through her at the coldly calculated threat, and she struggled to hold on to her control. "Y-you wouldn't shoot a child. A b-baby—"

"Don't bet on it."

She believed him then. She watched the edge of desperation tint his eyes a darker blue, and a flash of insanity deepened them.

Tori turned and reached for the doorknob.

Tanner set a plate of sweet rolls on the table and dropped wearily into a chair. Dusty watched as he dumped two spoonfuls of sugar into his coffee and carefully stirred it, his manner tense, preoccupied.

"You did the right thing," Dusty said gently.

"Yeah. I guess."

"You don't sound convinced."

He sighed heavily. "It's not that. But why would Kyle and Joey get involved with drug trafficking? They were both from good families, and families with money. More money than we ever had."

"I don't know what to tell you."

Tanner pinched little pieces off one of the sweet rolls, rolled them into tiny balls between his fingertips and dropped them on the table.

"Look, it doesn't matter why," Dusty insisted. "We'll probably never know the whole story. Maybe *they* don't even know why or how they got involved. But the important thing here is to get you off the hook."

The gray eyes darted up to his and he seemed a little startled. "I didn't think about that."

Dusty's grin was fleeting. "Your name will be cleared. You'll probably even get a written apology from the governor of Alaska," he added lightly, and Tanner laughed.

"Yeah. Right. And I bet the warden calls me up and invites me to his house for dinner."

Dusty reached for his coffee cup. "Stranger things have happened." He took a sip, his glance straying to the door, and he automatically tensed when he saw Zach Jordan enter Mooseheart. He set his cup down with a gentle thud and leaned forward to grin broadly at his brother. "What I'm waiting for is to see the look on Zach's face when he's finally forced into believing you're innocent."

Tanner didn't answer, he simply turned in his seat and followed Zach's progress into the room. His expression didn't change when Zach sauntered over to their table.

"You guys mind if I join you?" He shrugged. "It's crowded in here."

"Have a seat." Tanner was the one who answered him, much to Dusty's surprise.

"Have you talked to Caleb lately?" Dusty couldn't resist asking the question, although he knew Caleb wouldn't release any information before checking it out— even to his own brother.

"Not since last night."

"What about Joey? Have you seen him?"

Zach shook his head and then stopped abruptly, as if a thought occurred to him. "Actually, I saw him a few minutes ago. He was headed out toward your place."

Dusty jumped to his feet. His one thought was Tori. She was alone in the cabin. And she didn't know about Joey!

Dusty had a vague awareness of Tanner calling over to Suzi, "The sheriff and Caleb are at the hospital. Call them and tell them to meet us at Dusty's. Tell them we think Joey's with Tori."

Dusty pushed his way out into the street and then broke into a run. And only part of him registered the fact that he was being flanked by both Tanner and Zach. The other part was focused entirely on getting to Tori as quickly as possible.

"I need my boots."

"What?" Joey sounded more curious than outraged, and Tori looked down at her yellow socks.

"I need my boots." She turned once again to look at him, one hand on the doorknob.

Joey stared at her uncertainly. "You don't need them."

"We'll draw attention to ourselves this way. No one walks around Nome in their socks—"

"I'm telling you to forget it!"

Tori hesitated, and then opened the cabin door. She headed outside, only to pause on the front step when Joey ordered her to stop.

She felt the gun barrel resting against the small of her back, and heard Joey's voice, low and rough, against her ear. "No sudden moves. Walk slowly down the steps and toward the hangar." Then he laughed, a low, hollow sound. "Just two good friends taking the baby out for some air," he drawled. "Now move."

Tori walked down the steps and looked around. She noticed all four planes were lined up outside the charred ruins of the McKay hangar—the two floatplanes in the water, the other two on land—so that meant Tanner and Dusty must be around somewhere, but she didn't see them.

And she didn't want to see them. She closed her eyes momentarily, praying that both of them were safe in Mooseheart, playing pool or chatting with Suzi—anywhere but here.

Joey was teetering on the edge of control, on the brink of insanity, and she didn't know what he'd do if things didn't go the way he wanted.

Somehow she had to get out of this by herself. She had to get Dakota away from him.

"We're taking the blue and white one," he suddenly told her.

"Okay."

They passed the hangar and Joey urged her toward the blue and white Dornier DO 27 with his gun. And out of the corner of her eye, she saw three men reach the Cessna 185 ski-plane, which was parked next to the one Joey insisted they take.

She saw them briefly—Dusty, Tanner and Zach—just before they ducked behind the wing of the ski-plane. And she started praying.

Chapter 16

Tori stared straight ahead, her gaze fixed on the cockpit of the Dornier DO 27, her nerves taut, screaming for release. She didn't know how much more of this she could take. They were getting closer to the plane with every passing moment, and she could no longer see Dusty or the others.

What were they going to do? Surely they'd be careful. Wouldn't they? Joey was holding Dakota like a shield, the damned coward! If someone made the wrong move...

"Good girl," Joey said. "I always knew you were smart. Now let's get in the plane and then we can relax."

"Relax? With a gun in my back?" Tori stole a look at him over her shoulder. "Can't you put the gun away?"

"Get in the plane."

Dusty's gaze darted from Tori to Dakota, and then back again, his gaze lingering on Tori as he listened to this exchange. They were close enough for him to hear everything.

They were close enough for him to reach out and—

Dusty started to move forward when he was yanked back, and held against the body of the Cessna 185. Zach growled in his ear, "He has a gun—and the baby." When Dusty tried to wrench himself out of the iron grip, Zach added sharply, "You want to get them both killed?" And then his tone softened. "We have to stall him somehow until Caleb gets here—"

He broke off when they both realized Tanner was already moving around the edge of the wingtip.

"Tanner—" Dusty whispered furiously, but it was too late.

Tanner moved into Joey's range of vision, and Tori stiffened and closed her eyes, knowing he was going to squeeze the trigger. And she was stunned when he didn't.

"Well, well, the local hero to the rescue," Joey drawled.

"I'll fly you anywhere you want to go." Tanner's voice was calm. "Give Tori the baby and let them go back to the cabin, and then you and I can make a clean getaway."

He laughed. "Are you out of your mind?" And then, "Yes, I think you probably are." Joey shook his head slightly as though he couldn't believe what he was hearing. "You're a real piece of work, you know that, McKay? The innocent jailbird. The self-righteous dogooder who got his best friend killed. And now the hero who charges up, all hot to save the day. Where the hell do you get off telling me what to do?" he snarled suddenly, shoving the gun more firmly into Tori's back, causing her to jump in fear.

Dusty forced himself to remain in his crouched position, to remain calm. Zach had released him, and was closely watching the two men and listening intently to what they were saying.

Dusty's gaze swept over to Dakota. Why wasn't she crying or wiggling or something? he wondered in frustration. Something, anything so Joey would get tired of holding her and put her down. But lately, the toddler had been handled by so many strangers, what was one more to her?

His eyes lingered on the baby's little face. She was quiet and content, the coal black eyes—so much like Matt's— watching everything with interest.

"It's me you want," Tanner was saying, and Dusty swung his attention back to his brother.

"You're damned right about that!"

Dusty motioned to Zach that he was going to try to get behind them, and Zach nodded, moving under the wing and toward the back of the Cessna 185. Dusty circled around the front of the plane, slowly, his eyes on Joey, and then moved around the front of the DO 27. He could hear the entire exchange between Tanner and Joey.

If Tanner could just keep him talking long enough for Caleb and the sheriff to get there. Or if he could only keep him distracted long enough . . .

"You did quite a number on Kathy's face," Tanner said casually.

"You always did have the hots for her, didn't you, McKay? I saw the way you so gently escorted her to the hospital this morning—"

"You were watching?"

He laughed. "I knew she'd call you, or you'd come nosing around her house again. She gave you an earful this morning, didn't she?"

"You might say that."

"I saw you and Dusty hightail it over to the sheriff's office, so I thought it was time to get out of here. And I knew just the way to do it, too. What better hostages than your sweet sister-in-law and Matt's orphaned kid? Nice touch, wouldn't you say? Lends a little drama to the situation."

"A lot of drama," he replied evenly, and Tori saw him glance at her. The silver-gray eyes were calm, reassuring, and she looked back at Tanner, hoping she didn't look as terrified as she felt.

"Hop up into the cockpit, Tori." Joey's voice startled her and she moved to open the door of the DO 27, her eyes glancing toward the front of the plane, where she saw a flash of faded jeans and dark blond hair.

Dusty crouched down, his hands on the nose of the DO 27, and his deep green eyes locked on hers for an endless moment. She had so much to say to him. Too much.

She wanted to tell him she was sorry for this past year, that she didn't blame him for Shawn's death. She wanted to tell him she wanted to stay with him, here in Alaska, forever. She wanted to tell him she loved him. And that she wanted to be Dakota's mother; that in reality, she already was.

She wanted to tell him she was scared she'd never get the chance to get him back, and build a new life with him.

"Why didn't you cut me loose, McKay?" Joey was saying peevishly. "Why'd you make me do this?"

"Why'd you set me up?"

He laughed. "I couldn't resist."

"And Kelly?"

"Kelly had the two things I needed to expand my operation—a brother and a fiancé who were both bush pilots."

"So you used her to keep us in line."

"Why not?" He grinned. "It worked, didn't it?" Then his grin faded. "At least it worked with Kyle. But not you. No, you were too cool to work for me—even if it meant Kelly's safety."

"So you decided to get even."

"You persuaded Kyle to turn himself in—and me along with him."

"Is that why you killed him?"

"It was an accident."

"No, it wasn't, Joey," Tanner said softly.

"It was an accident!" he roared, and Tori flinched. She heard Dakota whimper in fright. Dusty's green eyes, gently holding her still, were the only thing that kept her from whirling around to offer comfort to the toddler.

Tanner was trying to keep him distracted . . . trying to stall for time—and it was working. Tori was still outside the cockpit.

But Joey was becoming more and more agitated. She could almost smell his fury . . . and his fear.

"Kyle was a featherbrain!" he said fiercely. "A wimp! He needed a damned keeper!" Joey's laugh was short and ugly. "Kyle came to me first, did you know that, McKay? He came to *me!* Wanted a little extra cash. Seems he couldn't keep his hands off Zach's girlfriend. So I showed him how he could get it."

Dusty cringed, wondering how Zach was taking this barrage of information he shouldn't be hearing. Zach was hidden from view, only the sleeve of his jacket was visible from where Dusty was standing, and he could only guess at Zach's reaction.

"But then you had to nose around and find out about it—and you wouldn't let go. Not even for Kelly. You were ruining everything, all my plans, *everything.* So I had to take you down. And something snapped inside of Kyle. He wouldn't listen to me. *He wouldn't listen!* He was going to turn me in to the cops, so I killed him." His voice lowered suddenly, and became almost gentle. "But I should have killed you, instead."

Joey turned and aimed his gun at Tanner, extending his arm straight out in front of him. Tori felt the sudden absence of the gun barrel in her back, and whirled. She turned just in time to watch in horror as Joey pulled the trigger.

But Zach was only a few feet away from Tanner, shielded by the body of the Cessna 185. When Joey turned his gun on Tanner, Zach executed a flying tackle, crashing his body into Tanner's lanky frame, and twisting to shield him from the bullet.

The impact of the bullet sent Zach sprawling and he landed in a heap on the ground, trapping Tanner beneath him.

Dakota screamed in fear at the sharp, popping sound the gunfire made, and kept on screaming in Joey's ear, reaching her arms out toward Tori and wailing pitifully. Joey was startled by the screams, and loosened his grip just enough for her to wrench the baby out of his arms. She turned and ran.

Dusty had started running toward Joey the instant he'd turned his gun on Tanner. He was on top of Joey just seconds after Tori got the baby away from him, and they both went down.

Joey made a vain attempt to ram the barrel into Dusty's stomach as they struggled, but Dusty was powered with sheer adrenaline. He possessed a strength he hadn't thought possible, but his entire life flashed before him the instant he felt the cold steel of the pistol against his belly.

He had to survive. He simply had to. Because if he didn't, then Dakota would once again be an orphan. And Tori—she couldn't take another major loss. He had to survive for her sake. And his.

He twisted Joey's right hand until he heard bones crack, twisted the barrel of the gun away from his body—

and then he heard the gunfire. A single shot. And time seemed to stop.

Joey stared at him for the longest time, shock and disbelief slowly entering his pale blue eyes, then he collapsed, and Dusty lowered him to the ground.

He died instantly, and there was nothing Dusty could do. Except kneel beside him, with Joey's gun in his hand, and remember that this man used to be his friend.

He tossed the gun aside and stood up slowly, his gaze drifting in surprise to the police car parked at an angle to the four planes. When had the cops arrived?

The sheriff was hustling toward him, and he stepped away from the body, his gaze moving, as if in slow motion, to where his brother sat on the ground, unharmed, Zach's head and shoulders in his lap, as he attempted to stop the flow of blood. He watched as Caleb dropped to his knees beside them.

Dusty heard a small noise behind him and he turned blindly, still feeling dazed, confused, and too disoriented for comfort, only to feel the slim figure throw herself into his arms.

His arms went around Tori and Dakota gratefully, and then tightened as his confusion cleared. They were safe. They were all safe.

Tori and Dusty stood at the foot of Zach's hospital bed. The bullet had gone through his shoulder, he had lost a substantial amount of blood, but he was okay—weak, and somewhat groggy from the painkillers, but no permanent damage.

They had stopped by his room to see how he was feeling, only to find Tanner in a chair by his bed. The two men were talking quietly when they entered, but all conversation ceased abruptly when they made their presence known, and Zach's deep blue eyes fastened on them.

"Rough day, huh?" he said weakly, and Tori laughed.

She circled the bed and placed her armload of magazines and books on his nightstand. "I thought you might like something to read while you're laid up." Then she bent and kissed him on the cheek. "Thank you."

"For what? Getting myself shot?"

"For saving Tanner's life."

Zach studied her a moment, the blue eyes on her face, and Tori thought he looked younger than he had in years. More relaxed, more at peace. Some might say it was because of the medication, but Tori knew better. The demons no longer rode on his back—or on hers, either.

He looked away, his gaze straying to Dusty. "Tanner was just filling me in." And then, quickly, "I already told Caleb that I'd testify or sign papers or whatever to get Tanner's name cleared. I can't fix what happened these past few months, but—"

"Don't worry about that," Tanner cut in gently.

Tori looked uneasily around the room, wondering why Jenna was not here with her husband, wondering what had happened between them, wondering what Zach was going to do about her. He had a reputation for being jealous and possessive where Jenna was concerned, but she knew how deeply he loved her.

Did he love her enough to forgive her affair with Kyle?

The silence lengthened and deepened, the tension evident, and then Zach said abruptly, "I already knew about Jenna and Kyle. I've known for years, long before I married her."

"You did?" Tanner looked stunned.

"Sure," he said quietly. "I was hoping that one day she'd trust me enough to tell me herself. I forgave her years ago. And forgave Kyle, too."

On that note they decided to leave. Zach looked exhausted and his eyes kept closing, as if sheer willpower was the only thing keeping him awake. But when they reached the door, Tanner hesitated, and then turned around and walked back to stand at the foot of Zach's bed.

"Why?" The question seemed wrenched out of him. "Why did you take that bullet for me?"

Zach's dark blue eyes opened and he looked straight at him. "It was the least I could do," he said softly, and then he was asleep. They left the room quietly, and Tori noticed Tanner was shaking his head slightly as if he didn't know what to make of Zach Jordan.

Outside in the hall they met Zach's parents, and they exchanged polite words, Geoffrey and Susan Jordan stealing bewildered glances at Tanner from time to time. But they didn't say anything and neither did Tanner. It was going to take some time, Tori knew, for the Jordans to digest this startling chain of events—and to assimilate the fact that Tanner was not guilty of killing their youngest son.

They found Jenna at the end of the corridor, near the elevator, and she was huddled against the wall taking swipes at her tearstained face with a pink tissue. There was nothing elegant or flirtatious about her manner, or her looks. Worn jeans, T-shirt, running shoes, red leather jacket, uncombed blond hair and huge blue eyes—scared blue eyes.

It hit Tori that Jenna didn't want to lose Zach...that in all probability he was her anchor and her one true love. She flirted outrageously, but Tori now suspected it rarely, if ever, went beyond flirting.

Kyle was probably the rare exception and that had been long ago.

"It's time you faced the music, kid," Tanner said bluntly, and Tori was startled at his choice of words, but even more startled when Jenna didn't get angry at him.

Instead, she gazed up at him, flicked an uneasy look at Dusty and Tori, then glanced back at Tanner. "He knows, doesn't he?"

"Yeah."

"What am I going to say to him, Tanner?"

He bent and kissed her lightly on the cheek. "Tell him the truth."

He straightened, pushed the button on the elevator, and they waited. A moment later, Jenna shoved her tissue into the pocket of her jacket, squared her shoulders and walked down the corridor toward Zach's room.

"Is she asleep?" Dusty asked as she entered the living room.

She nodded, smiling. "Dead to the world. It was a hard day for her."

"It was a hard day for all of us."

Tori dropped down next to him on the couch and glanced out the window. "It's almost dawn."

"And this time tomorrow morning, we'll be on our way to Fairbanks so you can catch your flight to Phoenix." He said it slowly, carefully, and she lifted her eyes to meet his.

"No, we won't."

The forest green eyes lit up and then caught fire. "We won't?"

She shook her head, steadily holding his intense gaze. "No, I'm staying here with you and Dakota. That is, if you'll let me."

"Let you?" Relief had flooded through him, rendering him speechless. But he did manage to blurt out the one question he needed an answer to. "Are you sure?"

"Yes."

"What made you change your mind?" The question was gently asked, but he was watching her intently.

"A lot of things. But the bottom line is that I love you and I love Dakota, and I want the three of us to be a family." She gazed into his eyes, saw the love deeply ingrained in their green depths and gathered enough courage to say, "When Joey was holding the gun on me and I was looking at you, not knowing if I'd ever see you again..."

"Tori?" he asked when her voice trailed off, and she looked at him uncertainly. "Are you okay?"

"I was just remembering this morning, and how cold you were when you gave me my plane ticket. I should have gone ahead and told you I'd changed my mind about leaving—"

"You had decided to stay? This morning?" He was staring at her, shock and disbelief in his deep green eyes. "Why didn't you tell me?"

"Stubborn pride, I guess."

"Pride?"

"You came out in the rain just to bring me my plane ticket to Phoenix," she said in a small voice. "And I'd hurt you so badly this year, I...I didn't think you'd like it if I told you I'd changed my mind."

He stared at her for the longest time before he stood up, and headed toward the desk in the corner. He returned with the plane ticket in his hand. He dropped it in her lap and sat down beside her. "Look at it."

"But it's just a ticket—"

"Look at it," he said softly.

Tori examined it carefully and then lifted her eyes to meet his. "It's a round-trip ticket."

"I was hoping you'd get there, change your mind and come home."

Tori laughed, sheer joy racing through her. If she'd had any doubts, this round-trip ticket had erased them. Dusty wanted her to stay.

She could see it in his eyes . . . hear it in his voice. . . .

Tori moved toward him, sliding one leg over him until she was sitting in his lap, facing him, her knees on the couch, her hands on his shoulders.

"There's one other thing. I never blamed you for Shawn's death," she stated matter-of-factly, stroking one lock of dark blond hair falling over his shirt collar. "I blamed myself."

"But why?" He looked genuinely perplexed. "You weren't even here."

"Exactly. I wasn't here—and I should have been."

His hands had been resting on her hips, and now he sat up a little, and drew her to him. "It wasn't your fault. You can't spend twenty-four hours a day with a kid. It's impossible, without driving yourself—and the kid—completely nuts."

"The part of me that's intelligent and logical knows that, Dusty. But the part that became a mother felt pure guilt. Especially after Shawn died," she said in a low voice. She laid her head wearily on his shoulder, and his fingers gently stroked her hair.

He had no words to comfort her, nor did he even try. They had time now, an entire lifetime, to work through her feelings, and his, and come to terms with their son's untimely death.

But the most important thing, to him, was that she had agreed to stay here and to try to build a new life with him and Dakota.

She raised her head and sat there staring at him, suddenly uneasy. "Do I have to . . . ?" Her voice trailed off and Dusty gently took her hands in his and held them reassuringly.

"What?" he prodded, and the brown eyes lifted to meet his.

"Have another child?" she asked softly and he grew still.

"Of course not."

"I'm worried about—"

"I know."

"What if it happens again, Dusty? What if—you know...crib death is something that runs in our family? What if it's in our genes? What if you and I can only make babies who can't breathe when they're asleep?"

"When it's time for us to think about having another child, then we'll go to a doctor, we'll read books on the subject, we'll gather all the information we need to make a decision, and we'll take it from there." Dusty didn't know what else to say to her, but she seemed to take comfort from his words.

They had a plan, some control over their lives, and she liked that idea.

"You want another baby, don't you?" she asked.

"Only if you do," he said honestly. "And only when you're ready. When *I'm* ready." He was cringing inside, but he said it. "I don't think I could take losing another child, either," he said quietly and she studied him for several long seconds.

Then she smiled. "You have to have faith." She said it lightly, her expression rueful, but to Dusty it was the budding of new life. Tori's new life. And his. "And in the meantime, whatever happens, we already have a daughter," she added firmly.

"That's right. Dakota Grace McKay."

"When can we file the papers to legally adopt her?"

"You really want to adopt her?"

Tori laughed. "Sure. Don't you? I don't like the sound of legal guardian. It sounds too cold. I like the sound of mom and dad a whole lot better."

He brought her head down and kissed her forehead, then both cheeks. "Then that's what we'll do. First thing tomorrow. The day after at the latest." And then, "Tori, are you sure you want to do this?"

"Stay with you or adopt Dakota?"

"Both."

"Why would I want to break up such an interesting marriage?"

He shook her once and she giggled. "And Dakota?"

"She's already our daughter. I just want to make it official."

He was staring at her with wonder in his eyes, but his expression was puzzled, too. "I can't believe you're this... calm about what happened."

"Alaska didn't kidnap me, Dusty," she said soberly. "A man did. One sick man, who would have been sick in New York or Hawaii. Alaska's a gorgeous place to live and my favorite place on earth." Then she grinned happily. "Because, you know what? I woke up from my nap and discovered I was truly a McKay—a full-fledged member of the third generation of bush pilots, complete with the rugged pioneer spirit of any true Alaskan." She nodded once and beamed at him.

"Is that so?" he murmured, shifting their bodies into a more comfortable position—she was flat on the couch and he was hovering over her, his arms braced on each side of her head. "From one rugged bush pilot to another—would you like to engage in a little flight training?"

Her denim-clad legs went up and around his waist, pulling his lower body into hers. "Oh, yes. Flying lessons. I'd like that."

Epilogue

Three Years Later

Tori peeked her head into Dakota's room, and the four-year-old was sound asleep, her long black hair spread out on the lilac pillow, one little fist clutching the quilt up around her chin.

Tori smiled and glanced around the room. Dakota loved stuffed toys and the color purple, and her bedroom reflected that. She gently closed the door and crossed the hall to the nursery.

She stood in the doorway and watched her sleeping sons. Their first birthday was tomorrow, and they had planned a large party for them. Tori sighed in relief when she thought about this past year. The twins had been born a month early, but they were healthy and they had thrived.

Their first six months of life had taught Tori the true meaning of the word *faith.* She had clung to hers each night when she put them to bed, and each time she put them down for a nap.

And each time they woke up, it was with lots of sunny smiles and huge appetites—and her faith was restored little by little.

Sometimes when Tori looked at her blond-headed, green-eyed babies, she could see Shawn. A crooked smile, or a tight fist around her thumb, and pain would flood every fiber of her being.

But it didn't last long, and she was more than grateful for what she had.

Steven Tanner was asleep with his thumb in his mouth, and Matthew David had kicked the covers off. Tori entered the room and covered him again, and then stood and watched the twin mobiles that hung over their cribs—a gift from Dusty.

Soft, sculptured airplanes in bright colors chased each other around in circles.

"You're too sexy to be the mother of three," Dusty said from behind her, and she smiled invitingly at him.

"Good. I'll race you to the bedroom."

She brushed past him and out the door, Dusty hot on her trail.

* * * * *

COMING NEXT MONTH

#601 CALLAGHAN'S WAY—Marie Ferrarella

American Hero Kirk Callaghan had returned home in search of peace. But he soon found himself playing surrogate dad to Rachel Reed's eight-year-old son—and playing for keeps with Rachel's heart.

#602 A SOLDIER'S HEART—Kathleen Korbel

Tony Riordan merely wanted to thank the nurse who'd saved his life so many years ago in a war-torn jungle. But that was before he saw Claire again—and the unresolved anguish reflected in her eyes. Now his angel of mercy needed *his* help, and Tony would never refuse her.

#603 SCARLET WHISPERS—Diana Whitney

His father was no murderer. And Clay Cooper would prove it once and for all to the closed-minded people of Scarlet, South Carolina. But that meant convincing Lainey Sheridan, the dead man's daughter. She alone held the key to the past—and to Clay's heart.

#604 FUGITIVE FATHER—Carla Cassidy

Sarah Calhoun had successfully kept her secret from the Clay Creek rumor mill—and Reese Walker—for six years. But once she returned home, there was no denying who'd fathered her child—and no keeping Reese from the daughter he'd never known existed.

#605 ONLY THE LONELY—Pat Warren

Giff Jacobs had one reason for living: retribution. And he would have it once he gathered the evidence to clear his name. But his agenda radically changed the moment he encountered Roxie Lowell, the woman who'd made him trust—and love—again. The woman he'd unwittingly placed in danger.

#606 JENNY'S CASTLE—Elizabeth Sinclair

He'd found her. Six long years of separation hadn't eased the pain of Jennifer Tyson's betrayal, but Devin Montgomery would have his revenge. But Jenny wasn't the ice princess he'd believed her to be. Instead, she was a victim of the past just like him—and their five-year-old daughter....

MILLION DOLLAR SWEEPSTAKES (III)

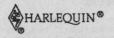HARLEQUIN® Silhouette®

The movie event of the season can be the reading event of the year!

Lights… The lights go on in October when CBS presents Harlequin/Silhouette Sunday Matinee Movies. These four movies are based on bestselling Harlequin and Silhouette novels.

Camera… As the cameras roll, be the first to read the original novels the movies are based on!

Action… Through this offer, you can have these books sent directly to you! Just fill in the order form below and you could be reading the books…before the movie!

48288-4	Treacherous Beauties by Cheryl Emerson	
	$3.99 U.S./$4.50 CAN.	☐
83305-9	Fantasy Man by Sharon Green	
	$3.99 U.S./$4.50 CAN.	☐
48289-2	A Change of Place by Tracy Sinclair	
	$3.99 U.S./$4.50CAN.	☐
83306-7	Another Woman by Margot Dalton	
	$3.99 U.S./$4.50 CAN.	☐

TOTAL AMOUNT	$
POSTAGE & HANDLING	$
($1.00 for one book, 50¢ for each additional)	
APPLICABLE TAXES*	$ _____
TOTAL PAYABLE	$ _____
(check or money order—please do not send cash)	

To order, complete this form and send it, along with a check or money order for the total above, payable to Harlequin Books, to: **In the U.S.:** 3010 Walden Avenue, P.O. Box 9047, Buffalo, NY 14269-9047; **In Canada:** P.O. Box 613, Fort Erie, Ontario, L2A 5X3.

Name: _____

Address: _____ City: _____

State/Prov.: _____ Zip/Postal Code: _____

*New York residents remit applicable sales taxes.
Canadian residents remit applicable GST and provincial taxes.

CBSPR

"HOORAY FOR HOLLYWOOD" SWEEPSTAKES

HERE'S HOW THE SWEEPSTAKES WORKS

OFFICIAL RULES — NO PURCHASE NECESSARY

To enter, complete an Official Entry Form or hand print on a 3" x 5" card the words "HOORAY FOR HOLLYWOOD", your name and address and mail your entry in the pre-addressed envelope (if provided) or to: "Hooray for Hollywood" Sweepstakes, P.O. Box 9076, Buffalo, NY 14269-9076 or "Hooray for Hollywood" Sweepstakes, P.O. Box 637, Fort Erie, Ontario L2A 5X3. Entries must be sent via First Class Mail and be received no later than 12/31/94. No liability is assumed for lost, late or misdirected mail.

Winners will be selected in random drawings to be conducted no later than January 31, 1995 from all eligible entries received.

Grand Prize: A 7-day/6-night trip for 2 to Los Angeles, CA including round trip air transportation from commercial airport nearest winner's residence, accommodations at the Regent Beverly Wilshire Hotel, free rental car, and $1,000 spending money. (Approximate prize value which will vary dependent upon winner's residence: $5,400.00 U.S.); 500 Second Prizes: A pair of "Hollywood Star" sunglasses (prize value: $9.95 U.S. each). Winner selection is under the supervision of D.L. Blair, Inc., an independent judging organization, whose decisions are final. Grand Prize travelers must sign and return a release of liability prior to traveling. Trip must be taken by 2/1/96 and is subject to airline schedules and accommodations availability.

Sweepstakes offer is open to residents of the U.S. (except Puerto Rico) and Canada who are 18 years of age or older, except employees and immediate family members of Harlequin Enterprises, Ltd., its affiliates, subsidiaries, and all agencies, entities or persons connected with the use, marketing or conduct of this sweepstakes. All federal, state, provincial, municipal and local laws apply. Offer void wherever prohibited by law. Taxes and/or duties are the sole responsibility of the winners. Any litigation within the province of Quebec respecting the conduct and awarding of prizes may be submitted to the Regie des loteries et courses du Quebec. All prizes will be awarded; winners will be notified by mail. No substitution of prizes are permitted. Odds of winning are dependent upon the number of eligible entries received.

Potential grand prize winner must sign and return an Affidavit of Eligibility within 30 days of notification. In the event of non-compliance within this time period, prize may be awarded to an alternate winner. Prize notification returned as undeliverable may result in the awarding of prize to an alternate winner. By acceptance of their prize, winners consent to use of their names, photographs, or likenesses for purpose of advertising, trade and promotion on behalf of Harlequin Enterprises, Ltd., without further compensation unless prohibited by law. A Canadian winner must correctly answer an arithmetical skill-testing question in order to be awarded the prize.

For a list of winners (available after 2/28/95), send a separate stamped, self-addressed envelope to: Hooray for Hollywood Sweepstakes 3252 Winners, P.O. Box 4200, Blair, NE 68009.

CBSRLS

OFFICIAL ENTRY COUPON

"Hooray for Hollywood"
SWEEPSTAKES!

Yes, I'd love to win the Grand Prize — a vacation in Hollywood — or one of 500 pairs of "sunglasses of the stars"! Please enter me in the sweepstakes!

This entry must be received by December 31, 1994.
Winners will be notified by January 31, 1995.

Name _____

Address _____ Apt. _____

City _____

State/Prov. _____ Zip/Postal Code _____

Daytime phone number _____
(area code)

Mail all entries to: Hooray for Hollywood Sweepstakes,
P.O. Box 9076, Buffalo, NY 14269-9076.
In Canada, mail to: Hooray for Hollywood Sweepstakes,
P.O. Box 637, Fort Erie, ON L2A 5X3.

KCH

OFFICIAL ENTRY COUPON

"Hooray for Hollywood"
SWEEPSTAKES!

Yes, I'd love to win the Grand Prize — a vacation in Hollywood — or one of 500 pairs of "sunglasses of the stars"! Please enter me in the sweepstakes!

This entry must be received by December 31, 1994.
Winners will be notified by January 31, 1995.

Name _____

Address _____ Apt. _____

City _____

State/Prov. _____ Zip/Postal Code _____

Daytime phone number _____
(area code)

Mail all entries to: Hooray for Hollywood Sweepstakes,
P.O. Box 9076, Buffalo, NY 14269-9076.
In Canada, mail to: Hooray for Hollywood Sweepstakes,
P.O. Box 637, Fort Erie, ON L2A 5X3.

KCH